DEADLY REPLY . . .

The Death Merchant was shoving the projectile into the front end of the launching tube when a voice, speaking Bulgarian, came through a loudspeaker attached to the top of the armored car. By the time the message was finished, Camellion had locked the projectile in the launcher tube and was preparing to look down the optical sight.

Again the harsh, demanding voice spoke, repeating the message, and Traikov translated. "They're giving us three minutes to come out the front door—backward, with our hands raised. They said the house is completely surrounded and that we'll be well treated if we surrender."

"Whoever that officer is out there, he should know that you never send a baby to buy a beer," Camellion said. On one knee, he saw the armored car, aimed at its side, and pulled the trigger . . .

Other titles in the **DEATH MERCHANT** series from Pinnacle Books:

#61
DEATH MERCHANT
THE BULGARIAN TERMINATION
Joseph Rosenberger

PINNACLE BOOKS NEW YORK

DEATH MERCHANT #61: THE BULGARIAN TERMINATION

Copyright © 1984 by Joseph Rosenberger

An original Pinnacle Books edition, published for the first time anywhere.

First printing/December 1984

ISBN: 0-523-42089-7

Can. ISBN: 0-523-43254-2

Cover art by Dean Cate

Printed in the United States of America

PINNACLE BOOKS, INC.
1430 Broadway
New York, New York 10018

9 8 7 6 5 4 3 2 1

This book is for D.L.K.
Shapis trav-gif

Special Dedication

Mitchell Livingston John WerBell III
Lieutenant
General
RFAA
1918–1983
(See you later, Mitch)

SPECIAL ADVISER
Colonel George Ellis
Le Mercenaire
Aurora, Illinois

CHAPTER ONE

The instant that Fedor Rykov shouted "Police! Surrounding the house!" from the top of the stairs—first in Bulgarian, then in broken English—the Death Merchant knew that his instincts had been right. The night before Camellion had warned Stephen Traikov that it would be unwise to spend a third day in this safe station of the NFC, that to do so would be courting disaster. Traikov had said there was no danger. "I am assured—on good advice from the main cell—that this house is not known to the police," Traikov had assured Richard Camellion—and it was Traikov's show. After all, he was even one of the leaders of the *Narodno Gorsiku Rakigla-denov*, the Bulgarian National Freedom Council that was determined to overthrow the legal Communist dictatorship governing Bulgaria.

No danger! And now the *Nersko-Tsopska*,[1] or militia, had arrived!

It only proves that "good advice" usually gets in the way of common sense! But why complain? This little "vacation" in Bulgaria was paid for by the Company!

The Death Merchant glanced knowingly at Carey Winkler, whose own eyes were saying: *All this time spent in getting our-selves smuggled into Bulgaria, all the way to Sofia. Now—this!*

Stephen Traikov stared at Fedor Rykov. "You are certain, Fedor? If the police are outside . . ."

---

[1] In communist nations there are no "local police departments." It's uniformed militiamen who carry out ordinary police duties. The militia is always under the strict control of the secret police.

Rykov, who had just come from the attic above the third floor of the large house, was always sulky, even under the best of conditions. Now, he looked almost angry that Traikov should doubt his word.

"*Dai*,[2] I know what I saw," he said bluntly. "There's a Zil parked out front, across the street. Several Kalotas are parked close to the southwest corner of Kirili and Zaimov. The cars are unmarked, but they're the police. To clinch it, there's an armored car on Evloggi Georgiev—and you ask me if I'm sure!"

"That's good enough for me," Mekhlis Kalojan said casually, in fairly good English. "We all know how the NT closes in on its victims." He picked up an Egyptian Maddi AKM assault rifle and turned to Traikov, expecting some kind of affirmative comment, but Traikov was hurrying to one of the tall windows of the parlor.

Verdo Yydasgrei pulled back the cocking knob of a Czech Vz-58 submachine gun. "Our only chance now is the tunnel to the other house. Even then the risk will be great. At least the van has an overcharged engine, and we do have two Soviet missiles."

The Death Merchant, the two Bulgarian Bidja pistols heavy in their shoulder holsters, followed Traikov to the window. Camellion went to the left, gently pulled back the dirty green shade, and peered out. Like the rest of Europe, Bulgaria was in the grip of an unrelenting winter, and the big yard in front of the rundown old mansion was covered with snow, although Kirili Avenue had been snow-plowed clean. The early morning sun had risen higher, its light starting to make the snow sparkle and flash with color, none of which interested Camellion and Traikov. Both could see the black Russian-built Zil parked across the street, its tinted windows making it impossible to see how many men were inside.

"How could they have known about this house," murmured Traikov, his voice shaking slightly. "It's impossible, but they obviously know we are here."

He moved to Camellion's side in order to get a look at the two cars parked on one corner of Kirili and Zaimov; however, due to the sharp angle, all he and the Death Merchant could discern was the front of the first Bulgarian-manufactured

---

[2]"Yes" in the Bulgarian language.

Kalota that would make an American automobile buff think of a 1958 Firedome De Soto.

"Yes, they're there," admitted Traikov. "We can count on their having men in the alley and on the east and the west sides of the house."

"So much for your security system," the Death Merchant said, and moved back from the window. "As we say in the States, there are termites in the woodwork. In this case, there's an informer in your overall network."

Stephen Traikov gave Camellion a worried look. "I do believe you are right, *tosvarkish*.[3] Right now, we have another problem. We will have to hold them off as long as possible. A short fight will make them move in with caution, very slowly. That will give us time to move through the tunnel and get to the van."

"Provided the traitor hasn't informed them about the tunnel," the Death Merchant reminded the freedom fighter leader. "If he—or she—has, then we're trapped like flies in a bottle."

Traikov lowered his voice to a whisper. "Only I and Georgi Charov and Todor Divjiguv knew about the tunnel. I would stake the soul of my mother on Georgi and Todor. They risked their lives to bring you and the other American this far. Todor almost acquired frostbite in the task. No, the spy is neither Todor nor Georgi."

"I presume the militia will give us a chance to surrender— not that it makes any real difference." Moving across the room with Traikov, Camellion came directly to the point. "The KDS[4] couldn't get answers from dead men, and either we'll escape or we're dead."

Carey Winkler spoke up. "We had better take up positions on all four sides of this house. We're too vulnerable, bunched up as we are. We're a helluva long way from being safe, even with that tunnel down there."

A man who could converse and write in eleven languages, including Bulgarian, Winkler was a well-built individual with curly cinnamon hair, heavy brows, wide walnut-brown eyes that no amount of whiskey could ever dim, and a red-hued face that not even a tropic sun could tan.

---

[3]The Bulgarian language is very similar to the Russian language. In Russian, *tovarisch* means "Comrade" and is also the equivalent of "Mr." In Bulgarian, *tosvarkish* is the equivalent of "good—and trusted—friend."

[4]Komitet Darzhavra Sigurnost, the state security apparatus.

Stephen Traikov acknowledged Winkler's advice with a nod, then said to Camellion, "The *Nersko-Tsopska* will give us plenty of time to surrender, especially if they know I'm in here. The secret police have been after me and the other two for almost four years. But it is as you said: we would be better off dead than to fall into the hands of Colonel General Zhivkov." He began to give orders. "Yavo, go to the living room. Fedor . . ."

By one of the east side windows in the study, the Death Merchant waited in the house with the other eight men, an Israeli Uzi SMG in his hands. The Hungarian National Freedom Council obtained its weapons by two methods: by stealing Soviet and Bulgarian weapons and by arms shipments from the CIA, the latter routed from northeast Greece through the treacherous passes of the Rhodope Mountains. All the weapons—handguns, SMGs, assault rifles—and grenades—were never of American manufacture, but were a hodgepodge gathered from many nations—often a difficult process since ammunition had to be included.

The study was cold, The Death Merchant buttoned the top of his heavy woolen *chivva,* a mackinaw-type coat, and thought of the dangerous situation facing him and the other men. In his own opinion, the decrepit mansion was a poor choice for a safe house because it was deserted.

Many years earlier, the houses on the 1600-block of Kirili had belonged to the well-to-do, most to professional people. However, the middle class had disappeared from Bulgaria. Either the wealthy had fled the country or had ended their days in one of the KDS's prisons. Now there were only the "masses" and "equality," which meant that the poor were still poor and that the Party bosses had all the power and privileges.

As yet, the Bulgarian Ministry of Housing had not gotten around to either renovating the nine houses on the 1600-block or Kirili or tearing them down to put up modern concrete cubes for the "happy people" of Sofia.

Only four of the nine houses were occupied, including the one next door to the "safe house." Two elderly sisters and their retarded brother lived in the house next door to the safe house, and they had rented the garage to a "Boris Gravtik," who was supposedly an engineer working for the Ministry of the Interior. Only Gravtik was actually a member of the NFC—the National Freedom Council.

As for the safe house, it had formerly belonged to a Jewish psychiatrist, who, with his wife and two sons, had disappeared. Since then, it had been empty, filled only with memory. There was no heat or electricity. The only heat came from two kerosene heaters, one in the parlor and one in the master bedroom on the second floor.

A poor way to spend a Tuesday morning! The Death Merchant let his eyes wander about the study. Most of the furniture was gone and so were the books from their shelves. The walls were badly in need of paint or new wallpaper, the high ceiling flaked and stained, the old rug filthy with grime. On the south wall were six color photographs of nude men and women, most of them in obscene poses.

The small group did not have long to wait. A Russian BTR-60 armored car moved north on Zaimov Street, turned west at the corner, and came to a stop on the side of Kirili Avenue facing the house, positioning itself between the yard and the Zil. An SGMB light machine gun protruded sinisterly from the turret that was turned toward the front of the house. On top of the turret was a large parabolic dish that resembled a small satellite antenna. Camellion stared at the dish, question marks popping around in his brain. *No, the dish wasn't for radar. Microwaves? No dice. What then was it?*

"How can we fight an armored car?" said Verdo Yydasgrei, who was by another window in the study. "God help us all."

Uh huh . . . pray to God but all the while keep rowing to shore! Still thinking about the dish—*an antenna of some kind?*—Camellion didn't answer. He did glance around when Stephen Traikov, who had been stationed in the kitchen, hurried into the study, his big face a field of worry.

"You both saw the armored car," Traikov said. "There are also two personnel carriers parked in the alley, right in back of the house, in full view. They have us surrounded, or they wouldn't be so open about their movements."

"That means they are also in the house next door," offered Verdo Yydasgrei. "We have no chance, none but the escape tunnel."

"Awhile ago I heard Verdo mention that you have two Soviet missiles," Camellion said to Traikov. "We'll need one to take out that armored car out front. That vehicle can roll right up to the front door if it wants to and blast us with its light machine gun.''

Traikov, looking uncertain, hesitated. ''He meant we have two launchers. We have six missiles. One of the launchers and two of the missiles are upstairs. The other launcher and four missiles are in the tunnel. Are you sure we need to use one on that armored car? I don't want to waste it.''

''Of course I'm sure,'' Camellion said with an aggrieved expression. ''I've been in situations worse than this, many times. Now get me that launcher and the two missiles. We can use one missile on a carrier.''

Nodding, Traikov turned and hurried from the study. Yydasgrei, clutching his Czech Vz-58 subgun, peered through a slit in the shade, cursed, then said, ''One of the personnel carriers has stopped on the far side of Zaimov and men are getting out the back.''

''Hold the fort here,'' Camellion said brusquely. ''I want to have a look from the dining room.''

Leaving the study, the Uzi loosely in his right hand, Camellion ran down the short hall and hurried into what had once been the dining room. Georgi Charov was at the east window, his RKZ Bulgarian submachine gun in his hands. Carey Winkler, armed with a Soviet PPsh chatterbox, was at one of the south-side windows, looking out through a tear in the shade.

''Camellion, all hell is going to explode any second,'' Winkler said without turning from the window and shifting the unlit cigarette to the other side of his mouth. ''There's so much firepower out there that we'll be lucky to even reach the cellar.''

The Death Merchant moved in close and stared through the horizontal rent in the shade. There it was, past the backyard, the storage shed, and the board fence by the alley—a dark green eight-wheeled BTR-60 armored personnel carrier. The rear door of the vehicle was open, and he could see faces, behind visors and underneath combat helmets, peering from the far side of the vehicle, at both the front and the rear ends. The top hatch was closed and so were the plates in the driver's compartment.

''How do you think they'll play it?'' asked Winkler.

''First, they'll demand that we surrender; then they'll open fire. Or maybe use tear gas before they start tossing slugs. Who cares. I'm going to demolish the AC on Kirili and the P-carrier on Zaimov. That will slow them up considerably. . . ."

"Or make them mad enough to blow up the house!" Winkler gave a tiny laugh. "I was told you're triple hell on wheels! It's your show."

"You speak with the tongue of a ding-a-ling," Camellion said good-naturedly. "See you later. Watch out for falling anvils!"

Camellion left the kitchen and, in the hall, found Traikov reaching the bottom of the stairs. He carried a RPG-7V rocket launcher and two 40mm. projectiles in a canvas bag, the straps of the bag over his left shoulder. Camellion relieved Traikov of the launcher and the two men made their way to the living room where Yavo Uglanov was waiting by one of the windows.

A very ugly man—he was built like a barrel but with a face that made one think of a toad—Uglanov grinned broadly when he saw the RPG and watched Traikov put the bag on the floor and pull out a projectile.

The standard anti-armor weapon of Soviet infantry, the RPG was basically a hollow tube, a small light antitank weapon that fired a 40mm. projectile with a HEAT warhead.

The Death Merchant was shoving the projectile into the front end of the launching tube when a voice, speaking Bulgarian, came through a loudspeaker attached to the top of the armored car on Kirili. By the time the message was finished, Camellion had locked the projectile in the launcher tube and was preparing to look down the optical sight.

Again the harsh, demanding voice spoke, repeating the message, and Traikov translated. "They're giving us three minutes to come out the front door—backward, with our hands raised. They said the house is completely surrounded and that we'll be well treated if we surrender."

"Whoever that officer is out there, he should know that you never send a baby to buy the beer," Camellion said. "Uglanov, when I—"

"A 'baby to buy the beer'?" intoned a perplexed Traikov. "I do not understand."

"An American proverb," explained the Death Merchant. Then to Yavo Uglanov, "When I tell you, pull the shade to one side. I want a clear view of the armored car."

Uglanov was startled. "American, you will have only seconds to aim and fire. Can you do it?"

The Death Merchant already had the RPG launcher on his right shoulder and was practically looking down the sight. "I can—"

The pain exploded in the very center of his brain, a searing agony akin to being touched with the tip of a red-hot rod. Traikov and Uglanov were similarly affected, as were the other men in the house.

The Death Merchant's first instinct was to drop the launcher and press his hands to the sides of his head, as if to squeeze off the pain. He didn't. He did look down the sight and manage to yell, "Rip off the s-shade and s-smash the window—quick!"

With sounds of agony coming out of his mouth, Uglanov jerked the shade from the window, then swung the stock of his Maddi AKM against the dirty glass in the bottom frame, some of the pieces falling to the floor, the rest to the porch on the outside.

On one knee, Camellion saw the armored car, aimed at its side, and pulled the trigger, all in the space of a few moments. There was a whoosh from the rear of the tube and the 40mm. projectile was on its way.

BLAMMMMMMM! A ball of smoke and fire and the armored car dissolved, along with its crew of three, concussion killing four of the six militiamen crouched on the street side of the vehicle. The turret, its SGMB machine gun, and the head and the right arm of the man preparing to fire the weapon were blown ten feet upward while other pieces and parts headed toward the dull gray sky, then began to fall within a fifty-foot radius.

Standing by one of the Kalotas parked close to the southwest corner of Kirili and Zaimov, Captain Peturi Riskilin gave a cry of rage when he saw the armored car explode. Neither he nor anyone else had considered the possibility that the traitors to the state might have tank-destroying missiles. An officer in the Third Directorate of the Bulgarian KDS, Riskilin snarled into the walkie-talkie, *"Fire!"*

The instant the Death Merchant fired, he dropped to the floor and yelled, "Down! Hit the deck!"

With the burning pain gone, Yavo Uglanov and Stephen Traikov complied instantly, Traikov muttering, "What caused that pain? My God! It felt as if my head were being pulled apart by a team of horses!"

"We were in a phaser pain field," Camellion said. "The 'dish' on top of the armored car as the 'sender antenna.' The generator must have been producing ultrasonic energy between two and three hundred kilohertz."

A former electrical engineer, Traikov nodded. "The KDS is becoming sophisticated. It's those goddamned East Germans who must have made the device. They—"

The firing from outside the house started. To the north, across Kirili Avenue, militiamen, in a deserted house on the other side of the street, opened fire with Zeff AKM assault rifles, hundreds of 7.62mm. projectiles stabbing into the front of the safe house. Glass on all three floors shattered. Splinters flew from the weathered boards and full metal-jacketed slugs slammed into rooms, striking furniture and walls. Simultaneously, NT militia gunners poured streams of fire from the ends of the BTR-60 personnel carrier on Zaimov Street while to the west and the south, Bulgarian militiamen cut loose from the house next door and from the BTR-60 PC parked in the alley. In less time than it takes to say "head for the hills, boys!" several thousand AKM slugs had ripped into the house: and then, from the second floor of the house across Kirili, a PKT light machine gun began chattering. Hundreds of 7.62mm. rimmed-type 54R projectiles chopped into the front of the house, many of them cutting through the cold air above the Death Merchant, Traikov, and Uglanov, all three of whom were belly-wriggling across the floor toward the hallway, their destination the study.

Mekhlis Kalojan, on the north side of the parlor—west of the living room—was not as fortunate. He had dropped, but now, crawling from the window, reared up slightly. A single PKT 7.62mm. bullet caught him high in the back of the head. He was dead before his face crashed into the pile of newspapers in front of him.

A storm of slugs rained into the house. In the study, three caught Verdo Yydasgrei, who had thrown himself flat at the sound of the armored car's exploding. Nevertheless, in spite of his "safe" position, the firing from the militiamen by the personnel carrier on Zaimov Street was so intense that projectiles had ripped out pieces of wood from the old boards on the outside of the eighty-year-old frame house. Another flood of slugs struck the east side of the house, and three, zipping through several of the outside openings, went completely through the inner wall and wasted Yydasgrei, who was struck in his left hip and left side. The first two slugs ripped out his colon, the second skidding to a bloody stop when it struck a rib on the right side. Yydasgrei cried out in pain, fell flat, and started to sink into unconsciousness.

It was the same kind of situation that pulled the life from Todor Divjiguv, who was in the parlor, stationed by one of the west windows, watching the house next door. He too had dropped to the filthy floor, and he too died when some of the Zeff AKM slugs, slicing through the outer and the inner walls, found him—in the right temple and the right side. A third projectile tore off part of the heel of his left shoe.

Having been in fourteen firefights in various parts of the world, the highly experienced Carey Winkler knew the situation was hopeless. To even try to fire through one of the dining-room windows would be tantamount to suicide.

"Let's get out of here," he yelled at Georgi Charov. "The only chance we have is to get to the tunnel. Traikov and Camellion aren't playing with a full deck if they think we can hold out for even five minutes."

Charov did not put up an argument. After all, enemy slugs were pouring into the dining room with such speed that scores of splinters were flying from the window frames. How could one possibly return the fire?

Dragging a Bulgarian RKZ submachine gun with him and wondering about strange American expressions involving "a full deck"—*a deck of playing cards?*—Charov snaked on his belly with Winkler toward the hall.

In the kitchen—west of the dining room—Fedor Rykov also realized that he would be an idiot to fight a battle he couldn't possibly win, although he had managed to fire off an entire magazine with his SIG assault rifle. At least, he reasoned, the *Nersko-Tsopska* militiamen in the alley would close in with extreme caution. Rykov began crawling to the trapdoor in the southwest corner of the kitchen.

By now, Winkler and Charov had reached the hall and could see Camellion, Traikov, and Uglanov. The Death Merchant and the two men with him had crawled to the door of the study, and Camellion, flat on the floor, was pushing a 40mm. missile into the mouth of the launcher.

There was a lull in the firing, and Winkler yelled in alarm at Camellion. "Don't try it. You'll be chopped into cutlets!"

Just then another swarm of slugs ripped into the house from all four sides. Many of the projectiles came through the doorway of the study and through the north opening of the hall, the high-velocity metal striking the walls with loud thuds.

Winkler shouted in anger at Camellion. "You won't even have time to sight in on that personnel carrier. Anyhow, what's the point? Let's get the hell out of here."

"The *Nersko-Tsopska* will start to close in soon," Yavo Uglanov growled, "and if there is another carrier blocking the west end of the alley, we will still be trapped." He watched the Death Merchant slip a leather glove onto his left hand.

Ignoring Winkler and his warnings, Camellion raised his head very slightly and listened to the firing coming from the east, fixing the position of the sound in his mind, picturing the militiamen grouped around the BTR-60 on Zaimov Street. He wasn't concerned about the missile's striking any glass in a window. All the glass had been shot out. The typhoon of slugs had even ripped the shades from the windows.

Camellion did not stand up to fire. He did raise the RPG tube from his prone position on the floor, holding it with the "muzzle" a foot and a half above, and a foot in front of, his head. His right hand was around the forward handle, his finger only a millimeter from the trigger. His gloved left hand was around the narrow rear end of the tube, the section in front of the funnel-mouthed exhaust.

He pulled the trigger. With a loud whoosh the missile streaked from the launcher and shot through a window. Fumes were pouring from the exhaust and Camellion was feeling the heat on his left hand when there were four loud pings in quick succession, the zings of Zeff AKM slugs striking the tube. Camellion and the other men automatically ducked to avoid the ricochets. Two projectiles, coming in at a sharp angle, had struck just inside the mouth of the tube. A third projectile also streaked in from the right, this one striking the right center of the tube, only inches from Camellion's right hand. The fourth bullet hit the perpendicular shoulder rest and shattered the plastic, the impact of the slugs almost tearing the tube from Camellion's hands.

BLAAAAMMMMMMMM! The missile exploded, but Camellion's aim—by mental estimation—had been off. The missile did not strike the right side of the BTR-60. Instead it struck the right rear tire of the personnel carrier and detonated with a crashing roar. When the smoke cleared, one could see that the entire rear end of the carrier had been wrecked. Not only were three of the tires and wheels on the right side missing, but the violence of the explosion had half turned the heavy vehicle around so that its front now faced the west. The rear of the vehicle was burning, and bodies—the militiamen killed by concussion and flying metal—lay around the vehicle. Three others were moaning, two crawling on their hands and knees.

If one could see! The Death Merchant and the others couldn't. They were too busy crawling along the east-west hall to the kitchen, all except Georgi Charov, who was squirming into the combination parlor and sitting room to get Mekhlia Kalojan and Todor Divjiguv.

Reaching the kitchen—slugs screaming over their heads—Camellion and the others saw that Fedor Rykov had opened the trapdoor and was preparing the *pjâsaci*—dynamite. He had inserted the caps into the eleven sticks of dynamite, had taped them together with electrician's tape, and was taping a Soviet RGD-5 grenade to the package of high-explosive that would be tied to the top step below the trapdoor. A strong cord would be fastened in the ring of the pin in the grenade and its other end secured to a metal screw-in eye on the underside of the trapdoor—a simple but effective trap. When the trapdoor was pulled open . . .

The sullen-faced Rykov, the package of explosive and its RGD-5 "detonator" in his hands, was the first to go down into the celler and to accept the missile launcher that the Death Merchant thrust down through the square opening.

"Get down there," Camellion said to Winkler. "One of us has to stay alive to kill the Russian 'Uncles' and blow up KDS headquarters."

"A 'Mission Impossible' and you know it," Winkler said, crawling toward the opening. "All we're proving is what happens to a couple of jokers—like us—who are too lazy to work and too nervous to steal!"

He swung a leg through the opening. Camellion, thinking that only the living feared death—*The Dead know better!*—checked his Uzi chatterbox to make sure it was free of debris. He had dragged it all over the house and wanted to make sure the muzzle of the stubby barrel wasn't clogged. *Good! It wasn't.*

He glanced toward Georgi Charov, who was crawling into

the kitchen on his hands and knees, pushing his Swiss SIG assault rifle ahead of him.

"The souls of Todor and Mekhlis are with God," Charov reported, his voice heavy, as he moved toward the open trapdoor.

Stephen Traikov, watching the south side shot-to-pieces kitchen windows, did not turn to Charov. He merely said, "We will be joining them soon unless we are very lucky."

Amused that Charov was positive that Mekhlis Kalojan and Todor Divjiguv were with God—*Some straight shot to heaven!*—the Death Merchant became extra alert when the firing to the south stopped. *They're going to close in!*

Camellion and Traikov, Uglanov, and Charov soon learned why the firing from the alley had stopped completely. Faster than a politician making promises before an election, five militiamen reared up from outside the windows to the south and thrust in the barrels of one RKZ SMG and four Ziff assault rifles. But the five *Nersko-Tsopska* were a fraction too slow, a mite of a moment off, losing time when they moved the barrels through the shot-out windows.

The Death Merchant fired as he rolled over on his back—to the right—Stephen Traikov's own RKZ spitting out 7.62mm. slugs at about the same time that the Death Merchant triggered his Uzi, moving the Israeli music box from right to left.

Yavo Uglanov, who had been crawling toward the trapdoor, and Georgi Charov, about to go down into the cellar, were caught off guard.

The Death Merchant's chain of 9mm. Parabellum slugs popped into three of the enemy almost at the same instant that a stream of Ziff projectiles stabbed into the section of floor to his left. A few of the 7.62mm. slugs punched their way through the outer left sleeve of his *chivva*, tearing through his sweater and "razor-blading" across his skin. Four other slugs cut through the heavy woolen coat—on the left, by his rib cage—but these didn't touch the sweater.

Yavo Uglanov and Georgi Charov did not fare as well as Camellion and Traikov. A stream of 7.62mm. RKZ projectiles rained down across the right side of Uglanov. He flopped like a fish out of water, but only once, then lay still, a pool of blood quickly starting to form under his corpse.

Georgi Charov was even more of a victim of calamity. At least Uglanov had died in less time than it takes to swat a fly. Georgi Charov did not. Most of the enemy slugs missed him, all except two. One bullet caught him in the left leg, just below the knee, and while it missed the vital arteries and major vessels, it did break the tibia. The second slug struck him high in the left thigh. It too missed the veins and the arteries but clipped the femur, fracturing the long leg bone.

As for the other two militiamen at the windows, they had given short cries of shock and had gone down, thrown violently into eternity by Stephen Traikov's slugs.

The Death Merchant, pulling the empty magazine from the Uzi, glanced across at Traikov, then at the moaning Charov, and finally at the bloody corpse of Yavo Uglanov. Camellion was icy calm, so was Stephen Traikov, the latter of whom wore his age well, his forty-four years neither hanging under his eyes nor over his belt. His angular face had boyish, innocent features . . . the kind of face God loves . . . the face of a man who would die young.

Camellion said, "Uglanov has had it." With Traikov, he started to crawl to the opening of the cellar. "What do we do with Georgi?"

"He goes with us," Traikov said with determination. "We never leave our men, under any conditions. . . ."

By then, Winkler had reared up through the opening and was covering the south-side windows with a Soviet PPsh submachine gun while Fedor Rykov finished fastening the package of *pjâsaci* to the top step.

Traikov started toward Georgi Charkov, who whispered weakly, "N-no, Stephen. There i-is n-nothing you can d-do. The pain—the p-pain in my leg is so great I-I can't m-move. I'd pass out if. . . if y-you tried to get me down the s-steps."

"But—"

"You-you can't c-carry me. We w-would a-all die. Move q-quickly. Escape while y-you can." He motioned with his RKZ. "Be sensible—go! I will die quickly w-when they storm the h-house. Better that t-than all of us. . ."

Without another word, Traikov followed the Death Merchant through the opening and down the wooden steps. Traikov reached up, gripped the large loose ring of the trapdoor, pulled up the square of wood, let the door fall into its frame, then slid the small bolt into its receiver, locking the trapdoor.

With the Death Merchant holding a penlight, its beam illuminating the top of the steps, Winkler tied the end of the cord to the eye in the screw in the underside of the trapdoor, making sure that the cord had only a slight slack. The pin would be pulled from the grenade when the door was pulled up only several inches.

Down in the cellar, Fedor Rykov had switched on a six-volt safety lantern, had placed it on the stone floor, and by its light had pulled aside an old wooden cupboard that had concealed the entrance to the escape tunnel, which moved, at a slight angle, 114 feet to the southwest and ended underneath the garage of the house next door. It had taken members of the NFC almost two years to dig the tunnel, shore up its sides and ceiling, and dispose of the dirt. "The dirt was scattered all over Sofia!" Todor Divjiguv had once remarked.

"*Dovoi! Dovoi!* Hurry! Hurry!" urged Traikov as Rykov picked up the lantern and moved into the tunnel that was only five feet high and four feet wide.

Once inside, Rykov turned around and, bent over, flashed the beam of the lantern downward. "Be careful, *tosvarkiski,*" he warned Winkler and the Death Merchant. "See the wide board at the bottom. It has slats across it so you will not slip. It slants downward for about three meters. We will then be in the tunnel. Come."

The last one through the mouth of the tunnel was Stephen Traikov, who was behind Camellion. Leading the way was Fedor Rykov; behind him was Carey Winkler, who, carrying both the RPG missile launcher and his PPsh SMG, was concerned not only about the dank, dead stink but also feared the possibility of methane, that odorless, colorless gas that could kill so very quickly. It wasn't likely that the "firedamp" of coal mines would be in a tunnel so close to the surface of the ground. Let's see . . . three meters is ten feet. Add to that about seven or eight feet and you get seventeen or eighteen feet below ground. Yet the potential for methane was still there, especially since the tunnel intersected a very old drainage tunnel unused for the past sixty years. The exception had been during the era of the Nazi occupation. Bulgarian partisans had then used sections of the tunnel to hide both men and arms.

The group of four had passed the slanting boardwalk and was another twenty-five feet into the tunnel and, within the confined beam of the lantern, moving as fast as possible when they heard intense firing behind them, from where the south side windows would be. Within the furious and vindictive roaring, they thought they could detect Georgi Charov's lone RKZ snarling very briefly in reply. Then, only silence, an eerie stillness that seemed to reach out for the four men creeping uncomfortably through the tunnel.

"They got him," Rykov said. "He's dead."

"Until we meet again, Georgi, old friend and comrade," murmured Stephen Traikov.

CHAPTER TWO

The Death Merchant told himself that since a good part of life involved getting used to things one didn't expect—*I must be dead!* He lived by Murphy's Law and almost always got what he expected: it was usually the worst. Yet he and the other three were still ahead of the Bulgarian militia and the KDS[1].

The first section of the low tunnel ended, and the four men stepped into the underground drainage canal that was eight feet in diameter and had been constructed of stone in 1877, during the Russo-Turkish War.

"We'll get the other launcher and the four projectiles," Stephen Traikov said, his voice hollow and echoing slightly within the rounded tunnel that was completely dark, except within the area of the beam from the lantern that Rykov carried.

Rykov turned and began to play the bright white beam over the stones, many of which were covered with green slime and fungi. He had moved thirty feet to the left, the other three behind him, when he stopped in front of a stone three feet above ground level. The stone appeared to be a two-foot square, seven inches of which was protruding from the tunnel wall.

"*Dovoi, tosvarkish* Camellion. Help me pull out the stone," urged Traikov. "We must work with all possible speed. In a short while—"

He stopped and jerked his head at the sound of the terrific explosion to the east, the concussion so severe that the stones underneath the feet of the group shook slightly.

---

[1]But usually only by the letters SD.

"It would seem that some poor soul tried to open the trapdoor," Winkler said lightheartedly. "The blast must have destroyed half the house."

"Let's get on with it," Camellion said. "We're not even halfway home." He stooped, reached for one side of the stone with gloved hands, and gave Traikov a penetrating look that was lost in the shadows. "I hope the next safe house we're going to—if we get there—will be 'safer' than the one we just left. This time we're staying only a day and a night."

Not giving a reply, Traikov grunted from exertion, and gradually he and the Death Merchant worked the stone loose, pulled it from the wall, and set it in the middle of the floor that was flat.

While Rykov directed the beam inside the square cavity, Traikov reached in and pulled out an RPG launcher, two bags of 40mm. missiles, each sack containing two projectiles, and a bag of grenades.

"Dragging this launcher along was a waste of time," Winkler said argumentatively, directing his words at Camellion. "The way the damn tube was hit by slugs, I doubt if we could have used it. The missile would have blown up in our faces."

"The tube you're carrying will still work," Camellion said. "I brought it along for another purpose. You'll see why shortly. So keep that launcher with you."

Fedor Rykov voiced his thoughts. "I hope the KDS doesn't take revenge on the two sisters and their brother who has the mind of a child."

"The KDS knows they are innocent," Traikov said, picking up the sack of grenades and a bag of two missiles. "The KDS will not do more than question them. But who knows? We did what we had to do. Even the innocent must suffer in the fight for freedom."

Buffalo bull! But the Death Merchant only picked up the other sack of projectiles and the launcher tube and began walking to where the other side of the low, narrow tunnel began, on the opposite side of the stone drainage ditch.

Once they had moved thirty feet inside the tunnel and had come to an area where one side had partially caved in, so that they had to squeeze through, Camellion ordered a full stop, explaining that he was going to leave an explosive "present" for the enemy.

"Think of what you are doing," warned Traikov. "If you

are wrong and the grenade goes off . . . or even later . . . the concussion within such an enclosed space as this would kill us.''

''We could have more fun with some C-4 of a det cord,'' mused Winkler. ''Damn! I feel like an actor in a grade-B movie!''

Camellion motioned Winkler to place the launcher he was carrying on the tunnel floor, close to a pile of clay that had oozed out from the wall. Camellion next took a grenade from one of the bags and sank to his knees.

''Fedor, shine the light down here,'' he said. ''Keep the beam a bit to one side. I don't want to work in a glare.''

''Ah . . . you Americans . . . you are a strange breed,'' said Traikov. ''You fight your enemies with the vengeance of a demon from hell.''

''We're only practical,'' Winkler said. ''Some of us . . . in certain areas.''

The grenade was a Turkish KOT-M7, a frag deal amounting to a lot of ''hard'' shrapnel wrapped around eleven ounces of TNT—a five-sec delay fuse.

The Death Merchant first moved the RPG launcher slightly and scooped out a hole in the clay, using the large blade of a pocket knife. He then inserted the grenade to make sure he had made the right depth and width. Not quite. A bit more clay had to be removed from the bottom and one side. He again tried the grenade. Good. Just right. With three pairs of eyes watching him intently, Camellion pulled the pin from the KOT-M7 and, his right hand tight around the handle, placed the grenade snugly into the depression he had scooped out of the clay. Still holding down the handle, he used his left hand to position the launcher tube so that its forward muzzle end covered the handle of the Turk grenade.

''Did I ever tell you about the time I terminated a target in D.C.?'' Winkler said lackadaisically. ''I used Coca-Cola and bleach[2] . . . dumped the coke in the bleach by timing it with a candle that would burn through a string. The hit went west in his sleep.''

''I've never liked to use gas; it's too unreliable.'' Very very gently, while leaning down so that the right side of his peaked cap was almost touching the ground, Camellion re-

[2] Soft drinks contain carbonic acid. Combined with bleach, the mixture produces chlorine gas.

leased the tube. Should the launcher not keep the handle depressed, he would still have time to grab the grenade, wrap his hand around it, and, if necessary, even replace the pin.

The RPG tube did not move. The handle of the grenade did not move.

"Let's move," Camellion said, "the faster the better."

"Faster" meant that it took only nine minutes more for the tiny group to come to the end of the tunnel underneath the northeast corner of the house next door. Rykov flashed the beam of the lantern on the short flight of wooden steps.

Stephen Traikov whispered, "See the trapdoor. There are three empty oil drums in front of it on the garage floor."

"What's your overall plan for getting us onto Boulevard Septemvri Totleben?" the Death Merchant asked, an edge to his voice.

Traikov frowned slightly. "We start the van, open the garage doors, and leave. If we are followed, we can fire missiles through the rear window. It's almost eight-thirty and Boulevard Septemvri Totleben will have a lot of traffic. We will be able to lose ourselves, but only for a time. But we have six blocks to go before we switch vehicles. We have a Kolota parked at an apartment house garage on Kuskiko Street."

Fedor Rykov turned to the Death Merchant. "I suppose you have a better way." He sounded petulant.

"*Dai!* I have." The Death Merchant was just as petulant. "In the first place, we don't even know if there's another armored car or a personnel carrier blocking the west end of the alley."

"We have to assume that the alley is not blocked," Traikov said quickly. "The police do not know about this garage or the van. Why—"

"You hope!" Winkler interrupted.

"Why should they block the west end of the alley? The other personnel is at the east end because the house is there."

Rykov interjected smugly, "And if the east end is blocked, a missile or two will clear the way enough for us to get by. Now tell us that you still have a better way, American!"

"I—have—a—better—way!" The Death Merchant spoke slowly and emphasized each word. "Our only transportation is the van and we don't want to risk losing it. I'll tell you the better way. One of us will stay inside and get the van

started—if it will start! It's twenty degrees above zero, and
how long has the vehicle been sitting there?''

"We have the engine wrapped and it is full of—you Americans call it antifreeze,'' Rykov said. "The engine is special. I
tell you it will start.''

"I tell you, it had better!'' Winkler said. "We can't fly
and we're too tired to run. If that vehicle doesn't run, we're
dead—period, comma, semicolon, the works!''

"Camellion, you said that one of us would start the engine?''
Traikov said, his tone curious.

"The other three—Carey and I and one of you—will go
outside with the launcher and missiles. We'll hit the P-carrier
to the east and anything we find to the west. We escape
before the militia recovers from the blasts and confusion.''

Traikov thought for a moment. "Do the unexpected! That
is what you mean.''

"The unexpected and the practical. Hit 'em hard when they
least expect it!''

"He is right. His plan is a good one,'' agreed Rykov,
surprising both the Death Merchant and Carey Winkler. "The
militia think we are fleeing in a tunnel. They will not expect
us to suddenly rear up and bare our fangs!''

The Death Merchant pushed up the wooden trapdoor, stuck
his head through the opening, and looked around. All he could
see were the rusted sides of empty oil drums. Carefully, he
pushed the trapdoor all the way up, let it swing back, and gently
lowered it to the floor, after which he crawled the rest of the
way up the steps onto the concrete floor and, pushing off the
safety of the Uzi, looked over one fifty-gallon oil drum.

There was the blue and white van, a walk-in job, an Italian
Rimezzo that must have been new about 1970, sliding doors
on only the passenger side. The front of the vehicle and part
of both sides were covered with thick pads, so many pads—
the kind used by movers—that the covers, combined, were
almost a foot thick. Other than various kinds of junk usually
found in garages, the little wooden building was empty.

The Death Merchant leaned to one side and called down
the opening, "Come on up; it's all clear.''

In only minutes, Stephen Traikov was cutting the cords
holding the pads to the van, and Camellion, Winkler, and
Rykov were preparing to leave the garage via the side door in
the northwest corner. The Death Merchant would fire the

missiles that Winkler would carry. Rykov would "ride shotgun" with his SIG AR.

Winkler clutched at Camellion's arm. "Hold it. We should wait to see if the van starts."

"Why?" Camellion gave him a hard look. "One: Stephen will have to race the engine to warm it up. The enemy will surely hear the noise. Two: we don't have time to wait. The dynamite might have blown up half the house and filled the cellar with rubble, but who knows who might have guessed about the tunnel? Some of the NT boys might be down there right now, headed this way. Three: if the van doesn't start, we're as good as dead anyhow. On that basis, we might as well go out there right now and see what we're facing. And that's what we'll do, as soon as Stephen has the pads off the vehicle and is ready to start the engine."

"I told you both that there would not be any difficulty with the motor," Rykov insisted. "Other than the padding, there is some kind of warmer on the engine that runs off a series of batteries inside the van."

"Now he tells us!" Winkler said in disgust, swinging his head upward and smelling burning wood from the safe house.

"I did tell you that the engine would start; you should have believed me," replied Rykov angrily.

A keep-your-trap-shut look from the Death Merchant was the only reason that Winkler (who considered the revolutionaries of the NFC a "bunch of yogurt yahoos") didn't tell Rykov what he thought of him.

When Camellion saw that Traikov was about ready to get inside the van, he put his hand on the knob of the door and turned to Rykov. "You first, Fedor. You have the submachine gun."

Expecting the worst, they moved outside, the chilling wind slapping them in the face, the bright morning sun shining on the snow to the north and the south of the small building.

They looked first around the northwest corner of the garage and across the yard at what had been the safe house. The explosion in the cellar had demolished the entire southwest corner of the house; the structure appeared to have a gaping wound. Second- and third-story rooms were exposed, the splintered ends of flooring and joists stuck out hideously in wild disorder. The lower floor was burning, the flames soaring upward and creating clouds of gray-black smoke that were carried in all directions by the wind. And through the smoke,

Camellion and Rykov and Winkler could see scores of militiamen moving around helplessly in the backyard. Camellion
and his two helpers could also hear sirens to the northeast.

"Fire trucks," Rykov whispered. "Their sirens are different from police vehicles."

"The house is not worth wasting a missile on," Winkler
said to the Death Merchant, his breath turning to steam, "not
the way it's burning."

"Let's check the alley," Camellion said, "but first we'll
load the RPG—and we had better hear that engine damn
soon!" He turned the mouth of the launcher tube to Winkler,
who took one of the 40mm. projectiles from a bag and thrust
it into the mouth of the launcher. Camellion locked the
missile in the tube, then moved along the west side of the
garage to the southwest corner.

From his new position, he and the other two men could see
that the west end of the alley was not blocked by any police
vehicle.

To the east, the BTR-60 P-carrier was still parked in the
alley, directly in back of the burning house. In front of it was
a black Zil that pulled into the alley, its front end facing the
front end of the personnel carrier. Parked on Zaimov street
was a dark blue four-door Kalota, its front bumper facing the
south and only ten feet, at an angle, from the rear of the Zil.
A dozen or more militiamen were milling around the two cars
and the BTR-60. Included in the group were two KDS officers in light blue greatcoats and bright red peaked uniform
caps with ear flaps.

The Death Merchant had raised the launcher to his shoulder
and was aiming at the BTR-60, Winkler was pulling out
another projectile, and Rykov was watching their rear and the
alley to the west when Stephen Traikov started the engine of
the Rimezzo van and began to race the engine. Immediately
the militiamen around the two cars and the BTR-60, as well
as police in the backyard, jerked their heads toward the
sound. It was too late. The Death Merchant pulled the trigger
and the personnel carrier exploded into torrents of flame,
much of the armored steel turning into blobs and balls of
burning metal that were thrown outward and up to the wide-
open sky as the BTR-60 dissolved into twisted, burning junk.
Seven militiamen were killed outright by the blast—by concussion and flying metal—three of them picked up by the
terrific pressure and thrown twenty feet, like dead leaves in a

high wind. What was left of the personnel carrier began to burn, the black oily smoke teased by the wind.

The only thing that had saved Captain Peturi Riskilin was that he had been standing to the rear of the Kalota on Zaimov Street, getting a report on the explosion in the cellar from Leiutenant Johan Bisru of the *Nersko-Tsopska,* when the missile destroyed the personnel carrier. Concussion knocked the two men to the ground, but they were only stunned.

By the time the fuel tank of the BTR-60 exploded—ten seconds after the explosion—Winkler had shoved another missile into the launcher tube, Camellion was sighting in on the Zil, and Rykov had raced back to the northwest corner of the garage to waste any militiamen who might come across the yard to the north of the garage. Inside the garage, Traikov had removed the wooden two-by-four from the doors and was preparing to push them outward toward the alley.

"To the west!" Winkler had warned Camellion in the nick of time, before the Death Merchant could pull the trigger. The launcher still on his shoulder, Camellion swung around very fast and saw that another BTR-60 was coming down the alley, a militiaman hurriedly fastening a SGMB light machine gun to a mount in front of the top hatch. He never completed the task.

The 40mm. projectile hit, exploded, and turned the personnnel carrier into an instant hell on earth, the concussion alone killing all the occupants, the jagged chunks and sharp pieces of metal of the ripped-apart vehicle butchering the corpses. The stench of burnt flesh and burnt metal and what was left of the blackened corpses, with their charred death's-head grin, was already drifting to Camellion and Winkler by the time Winkler was thrusting a third missile into the RPG tube and Stephen Traikov was pushing open the garage doors. From the northwest corner of the garage, Rykov had killed three militiamen who had tried to come across the yard. He was getting worried; he had only one magazine left, plus a Walther P-38 automatic.

There was screaming from the east, from the area of the alley where the other BTR-60 carrier had been destroyed, the cries of the wounded a nightmarish cacophony. On man was slumped against the Zil, its glass blown out by the explosion, his left arm hanging in shreds from his shoulder. Six other men had broken bones and others were wounded. One had been blinded by flying metal. Another had part of his intestines hanging out.

The remaining junk in the west end of the alley had to be cleared away so the van could get through. Camellion moved the optical sight to what was left of the carrier—the frame, side metal, and three wheels—and fired. Another big blast, and when the smoke and fire cleared, the rest of the junk was gone and there was only a large depression in the oil and blood stained snow.

The blue and white van leaped from the garage, Traikov braking expertly, without spinning the tires, to let Camellion, who yelled at Fedor Rykov, and Winkler get aboard. Then Rykov was scrambling into the van, almost falling to the rear as Traikov, sitting grimly in the high driver's seat, gave the van the gas and began turning the steering wheel to his right.

"Watch that spot in the alley," yelled Camellion, the momentum of the vehicle shoving him to the rear. "You'll have to center the van over it."

Traikov did just that, the boxlike vehicle racing over the small crater, the wide tires crunching over assorted small wreckage and a gloved severed hand, mashing the mess into the hard-packed snow.

In the back of the van, Camellion, Winkler, and Rykov were doing their best to keep their shins from being banged by seventeen deep-cycle 25-volt, 75-amp batteries, which, with relay isolators, had been used to keep the coils around the engine warm and which Traikov had not taken time to throw out. The batteries kept sliding around the wooden floor while Camellion and Winkler loaded the launcher tube with the last 40mm. projectile. All the batteries slid to the left when Traikov left the alley and turned onto Way Felszarut, a two-lane street that led to the wide, well-traveled Boulevard Septemvri Totleben.

At the rear window, Camellion stared toward Kirili Avenue. No police cars were following. *We might still make it to Septemvri Totleben!*

Five minutes later they did.

Now the van was only six blocks from the apartment complex on Kuskiko Street and the first switch-over car.

But we're still a thousand miles from the targets!

Those targets were the file-room section of the *Komitet Darzhavna Sigurnost* and the five Soviet "Uncles." The file section and the five Russians were the goals of the mission that had begun five weeks ago, after the Death Merchant had completed a job in West Germany.[3] From London, Camellion had flown to Madrid, then on to Rome, where, in Vatican City, he had met Carey Winkler and two briefing officers of the Central Intelligence Agency.

Target nation: *Narodna Republika Bulgaria*—Bulgaria, in the Eastern Bloc. The actual targets themselves were not only the file rooms of the DS but also the five Soviet advisers who actually controlled the DS through Colonel General Grigor Shopov,[4] the first deputy minister of internal affairs and, ostensibly, the boss of the secret police.

The reason for the termination (with extreme prejudice) of the five Soviet experts was simple: the CIA intended to teach the Bulgarians and the Russians a lesson they would remember well into the next century, and not because of the attempted hit on Pope John Paul II. The reasons were more pragmatic.

Over 50 percent of the heroin consumed in Europe and much of that in the United States first flowed across the borders of Bulgaria[5], the drugs coming originally from Turkey and from gun-hungry Middle East nations such as Iran, Iraq, Lebanon, and the Soviet front organization, the PLO, and other dangerous terrorist groups—and all of it done with the full knowledge and the direct participation of the Bulgarian government, which paid for the drugs with Warsaw Pact weaponry. Through KINTEX, the Bulgarians distributed the heroin that found its way to Paris, West Berlin, Rome, Madrid, and other cities in Europe, and to London and other metropolitan areas in Great Britain. There was the "Sicilian Connection" by which H found its way to the United States and was distributed by several Mafia families in New York City.

On the surface, KINTEX was a Bulgarian state enterprise whose official role was the generation of badly needed foreign exchange through the import and export of commercial items and products. The real business of KINTEX was smuggling—cigarettes and booze to Italy and Turkey; weapons of all kinds to the Middle East and to Soviet-supported insurgencies in Africa.

KINTEX was bossed by and staffed with DS officers.

---

[3] See *Death Merchant #60: The Methuselah Factor.*
[4] This is the real name of the Bulgarian slop-face who runs the DS.
[5] This is fact.

"The first hard facts came out of Bulgaria thirteen to fourteen years ago," Jason Mark Adams, one of the Company men, had explained to the Death Merchant in Rome. He went on to say that this came about when, on February 10, 1971, Colonel Stefan Sverdlev, an official in the DS, slipped across the Bistritza River, in southern Bulgarian, into Greece, taking with him his wife, two children, and 496 sensitive documents from the DS's most sensitive files.

William Boslough, the other Company man who was also traveling under the cover of a free-lance journalist, explained that "back in those days the Greeks weren't too fond of our Uncle. It wasn't until 1974 that we learned about the documents, in particular document coded M-120/00-0050."[6]

The subjects of this document was the destabilization of a "corrupt" Western society by means of two methods: 1) Groups, affiliated with organized religion, that would "promote and work for World Peace"; 2) The use of hard drugs, especially heroin, in Europe and in the United States.

Bulgaria, which is about the size of Tennessee, was chosen because the majority of all land-transported goods shipped between Europe and the Middle East passed through the nation. Bulgaria is strategically located in the Balkans to oversee the flow of contraband: drugs *from* the Middle East, and weapons *to* the Middle East. The setup was perfect for the Russians, if for no other reason than that Bulgaria was the most trusted of all Moscow's stooge nations,[7] even the Bulgarian man on the street having a fond affection for the uncivilized trash born of the whore that was "Mother Russia." Accordingly, Soviet KGB officers were staffed in all DS directorates, especially the first directorate: intelligence and counterintelligence.

"That's where KINTEX comes in," Jason Adams had said. "For all practical purposes, the DS, the KGB, and KINTEX are one and the same."

Adams had then said that the director general of KINTEX was Radoslav Todorov, an official high in the Bulgarian Communist Party's Central Committee. The chief of contraband operations was a high-ranking DS officer named Ridan Terziev.[8] It was Colonel Terziev's deputy who handled

---

[6] This is fact.

[7] So much so that Bulgaria is called the "sixteenth Republic" of the Soviet Union.

[8] Although this book is pure fiction, Todorov and Terziev are real.

the direct buying and selling of the heroin or morphine base.

"One can see Terziev and his deputies lounging about in the lobbies of Sofia's best hotels," Bill Boslough had said. "That's where they meet and confer with international drug traffickers. Hell, it's like a regular bazaar. The way KINTEX works it is that it permits selected smugglers to purchase heroin and morphine base that has been supposedly destroyed by custom officials—after being seized from smugglers who did not have an 'arrangement' with KINTEX. If supplies run low, KINTEX obtains the drug from a state-owned pharmaceutical factory. As we understand it from DEA, most of the H produced at this factory is sold to Arab scum based in Sofia."

The second method employed by KINTEX was only good business: it exchanged drugs from the Middle East for weapons—all the way from AKM assault rifles to RPG-7 rocket launchers to trucks and Soviet ZSU-23 anti-aircraft guns.

Boslough had said, "We learned that by late 1982, KINTEX had narrowed the field of preferred customers to some twenty-five international drug traffickers. Most of them were Turks, but two were Sicilians. The Mafia buys big for import into the States. Two of the biggest Turks still in business are Bekir Celenk[9] and Melih Demirbulak. Another biggie is Sallah Wakkas, a Syrian."

"How does the U.S. Drug Enforcement Administration fit into this?" the Death Merchant had asked.

"The DEA has been very effective, considering that it has so much to do and lacks manpower, thanks to a stupid Congress.[10] Back in eighty-three, working with the Italians, the DEA helped smash Wakkas's ring in Italy. The son of a bitch was supplying more than half of all the 'horse' imported into the States. When things got hot, he fled to Bulgaria."

"Let's get down to the mission," Camellion had said, "down to the nitty gritty without any dialectical nonsense— and if Turkish intelligence is involved in any way, count me

[9] Agca named Celenk as the man who offered him a million dollars to kill John Paul II. After Celenk's exposure, Bulgaria "detained him for investigation." He is living like a king under the protection of the DS.

[10] Readers are advised to read *Death Merchant #69: Operation Nose-Candy*, to be published in the future.

out. Turkish intelligence is riddled with KGB officers and informers.''

Adams and Boslough had been greatly surprised. ''What makes you think that the Turks might be in on this 'termination for effective policy operation'?'' Adams had asked.

''I know about the trouble that KINTEX has caused the Turkish government,''[11] Camellion had said, thinking, *Because I have good friends in England.*[12] ''How I know is not important. But I do insist that the Turks be left out of the operation.''

''Only the *Narodno Gorsiku Rakigladenov,* the Bulgarian National Freedom Council, will be assisting you and Mr. Winkler. The NFC—or the NGR—whichever you prefer—is the only organized and effective underground anti-Communist force in Bulgaria. We have arranged to have members of the NGR meet you and Winkler at the Greek-Bulgarian border and smuggle you to Sofia, then back to the border after your task has been completed.''

And the CIA, operating from the United States Embassy in Sofia? The Company network would give all the help it could, which would be very little. Day and night, the DS/KGB kept a constant watch on the U.S. Embassy compound on 1 Boulevard Stamboliisky—front and back entrances—photographing every person who entered and who left the embassy. Nonetheless, the CIA station at the embassy did have its methods, its ways of making contact with the National Freedom Council and with intelligence agents from other nations in the West.

The Death Merchant had reminded the two CIA ''carriers of secrets'' that ''the Company is expecting me to accomplish the impossible. Assassinating the top five Soviet advisers, all at one time, is a tall order that borders on the ridiculous. Destroying the DS file section is total stupidity.''

''We agree,'' Bill Boslough had agreed with a good deal of smugness. ''Many of us feel that the operation is pure suicide. However, Mrs. Goldblum maintains that you're a kind of miracle man who can get the job done—and she ordered

---

[11] Between 1968 and 1972, it is estimated that from 70,000 to 80,000 weapons, purchased with narcotics, were smuggled into Turkey—the vast majority via Bulgaria and KINTEX.

[12] The Death Merchant is thinking of *Intelligence Digest,* probably the best intelligence newsletter in the world. It is published by Intelligence International Limited— 17 Rodney Road, Cheltenham, Glos, GL50 1HX England.

us to inform you that you will receive double your usual commission.''

"We do have the names and the photographs of the five Soviet Uncles,'' Jason Adams had offered. "Frankly, I think you'll be courting death in the worst way. We shall also supply you and Winkler with the proper pills which would assist you in terminating your own existence. . . .''

Contemplating his meeting with Adams and Boslough, the Death Merchant thought how all governments insisted on a language rule. Not once had Adams and Boslough used the words "kill,'' "murder,'' or "assassination.'' Career Company men wouldn't dream of calling a spade a spade. Killing the five Soviet advisers was "termination for effective policy operation.'' Nor would anyone dare say Courtland Grojean! Horrors! The language rule demanded a code name, and so Courtland Grojean, on this mission, had become a Jewish mother! Camellion smiled ever so slightly. Adams could have said, "L pills so that you and Winkler can commit suicide.'' Instead there had been "proper pills'' and "terminating your own existence!''

Piss on pyroclastics! The CIA is as bad as the Nazis[13] were in regard to the stupid language rule! Even the phrase itself is a code name that means what in ordinary language would be called a lie.

He stared through the dirty window of the van's rear door, his cold eyes on the other cars on Septemvri Totleben—people going to work—and there were trucks, mainly trucks of SOMAT, Bulgaria's own state trucking firm. SOMAT operated a fleet estimated at over 5,000 vehicles. SOMAT was also helping in the transportation and/or the smuggling of drugs and other illegal goods.

Thinking about it filled the Death Merchant with rage. *Those idiots in the United States. The lunatics have partially taken over the funny farm! Which proves how "intelligent" those idiots from Yale and Harvard are!*

Until September 14, 1983, the CIA, through a series of dummy companies and via a West German broker, had pur-

---

[13] The Nazis never used such bald words as "extermination," "killing," or "liquidation." Language rule demanded code names—*Final Solution, Special Treatment, Evacuation, Deportation, Change of Residence,* and *Resettlement* were other common words demanded by the Nazi *Sprachregelung,* the Nazi language rule. Another favorite was *Arbeitseinsatz im Osten*—"labor in the East."

chased millions of dollars of Eastern Bloc weapons to equip anti-Sandinista guerrillas in Nicaragua.

The weapons had been supplied by KINTEX.

The millions of dollars had gone to KINTEX.

Fedor Rykov said to Camellion and Carey Winkler. "We are almost to the Chuminka apartment complex. Another half block and Stephen will turn off on Pazardzhik Kardinskzo."

In the semidarkness of the van, Rykov was loading five Soviet 9mm. Vitmorkin machine pistols that had been in a suitcase tied inside the vehicle. Busy with his work, he did not see the look of pessimism given him by Winkler.

"Uh huh, and how long will it take us to get to the getaway car?"

"Only five minutes. All we have to do is go into the garage on the lower level." Rykov shoved a full magazine into the third Vitmorkin.

The Death Merchant continued to watch the traffic through the window. He despised the Russians, whom he considered lower than sick cockroaches. He had even a lower opinion of the Bulgarians. They were not even filth. Camellion told himself he was going to take great delight in blowing up the DS file section and killing the five main Soviet advisers—and more!

Whatever pig gods you Russians and Bulgarians pray to, you had better get down on your knees. I am going to destroy the entire DS headquarters building!

Camellion had only one other major ambition, one that took precedence even over his own life: to live long enough to see the entire Soviet Union, all of Red China, and the rest of the filth nations turned into a radioactive wasteland.

I want to see three and a half billion ghosts on this little cinder of a planet. And I will—as one of the ghosts—in less than thirteen years. . . .

CHAPTER THREE

In a quiet neighborhood in north Sofia, the building at 66 Boulevard Anton Ivanova was ultra-modern, all white stone and smoked glass. There wasn't anything sinister about the six-story structure, nor the nine-foot decorative barrier surrounding the building and the grounds. There was, however, something vaguely menacing about the two guards behind the double gate. Night and day the gates were guarded by two men in blue uniforms, with white stripes on their trousers, green shoulder boards, and red peaked caps.[1]

People passing on the sidewalk of Boulevard Anton Ivanova didn't even glance at the guards or the building. They often quickened their pace, for this was the headquarters of the Bulgarian State Security apparatus, the *Komitet Darzhavna Sigurnost*. The dreaded DS.

That something of importance was connected with the building was obvious to even the most innocent tourist. Not frequently, passers-by could hear the faint roaring of automatic weapons beneath their feet, from the underground range where KINTEX clients were testing Soviet and Warsaw Pact weapons. Then there were the long black Zils, other cars, and prisoner vans that were constantly coming and going through the gates. Another sign was the helicopter pad on the roof, on or from which coppers would land or take off. On the other side of the roof, across from the pad, were the series of mirrors, arranged on triangular frames, of the heliostat light-

[1] The Bulgarian national colors are white, green, and red—three horizontal strips is the flag.

ing system. Daylight penetrates to only twenty-five feet in a building. Lighting the rest of the floor space produces so much heat that air conditioners must be used to cool skyscrapers even in winter. To "pipe in" more sunlight, Bulgarian engineers had used a heliostat—aluminum mirrors placed on the roof. Some of the mirrors moved and followed the sun's path across the sky, reflecting sunlight onto fixed mirrors, which, via a periscope arrangement, shot the strong beam of light down a shaft that passed through the center of each floor. Each fifteen-square-foot polished aluminum mirror lighted up 1,500 square feet of floor space—when the sun was shining.[2]

It was the rotor noise from the helicopters, taking off and landing, that bothered Colonel General Grigor Shopov, the director of DS, even though the irritating sounds from the eggbeaters were infrequent and minimal in his fifth-floor office in the northwest corner of the DS building, overlooking the Ion Mincu, the wide road that led to Sofia Airport.

At the moment, Shopov was not concerned with noise. He was listening intently to Lieutenant General Frein Cherfesky, who, as the senior Soviet adviser, was talking about the disaster that had occurred that very morning.

Comrade Cherfesky was saying, "I feel that the American CIA is supplying the terrorists with weapons, or else those murderers of the *Narodno Gorsiku Rakigladenov* stole them from some army unit inside Bulgaria. What distresses me is the efficiency with which the terrorists destroyed the armored car, the two personnel carriers, murdered a score of militiamen, and then escaped so very easily." His weak eyes drifted to Major Ivan Mikolov, the boss of the DS's Third Directorate, of which the *Subranie-Kozivcho*, or border guards, and the *Nersko-Tsopska*, the militia, were sections. Therefore, the militia was the responsibility of Major Ivan Mikolov, who, sitting to the left of Cherfesky, was between Major Stanko Divuncha and Colonel Georgi Kraisin.

A tough man, physically and mentally, Mikolov didn't flinch as he turned to Cherfesky, who had weak eyes, thinning brown hair, and had been a close personal friend of Andropov before the death of the Soviet leader. Like the three

---

[2] This is why smoke smudge from torches has never been found deep within the Egyptian pyramids. The builders used polished bronze shields to reflect sunlight deep into the recesses of the tombs.

other Soviet advisers at the highly polished conference table, Comrade Cherfesky was dressed in civilian clothes.

"I placed Captain Riskilin in charge of raiding the house. He's an excellent officer," Mikolov said firmly. "It was I and Comrade Riskilin who planned the attack on the house, in accordance with the information we received from a member of the terrorist NGR. This—"

"You are referring to Verdo Yydasgrei," inserted Colonel Mikhail Isakov, another Soviet adviser.

"That is correct, Comrade Isakov," answered Mikolov. "We are holding his mother and father, and his sister. We made it clear to the swine and traitor Yydasgrei that they would spend long years in Darvo if he didn't cooperate with us. It was Comrade Colonel Kraisin's counterintelligence department who 'turned' the traitor."

"It was a week ago that we got the last report from Yydasgrei," declared Colonel Georgi Kraisin, who was chief of the DS's First Directorate. A small man, his uniform was very neat, and one got the impression he was a precise, meticulous individual in his personal habits. "A week ago he did manage to leave us a report at a 'drop.' His report didn't mention Traikov and his cell having rocket launchers. At the time, he was a member of another group of terrorists and hadn't made contact with Traikov's cell. No doubt the rocket launchers and the missiles were already hidden in the old mansion that Traikov used as a layover station. I do not feel that the failure is the fault of either Comrade Major Mikolov or Comrade Captain Riskilin. And of course Comrade Riskilin had no way of knowing about the cleverly built tunnel and the vehicle hidden in the garage next door. The cold truth is that the revolutionaries outsmarted us."

"I never said that either Major Mikolov or Captain Riskilin was responsible," Lieutenant General Cherfesky said mildly. "If anyone is to blame, it's the two CIA agents that were smuggled into the country. More importantly, the fact that the rebels succeeded in getting the two CIA people to the capital reveals that the NGR is better organized than we previously estimated. What we must concern ourselves with now is intensifying our search for the two American agents and the leaders of the NGR. Once we have the two Americans in custody, we'll know why they came to Bulgaria. Traikov will be able to give us the names of the two other leaders of the NGR."

Colonel Evgeny Tovma, a KGB specialist in "Extreme Action to Demoralize Populations"—terrorism—folded his big hands on the green cloth of the table. "Comrade Major Mikolov, how did your people manage to get the tracker transmitter to the traitor Verdo Yydasgrei. It is my understanding that the *Nersko-Tsopska* were able to find the mansion on Kirili because of the device."

It was Colonel Georgi Kraisin who answered. "Yydasgrei picked up the transmitter at the drop when he left his report. My department attended to that part of the operation. We instructed Yydasgrei not to turn on the transmitter until he was with Traikov's group and was actually in the house. The transmitter only had a battery life of nine hours and a range of only half a kilometer. My people worked frantically to triangulate the spaced signals. They had to drive all over the city and its suburbs. But they succeeded within four hours that first day."

Inwardly, Colonel General Grigor Shopov winced. That idiot Kraisin should have kept his mouth shut! But did it really matter? No, it did not. The KGB had its own picked and loyal informers within all the Directorates of the DS. Shopov was almost certain that the five phones in his office were tapped as well as his personal phone at home.

Colonel Tovma drew back in surprise. "That first day!" He turned his head and gave Comrade Cherfesky a quick glance, then turned back to Colonel Georgi Kraisin. "Do you mean that the militia didn't close in immediately?"

"How long did the *Nersko-Tsopska* wait?" asked Lieutenant General Cherfesky, frowning.

"It was I who ordered Comrade Major Mikolov to wait," said Colonel General Shopov from the head of the table. "After he reported to me that Traikov and his group, and the two CIA agents with them, had been pinpointed in the mansion, I ordered him to have Captain Riskilin wait. I wanted to see if any more *Narodno Gorsiku Rakigladenov* scum would put in an appearance. The NT had the house surrounded on all sides. At the time, we didn't know about the escape tunnel to the garage next door."

"How long did you wait, Comrade Shopov?" asked Cherfesky.

"The rebels were there an afternoon and a night and all the next day. No one else arrived. I ordered Mikolov to have

Riskilin close in this morning. You Comrades know the rest. . . ."

Shopov, who would have resembled a rawboned, wind-kissed farmer if he had been an American, was not fooled by Cherfesky's amiable manner. The senior KGB official was a son of a bitch who would have gladly sent his own wife and children to prison if he could have benefited from it. An organization man, that was Cherfesky, and a details and disinformation expert. He was not, however, the most intelligent of the five advisers.

Lighting a cigarette to cover his scrutiny of the three Russians from the corner of his eyes, Shopov did some thinking. The lean, sleepy-eyed Colonel Mikhail Isakov was the watchdog of KINTEX. It was Isakov who kept track of every single weapon, every carton of cigarettes, every ounce of perfume, every gram of heroin and heroin base. It was Isakov who gave orders to Radoslav Todorov, the director general of KINTEX, and to Ridan Terziev, the DS contact man of KINTEX.

No . . . Isakov was not dangerous to Shopov. He didn't have any imagination and was not subtle like the Machiavellian Lieutenant General Cherfesky. But he was a master salesman with a genius for wheeling and dealing.

Then there was Colonel Evgeny Tovma, as tanned and healthy looking as an athlete and whose face did not reveal his love of hard liquor and other men's wives. Nor was he dangerous. His imagination expressed itself only in new methods of violence.

Farthest from Shopov and closest to Comrade Cherfesky was the overweight Colonel Anatoly Tretyakov, the political theorist, who made weekly reports to *Moscova* on the loyalty of the Bulgarian Communist Party. He was not a threat either. He and his *Sluzhba* Political Service boys were too busy watching the members of the Bulgarian politburo and the National Assembly.

The most intelligent of the five advisers was not even present in the special meeting room. Colonel Josef Gavva had flown to Moscova to give the quarterly report to the head office of the KGB. A psychiatrist who was a behavorial specialist, Dr. Gavva had a mind that was almost a window into the future. He had accurately predicted the American action in the Caribbean and had been 100 percent against the operation to terminate Pope John Paul II, maintaining it was too daring, too prone to failure, and that using Bekir Celenk as a contact man was sheer stupidity.

It was Dr. Gavva who was convinced that, because of KINTEX, the Americans would take some kind of harsh measures against the DS and the KGB in Bulgaria.

Dai . . . Comrade Dr. Gavva was a very intelligent man. It was the meek-looking, stooped-over Gavva who had used hypnotism on Bulgarian prisoners at Darvo, the main Bulgarian prison for political dissidents, to drive the subjects into insanity, achieving this by telling the hypnotized subjects they had no *past* and did not have a *future*. When they awoke, with the posthypnotic suggestions deeply implanted in their minds, the victims were in a psychological time warp. Being robbed of a past brought on a semi-infantile, torpid state. Being robbed of a future, the subjects lost their sense of identity. Some lost their power of speech and became completely infantile. The methodical Gavva then proceeded to tell the subject they had no *present*. Stopping subjective time altogether produced an eerie sensation of being trapped between life and death. The subjects knew they were not dead. Neither were they completely ''alive.'' A few became raving lunatics; the majority became catatonic.

Dr. Gavva deemed the experiments a success. He reported to the Moscova Neuropsychiatric Institute that his experiment ''proves that time is a prime factor in the control of the individual,'' whom he referred to as ''a tiny cog in the machinery of the masses.''

What worried Grigor Shopov was Gavva's conviction that the United States would eventually take firm executive action against KINTEX. His analysis was logical. Four different times the United States had warned the Bulgarian government about KINTEX's smuggling heroin and morphine base into Europe. The diplomatic message was extremely strong in regard to KINTEX's dealing with Sicilian hoodlums.

''Eventually, the United States is going to take strong action,'' predicted Dr. Gavva. ''Their reelected president is not a timid Carter or a naive Ford. As they say in the American West: he shoots from the hip and knows that sometimes force is the only solution to a vexing problem.''

The other four advisers had not agreed with Dr. Gavva. They were convinced that there wasn't anything the Americans could do.

''President Reagan is a violent man,'' Comrade Cherfesky

had said. "But he is not a fool. He knows he can get away with military action in his section of the world, but Europe is quite a different matter. What did he do when we shot down the Korean airliner? Nothing! He only condemned the action as barbaric! What do we care about insults, mere words uttered by a *chernozhokski*. That's one of the major difficulties with democracy. It limits firm action. It is the creed of fools who will consider a hundred viewpoints and try to satisfy them all."

Moscova had not agreed with Dr. Gavva, who, in a report, had written that "CIA action of some nature could be directed against the Bulgarian ports of Varna and Burgas. We must assume that the American Central Intelligence Agency is aware that KINTEX is using these ports on the Black Sea for the exportation of products."

The possibility that Dr. Gavva might be right worried Shopov. Should any catastrophe occur, should the CIA succeed in doing harm to KINTEX and/or the DS and/or the KGB . . . as head of the DS, he would get the blame. To satisfy the excuse makers and the bureaucracy, some high head would have to roll from the neck supporting it and that head would be his.

Lieutenant General Comrade Cherfesky was saying in a grandfatherly tone, "Holding Comrade Mikolov and Comrade Riskilin in check was an honest mistake, Comrade Shopov." He smiled ever so slightly and inclined his head toward Colonel Georgi Kraisin. "However, I do feel that the First Directorate could have done its homework better. If DS counterintelligence had been on the alert, it might have learned about the escape tunnel and the vehicle in the garage next door."

Colonel Kraisin's reply was prompt, his voice as steady as his dark eyes. "There is a lot of truth in what you say, Comrade Cherfesky. We should have done better, and your own people, monitoring our progress, working with us—they should have been more efficient. In my opinion, the KGB, as well as the DS, failed to fully comprehend the true situation."

Not a single wrinkle changed in Cherfesky's face, and he maintained his expression of fatherly concern. Not the least bit frustrated in his cunning attempt to discredit the DS, Cherfesky took another tack. "Comrade Kraisin, you're forgetting that the KGB only advises," he said gently, "and is subservient to the DS. After all, we Soviets are only guests in your splendid nation!'' He spread his hands in a conciliatory gesture. ''Of course, you understand that . . . .''

Colonel Georgi Kraisin retained his composure in spite of Cherfesky's outrageous lie, one that was an insult to the intelligence of the four Bulgarians at the table. Above all others, they knew that the Soviet KGB controlled the DS, just as the KGB was boss of Fidel Castro's DGI. Cherfesky's brazen lie only proved the arrogance of Russians in general and the five advisers—who were ''guests!''—in particular.

''My memory is excellent, Comrade Cherfesky,'' Colonel Kraisin said agreeably. ''By no means have I forgotten that you and the other advisers are guests in our nation—and we are most grateful for your advice and the help and encouragement of the Soviet people. Apparently, it is your memory that is at fault, in that you have failed to remember that the KGB gave a rating of excellence to the DS in its last quarterly report. As I recall, Comrade Cherfesky, you even referred to the speed and efficiency with which the DS smashed the plot by Greek smugglers to secretly export heroin and weapons across the border.''

''I recall your even mentioning the resourcefulness of Comrade Mikolov's *Subranie-Kozivcho*,'' Major Stanko Divuncha, the chief of the DS's Third Directorate, mentioned casually.

It was Colonel Anatoly Tretyakov who saved Lieutenant General Frein Cherfesky from having the Bulgarians defeat him at his own game.

''Comrades, Comrades . . . let us profit from the mistakes of the past,'' he said cheerfully, his double chins shaking. ''The logical course now is to intensify our search for the traitor Stephen Traikov and the two American agents.''

Secretly pleased with Kraisin and Divuncha, Colonel General Shopov nodded in the Western manner[3] and said with exaggerated seriousness, ''Comrade Colonel Tretyakov is right. We can't undo what happened this morning. We can, however, use all our resources to capture Traikov and learn from him the identity of the other two leaders of the *Narodno Gorsiku Rakigladenov*. In theory, once we find the traitor Traikov, we'll find the American agents.''

''They are most probably non-Americans, or at least they

---

[3]When a Bulgarian nods his head up and down, he is saying no. It is when he shakes head *horizontally* that he is saying yes.

will not be career CIA personnel,'' announced Colonel Evgeny Tovma. "Professional CIA agents would not be involved directly in such a very dangerous undertaking. The two agents are surrogates—'contract agents,' or 'independent operators,' as the Americans call such brutal mercenaries.''

"That's reasonable," agreed Major Mikolov. "Good desk people always do poorly in the field, and often substitutes perform poorly—for instance, the Cubans in Africa."

"And I say another thing," Tovma went on, ignoring Mikolov's sly insult. "One of those independent operators, or contractors, will be that *ne kul'turno*[4] butcher, the *Cempt Tobtocpam*!''

At Tovma's mention of the dreaded name, the other men at the table stared at him. Instantly, they deduced that he almost certainly was correct. The American CIA would send the best, the deadliest man available. That man would be—the Death Merchant!

"I hope you are wrong, Comrade Tovma," Shopov said, keeping the uneasiness out of his voice. "I suggest we put the problem into its proper frame of reference. The Death Merchant is only one man, and I for one believe that most of his exploits are nothing more than CIA exaggerations. On the other hand, if one of the agents is that murderous maniac, the Death Merchant, think of what a blow it would be to the CIA if and when we capture him and put him on trial! Why there are all sorts of possibilities.''

Colonel Isakov mused aloud: "With Dr. Gavva's expertise in mental conditioning, it is possible that he could force the Death Merchant to confess that it was the CIA that tried to kill that *chernozhokski* Pope John Paul Two! That, Comrades, is something to think about.'' He stabbed his finger toward Colonel General Shopov, poking holes in the air. "First we have to capture the son of a bitch—provided one of the agents is the *Cempt Tobtocpam!* We don't know that one of them is he.''

"Who else?" insisted Tovma, swinging his gaze toward Isakov. "You know as well as I that the CIA would send the best its money could buy.''

Cherfesky's watery eyes mirrored disapproval. "Comrades, you cannot have the skin twice from the same bull! What we are doing is assuming that one of the agents is the Death

---

[4] Translated it means "uncultured."

Merchant and that the two came to Bulgaria to perform some great mission. Come now! All of you are thinking of Comrade Gavva's theory about CIA retaliation! Am I not correct?"

The four Bulgarians did not answer.

"He's been right too often to have made only lucky guesses," Colonel Isakov finally said, looking at Cherfesky. "In this case, I believe Comrade Gavva might be correct. After all, the Americans do know that KINTEX is responsible for a good deal of the heroin that comes into their country. Sooner or later they have to take action or lose their credibility."

Cherfesky shook his head, with a smile of superior amusement.

"You'll be telling me next that Comrade Gavva is psychic. Or perhaps he had a telephone line directly to God, like the Polish pope!"

Isakov hunched a shoulder. "My only concern is KINTEX. What Comrade Gavva said makes sense. The ports of Burgas and Varna are vulnerable; and since our vessels an only leave the Black Sea by passing through the Bosporus, that makes KINTEX all the more assailable."

"The CIA isn't working with Turkish intelligence in that direction, or we'd know it," Cherfesky said smugly.

Colonel Tovma came directly to the point. "We can't ignore the possibility that the two American agents have come to our country on some mission involving KINTEX. Whether the Death Merchant is one of them is a moot question. Frankly, I think it's irrelevant. Comrade Shopov has placed him in the proper frame of reference. He is, after all, only one man."

"I didn't say we would close our eyes completely to the possibility of American action against KINTEX," Cherfesky said carefully, slightly annoyed. "But to talk of capturing the *Cempt Tobtocpam* at this point, to speculate about making him confess to anything—all of it is premature." He directed his attention to Shopov. "Comrade Shopov, since the debacle this morning, what steps has the DS taken to ensure the capture of Traikov and the two Americans?"

"We have intensified our efforts in all areas," Shopov said evenly. "We did find the vehicle the survivors escaped in. We assume the terrorists had an entire series of cars to effect a rapid escape. We know that none of the dead terrorists were Traikov or the Americans. Their fingerprints were on file.

Two were known political traitors. I assure you, Comrade Cherfesky, the DS is doing all that can be done.''

"I have also doubled the border guards along the Bistritza River and in the Rhodope Mountains," reported Major Mikolov. "But it is difficult. At this time of year, the mountains are a frigid hell, and we are having an exceptionally cold winter. The *Subranie-Kozivcho* not only has to contend with Greek bandits and our own mountain people—and they hate us—but the weather as well."

Colonel Kraisin took a long cigarette from a red and white package and held it loosely in his fingers. "The people in the rest of the country are not too fond of us, especially here in Sofia."

"In spite of our propaganda," tacked on Major Stanko Divuncha. "Part of it is the Americans and their damned missiles in West Germany. The people are afraid of nuclear war and they blame us." He glanced at Cherfesky. "And you Russians."

"It's the attitude of the general populace that makes any investigation difficult," said Kraisin.

Cherfesky's eyes narrowed. "Surely, Comrade, you are not suggesting that the majority of people is disloyal to the state?"

"The DS counterintelligence department does not conduct polls," sighed Kraisin. "We are confident that the majority of people is not disloyal to the state. We also feel that while most people will not actively give aid to the terrorists, a large number will look the other way and conveniently have failed memories when they witness anything that could be of value to us. This morning was a good example."

Cherfesky inclined his head toward Kraisin. "The two sisters and their brother who lived next door—you're referring to them?"

"Those three should have been taken into custody and subjected to intense interrogation," intoned Colonel Tretyakov. "They can't be considered politically reliable."

Irritated, Kraisin stared intently at Colonel Tretyakov. "Those two old women and their brother were innocent. They were duped, used by Traikov and his murderous cutthroats. To have arrested them would have been counterproductive. With citizens looking on after the battle, what would they have thought if they had seen Captain Riskilin arresting two women in their seventies and their baby brother—feeble-minded and in his sixties?''

"Age does not matter when it comes to the security of the state," insisted Tretyakov. "The masses must always be aware that the state has full authority over their lives—for their benefit."

Kraisin turned away from Tretyakov. The Russian fat-ass gave new meaning to the word "pig."

Major Divuncha said with a straight face, "If we arrested every person suspected of being politically unreliable, we'd have to build a wall around the entire country."

"About this morning, Comrade Kraisin," said Cherfesky, ignoring Divuncha's remark.

Colonel Kraisin closed his cigarette lighter and blew out a cloud of smoke. "The van was parked to the rear of a state apartment house. We did find three eyewitnesses who saw four men leave the vehicle and go into the apartment house. We accounted for all the identities of the residents; we know that Traikov was not one of them. We think that he and the other three—two of them were probably the American CIA mercenaries—had a car in the garage of the apartment house. The paradox is that the garage attendant on duty is positive that there were no strange vehicles in the garage. He showed us the record book and explained the system in use, proving to us that it would have been impossible for a car to have been in the garage if it didn't belong there. The attendant could account for the two hundred and twenty-one cars that are normally parked there, all, except four, parked during the night."

Cherfesky sat up straight, surprise dropping over his face. "Two hundred and twenty-one cars? In the garage of one apartment house?"

"Comrade, there are more than seven hundred people living there," Kraisin said. "The cars belong to men and women in the managerial class, many of whom are Party members. My point is that the attendant is either lying or else we are wrong and the four terrorists didn't have an escape vehicle in the garage. My second point is that the attendant has a clean record; there is not one shred of evidence that he didn't tell us the full truth."

Cherfesky thought a moment. "I gather the three eye-witnesses didn't see the four men going into the rear of the building."

"They walked from the rear to the front entrance. So you see, there isn't any direct evidence to prove that they were even in the garage."

Colonel General Shopov wrinkled his forehead, feeling that Kraisin was placing him, as director of the DS, in a defensive posture, one that could compromise his position with the Russian advisers. The KGB would have placed the attendant under arrest and have broken him down with round-the-clock questioning. "Comrade Kraisin, I trust you brought the file on the attendant," he said easily.

"Yes, Comrade, I did." Almost daintily, Kraisin carefully placed his cigarette in one of the holders in the middle of the ashtray, leaned to one side, and opened the briefcase next to his chair. He pulled out a bright green plastic folder, placed it on the table, opened it, and began to read. "The attendant's name is Dobri Zlanti. He is twenty-eight years old and unmarried. Zlanti was a member of the Young Communist League and later joined the People's Democratic Union of Industrial Workers. In this organization, he was noted for his patriotic speeches at union meetings, at the State Steel and Foundry Works in Jubisk. He dropped out of the union when he took the job as daytime attendant at the apartment house. The—"

"He left the union!" Cherfesky's expression was one of anger. "Why that in itself was enough to have him arrested for antisocial action against the people!"

"Comrade, please permit me to finish," Kraisin said coldly, looking up from the folder. He turned back to the folder on the table. "Zlanti left the union in December of 1983 because of a severe illness—chronic myelocytic leukemia. The State Employment Directory permitted him to quit his job at the steel and foundry works and take the less physically demanding job as an attendant at the apartment house. He is being treated for his illness at the Plovdivi Medical Institute here in Sofia. He is expected to live only another year, a year and a half at the most." Kraisin closed the file and looked slyly at Lieutenant General Cherfesky. "I'm sure you can see, we could not have subjected Dobri Zlanti to intensive interrogation. Not that we aren't watching him. From now on, he won't be able to go to the toilet without our knowing about it. If he's connected with the terrorists in any way, we'll find out, sooner or later."

Mollified by his hasty conclusion that had been incorrect,

Cherfesky was quick to agree with Colonel Kraisin. "Good. Your department has taken the proper action. A constant surveillance is the proper procedure. By the way, Comrade, those cigarettes you have. I don't believe I've seen that kind of pack before. American?"

"*Dai*—American." Kraisin shoved the pack down the table toward Cherfesky. "They're called *Carlton 120s* and are extra long. Keep them. I have more."

"They from a new shipment that KINTEX received," said Colonel Isakov, "smuggled in from France via SOMAT. I'll get a dozen cartons for you, Comrade Cherfesky."

Colonel General Shopov leaned back, feeling elated over how Georgi had subtly made Cherfesky appear to be an overanxious fool. As the Russians would say, Georgi had *ochkovtiratel stvo*—he had "thrown dust" in Cherfesky's face. One of the major habits of that damned Cherfesky and the other "advisers"—indeed, with the whole Soviet leadership— was their habit of pointing out the inefficiencies in other governments while remaining silent about their own complex problems in the Soviet Union; and the Soviets were having any number of difficulties with their own restless masses. Shopov had intimate knowledge of such matters, all due to Colonel Josef Gavva, who often dropped by with several bottles of *slívova*[5] and always—after he requested that the DS find him a woman, often several, and the younger the better—became talkative and revealed bits and pieces of information about the problems at home. The drunker he got, the more he revealed—while Shopov took it all down on a hidden tape recorder for future use, and self-protection.

One of the problems facing the Soviet government was explaining the American system to the Russian people. Pravda was constantly publicizing all the criticism of the American president to justify the position of the Kremlin. In doing so, Pravda had to explain that the American system was not free because Americans were "brainwashed and manipulated by the capitalist press." How else could Pravda explain the determination of the American people—whom Shopov secretly admired—to defend themselves against Communism? The irony was that Pravda was caught in the quagmire of having to explain that the American people were free to criticize their president while no one in the Soviet Union

[5] Plum brandy.

would dare question the policy makers in the Kremlin—and remain free!

Another problem for the Soviet leadership and the KGB was the thirty or so foreign broadcast stations that beamed programs into the Soviet Union from stations based in the U.S., Munich, Manila, Guam, and Japan. Despite the radio-jamming network, maintained at considerable expense, and despite the fact that it was a serious offense for any Soviet citizen to be caught listening to unauthorized foreign broadcasts, a vast audience listened to the illegal broadcasts, and the KGB knew it. And was powerless . . .

Only recently, before he had left for Moscova, Gavva had let slip that the KGB could no longer "count on honest citizens to inform on their neighbors who are traitors to the state." The half-drunk Gavva had not explained why "honest citizens" no longer tattled to the militia and/or the KGB. Any idiot knew the answer. The "honest citizens" were disenchanted with the Soviet government.

Shopov studied Colonel Anatoly Tretyakov, who was saying, "Comrades, we should discuss making arrangements to receive *Tovarisch* Oleg Skarbovenko. He will be flying from Moscova with Colonel Gavva."

"We can hardly give him a parade, not in this weather," said Colonel General Shopov. "As usual, we'll meet him at the airport and escort him to the Vitosha New-Ontani. What more can we do? It's the best hotel in Sofia. For reasons of security, all our meetings will be conducted here at headquarters. I ask you, Comrade Tretyakov, what other arrangements are we to make?"

"I was thinking of amusements, sights of interests for him to see," Tretyakov said stiffly. "He is not only a representative of the Central Committee, he is a close personal friend of Marshal Ogarov."[6]

"I am acquainted with Skarbovenko." Cherfesky tapped ash from the Carlton 120 cigarette he was smoking. "His tastes are simple. Good food, good wine, and a hard bed is all he requires. He retires early and rises early. He works hard. He does have one interest—ancient art, murals and that sort of thing."

---

[6] Marshal Nikolai Ogarov, the number-one military man in the Soviet Union. Neither flamboyant nor charismatic, he is chief of the Soviet General Staff, a position equivalent to the U.S. Chairman of the Joints Chief of Staff.

"Why a hard mattress?" Major Divuncha was curious.

"He has a bad back, something to do with his spine. He carries a folding board with him when he travels." Cherfesky studied the end of his cigarette for a moment and added, "It is odd about Comrade Skarbovenko. His grandfather was a die-hard Menshevik[7] and was executed by Dzerzhinsky's[8] firing squads in the old days, but that black mark in his ancestry did not hurt his career."

"We might take Comrade Oleg Skarbovenko to the Alexander Nevsky Memorial Church," suggested Shopov. "It would be ideal. The church was built during the early years of this century as a token of gratitude of the Bulgarian people for Russian help in gaining independence from Turkey. The interior of the church incorporates the work of many Russian and East European artists. Comrade Skarbovenko should enjoy such a tour."

"Splendid, splendid." Cherfesky beamed. "A fine suggestion, Comrade Shopov."

Shopov permitted himself a smile, not only for the benefit of General Cherfesky and the other three Russians, but also for his own DS officers. A man who had survived by listening to his hunches and to instinct, Shopov was convinced that if one of the American CIA mercenaries was the Man without a Face, the man that the world's intelligence agencies called the Death Merchant, then all hell was about to break loose. Far better that Satan himself descend on Sofia than the deadly *Cempt Tobtocpam*. . . .

---

[7] A member of the less radical faction—the *Mensheviki*—of the Social Democrat Party that opposed the Bolshevik government after the 1917 revolution.

[8] Felix Edmundovich Dzerzhinsky, the father of Soviet intelligence and espionage. He founded the KGB on December 20, 1917, only then the secret police was called the *Chrezvychainaya Komissiya po Borbe s Kontr-revolutisiei i Sabotazhem*—or Extraordinary Commission for Combating Counterrevolution and Sabotage. This was the CHEKA. Today KGB men are still known as Chekists.

CHAPTER FOUR

Todor Jiguv had a broken jaw. At least it appeared that his mouth was wired shut, and to a certain extent it was. Yet just as concepts of time and space are not applicable to ideas, it follows that an appearance is not necessarily a true representation of reality. The truth was that Todor Jiguv did not exist. He was only a man on paper, a fiction made "real" in his *Vanchikvobla,* his identity book, an internal passport carried by all Bulgarian citizens, giving the complete history of the individual. Todor Jiguv's *Vanchikvobla* listed his residence and place of employment as the State Collective Farm outside of Cistatii, a village twenty-five kilometers north of Sofia. Occupation: mechanic.

Todor Jiguv was Richard Camellion. His "broken jaw" was necessary in case, for some remote reason, he and Miss Brokariev, the woman driving the small Soviet made Zaporozhets-968, were stopped and questioned by the *Jokka,* the militia traffic police.

It was actually a matter of accent. The Death Merchant spoke perfect Russian; he could also partially understand the Bulgarian language, which, also Slavic in origin, was similar to Russian. But he could speak only broken Bulgarian. There wasn't any way he would be able to fool an officer of the *Jokka.* He would not have to try. His jaw was broken. He could only mumble.

It wasn't likely that Camellion and the woman would be stopped. Russian Zaporozhets and Volga M-124 cars were as common in Sofia as bikinis on a Los Angeles beach in July.

Just in case the *Jokka* stopped the gray Zaporozhets, the

police would find that the mannish-looking Narda Brokariev, who had hair on her upper lip, was a nurse stationed at the collective farm outside of Cistatii and was taking Jiguv to the Plovdivi Medical Institute to have his jaw X-rayed. The bone was not knitting properly.

Narda Brokariev was neither Narda Brokariev nor a nurse. She was Katherini Nocheki and a conductor on one of the *elektrichka,* one of the electric commuter trains that came in from the suburbs. She was also a widow, her husband having died under interrogation by the DS, in 1979.

"More twenty minutes and we get to house that be secret," she said in broken English, and slowed the small car for a red light on the wide Aleksandar Stambolijski.

Camellion grunted. He could speak clearly if he had to, but it would have been difficult. While the broken jaw could be faked, the clamps and wire were genuine and were in place, holding his mouth shut. Under ordinary circumstances, one can speak while his teeth are together, provided he can move his lips. Because of the clamps, one on either side, Camellion could only partially move his lips, and part of a silver wire rested across his tongue.

He and the woman stared at the traffic facing them and watched the cars moving diagonally to them on Mesemebur Kur, the avenue that intersected Aleksandar Stambolijski.

"Be ready you with guns," the woman warned just before the light changed to green, "in case we stopped and no believe they our identification books. Prisoner of DS no good. How you say in America—worse than hell? To be dead better."

She took the car across Mesemebur Kur—a small-boned woman with a broad face and faded blond hair . . . grimly determined to get her important passenger to his destination.

Camellion glanced to the right as Katherini Nocheki increased speed to the mandatory thirty-five mph. To his right was the north side of Lenin Square—all a dirty gray under several feet of snow, with the exceptions of the sidewalks.

No . . . she and I will not be taken alive . . . should it come to that. . . .

Feeling very secure with the two Bidja autoloaders in shoulder holsters and a Vitmorkin machine pistol under the seat, Camellion considered most of the previous day and night. He and Traikov, Rykov, and Winkler had switched vehicles three times before using the last car to drive to the safe house in the eastern outskirts of Sofia, an old house of stone and wood, snow sagging in frozen sculptured splendor from the edges of the tiled roof. For the remainder of the day and all that night the four had remained in the large mushroom cellar: "Rats running around at the bottom of a steel barrel!" as the cynical Carey Winkler had phrased it.

It wasn't until the four were almost ready to leave the next morning—this same day—that Stephen Traikov had revealed to Camellion and Winkler that the house belonged to Nivka Koleza, a member of the *Nersko-Tsopska*. The Bulgarian NFC leader had then said that fourteen members of the revolutionary organization were in the militia. None, however, held rank. He finished with, "Not every man and woman who wears a uniform believes in a Communist dictatorship. They love their country, but regard Communism as the real enemy of the Bulgarian people."

For security purposes the four would not travel together to the next safe house, which was special in that it would be there that the Death Merchant and Winkler would meet the other two leaders of the NFC: "And we will be there a week or more," Traikov had said firmly. "For the time being, we have nowhere else to go. The DS is overturning the city looking for us."

The Death Merchant, without flicking an eyelash, had said, "We must meet the contact from the station at the embassy. We can't proceed until we do. I refer to the plan to blow up the file section."

"It may be weeks before you're able to meet the contact. We'll discuss it when we get to our destination. First things first."

All the arrangements had been made. Winkler and Rykov would ride in—of all things—a SOMAT truck, a tractor-and-trailer job loaded with refrigerators that would be delivered in Hungary. On its route out of Sofia, the truck would stop five blocks from the scheduled safe house.

Winkler had expressed his surprise. "So even some SOMAT drivers are in your organization!"

"That is not your concern. I have told you both as much as I have only to reassure you that the route has been carefully prepared. Experience has taught us many tricks; you are not in the hands of rank amateurs."

Traikov had then explained that he and Mrs. Koleza would

drive Rykov and Winkler to within two blocks of where they would meet the truck. "Fedor knows what to do."

"I get it," Winkler had replied. "It is none of my concern."

Traikov had been blunt. "In case of capture, one cannot reveal what he does not know. And now you, *tosvarkish* Camellion—"

The Death Merchant would leave the house and walk a block, going south. "You will leave at exactly eight-thirty." A woman in a Zaporozhets-968 would pull to the curb and pick him up. They would then drive to another location where—surprise!—Camellion would have his jaw wired by a physician. Traikov explained why.

Camellion had strapped on the shoulder holsters with their blue-black 9mm. Bidja autopistols. "I suppose I'm on my own during that stroll of a block and before my jaw is wired? Either run or pray, right?"

"You should complain!" Winkler had mocked. "Fedor and I have to walk a total of seven blocks. We'll be too cold to shoot if anything goes wrong. I heard someone say it's five below outside. Man, that's cold enough to make a corpse leave its grave and dance to get warm!"

Winkler's dull humor had not amused either Camellion or Traikov.

"It will be a risk for all of us," Traikov had said. "The routes we'll take are the best we can do under the circumstances. We live from day to day, with death—or worse—only a few lengths behind. At this time of the morning the danger is not too great. We are all poorly dressed. On the streets, we will look like workers, or what we Bulgarians call *anonymkas*. . . ."[1]

Camellion didn't mistrust Katherini Nocheki. Yet he was too experienced to fully trust her. So be it. If she was not what she was supposed to be, her soul would never sing with the wind. Should she be leading him into a trap, she would be the first to die. He was certain that the safe house was farther than twenty minutes away. *If I'm right, has she lied to me for security reasons—or? We'll find out, won't we?*

His feeling about the woman was more than gut instinct. It was his awareness of where he was, his location in Sofia. He was not familiar with the city in the sense that he had previously visited and walked its streets; nevertheless, back in

---

[1] The "anonymous ones".

Rome he had studied a detailed map of Sofia and, due to his photographic memory, could see the entire city in his mind—as clear as a three-dimensional model.

The "main street" of Sofia was Ruski Boulevard on which were the pride and joys of the Bulgarian government: September 9 Square, the Clement of Ohrid University, and the Bulgarian Communist Party headquarters. The National Assembly and several first-class hotels were also on Ruski Boulevard—and the hotels did have genuine toilet paper![2]

Nivka Koleza's house was on Pirovja, a short street on the eastern edge of the city and only a few kilometers from Ruski Boulevard. In theory, Katherini Nocheki should have driven to Ruski Boulevard to reach the next safe house; she could have saved time on the boulevard where one could drive forty-five mph. Instead, she had driven through a jigsaw puzzle of streets to reach Aleksandar Stambolijski, which was another major artery leading northwest to the suburbs. Unless she turned off within the next five blocks—*Or is it six? No. Five. We'll be going into the suburbs and the first stop will be Boyana. Another six miles—nine klicks—from the city limits!*

Katherini Nocheki did not turn onto any side street. The small Russian car continued on Aleksandar Stambolijski. The Death Merchant was not concerned. After all, the secret of being miserable is to have the leisure to bother about whether you are happy or not. He passed the time by thinking of Sofia and came to the conclusion that one's first general impression of the city was neither of great age nor of great beauty, although in fact it was very old, the area having been inhabited over 5,000 years. It was difficult to conceive that just about a century ago, Sofia was a down-and-out Oriental town, the capital of the Turkish province of Rumelia. At that time, it had only 3,200 houses and 15,000 inhabitants living in narrow twisting streets punctuated by mosques and little churches crouching half underground, for their roofs were not allowed to reach higher than a man on horseback, but otherwise most of central Sofia had its origins in the first town plans drawn up in 1880.

The first people of what is now Sofia were the Serdi, a Thracian tribe, who gave Sofia its first name, Serdica. Even

---

[2] The Russians may have been the first to put a man in space, but the best hotels in Moscow are still without rolled toilet paper. Instead, one finds small squares of rough paper, similar to American paper towels.

in those ancient days the site lay on one of the main routes between East and West. The Romans made the city the capital of Dacia, and it was one of the favorite cities of Constantine the Great. Attila the Hun destroyed the city in 447 A.D. From the ashes came a brand-new city, rebuilt by Justinian in the sixth century. It was also Justinian who began building St. Sofia Church.

It was the Slavs, in the seventh century, who changed the name from Serdica to Sredets, but by the end of the fourteenth century the city became Sofia.[3] In modern Sofia the streets are broad, except in the very old sections on the outskirts. There are spacious green parks, open-air cafes, museums, and, of course, many massive monuments depicting the "glory" of Communism.

A better-than-average amateur archaeologist and historian, the Death Merchant would have enjoyed touring Sofia in warm weather. There were so many intriguing sights, such as the little Church of Sveti Georgi on the west side of Lenin Square. Built in the fourth century, the church was destroyed by the Huns. Justinian rebuilt it. The Turks turned it into a mosque. The Bulgarians, ever conscious of history, restored it, and now, with it frescoes from the eleventh to the fifteenth centuries, the church was a tourist attraction.

North of Lenin Square, on Georgi Dimitrov Street, was Banya Bashi Mosque, one of the few major buildings left by the Turks, dating from the sixteenth century and rich in interior decorations.

To the east of Lenin Square was an underpass that would take one back 2,000 years—to the Sredica of Roman times. Here were Roman walls, a stretch of Roman-paved street, and a collection of stone blocks and carvings from those long-ago times.

On September 9 Square was the monolithic Georgi Dimitrov[4] Mausoleum that contained the body of the revered Bulgarian revolutionary leader, who died in Moscow in 1949. Across from the tomb was the National Art Gallery in the former Royal Palace. Next to the palace was the Russian Church of St. Nicholas.

The largest church of all was on Moskovska Street. This

---

[3] The name actually means wisdom.

[4] This dummy was poisoned by the Soviet secret police, which, in 1949, was known as the *Ministerstvo Vnutrennikh Del*, or Ministry of Internal Affairs—the MVD.

was the church from which Sofia derived its name—Sancta Sophia, that stately Byzantine basilica with its cruciform cupola-topped structure.

More historical monuments were in Boyana, and by now it was clear to the Death Merchant that he and Katherini Nocheki were going to Boyana. Anyhow, they would have to pass through Boyana, unless the safe house was between Sofia and Boyana.

"Katherini Nocheki, you should have told me that we are going to Boyana," Camellion said offhandedly, employing the Russian and the Bulgarian custom of using the full name. "I suppose you had a good reason for telling me we'd reach our destination in twenty minutes. I shouldn't think our destination is one of the public buildings on Aleksandar Stambolijski!"

She was surprisingly candid and direct. "No man know was supposed to about house on Kirili," she said in her fractured English, looking straight ahead. "An informer he told DS. All you almost die because he did. How we know that you and other American no be spy? *Tosvarkish* Traikov and two other leaders they worried. We no chances take. Safe house you know when we get there."

"I don't blame the NFC for tight security," Camellion said. "Stephen has reason for concern. We all have."

"You be right," the woman admitted. "We do go to Boyana."

From the corner of his eye, Camellion watched a bright blue jeeplike vehicle pass them on one of the opposite lanes, going in the other direction. The jeep was a Soviet Chor-7 and carried two members of the *Jokka*.

Enough time had passed so that it was obvious that the Zaporozhets was almost on the open highway on which the speed limit was eighty kph (fifty mph). Accordingly, Katherini Nocheki increased speed, saying, "We soon reach motorway and speed we make. Surprise you be when you see where we go."

At this point, nothing would have surprised Richard Camellion—unless he spotted Courtland Grojean wearing overalls! Not even the reckless way in which Bulgarian drivers drove had given Camellion a start. It was the Bulgarian system to go past the street you want, make a legal U-turn, and then come back. Only legal U-turns were few and far between. No problem to the Bulgarians, who made illegal U-turns.

Gas stations would have made an American think he had died and gone to hell. Not only did gas stations operate on a pump-it-yourself basis, but no one popped up out of nowhere to wipe the windshield and to check the tires. Psychologically, gas stations were self-defeating, for one had actually to pay to service one's own car, and such signs as "front glass wiping—20 *stotinki*," "side glass wiping—15 *stotinki*," and "tire pumping and pressure checking, per wheel-10 *stotinki*" were common.[5]

Another peculiarity of Bulgarian drivers—similar to the Russian custom—is driving at night using only parking lights, even on intercity roads, none of which could really qualify as a highway in the Western sense. As for finding spare parts—a *kashmiri* . . . a nightmare!

Soon the Zaporozhets-968 was on the "motorway," the open highway, and Katherini Nocheki pushed a big foot down on the gas pedal, increasing the speed to almost seventy mph. Gradually, on either side of the highway, buildings became sparse, and there were more and more fields covered with snow that, instead of sparkling with color, was a dirty off-white. There was no sun, the sky a solid ceiling of gunmetal gray.

It was eleven-thirty A.M. when Katherini Nocheki, who looked like a typical Bulgar[6] peasant woman, guided the car into the southern outskirts of Boyana, one of the main villages in the Sofia *okrug* (or district) and a must on the itinerary of any tourist. Some of the most ancient historical monuments were in Boyana. There were the Church of the Five Martyrs, built in the thirteenth century, the ruins of a Roman temple, a few museums, and the house of Baba Tonka, a national hero who sheltered anti-Turk revolutionaries.

Nocheki slowed to a proper thirty-five mph, entered the town, and turned to the right. Another four blocks, a left turn, and the little car was approaching a large Byzantine church at the end of Minur Govgu. Snow had been removed from the wide steps of the imposing building and from the square in front of the church. A dozen green buses of Balkantourist were parked in the square as well as a score of automobiles of various makes and sizes.

---

[5] The monetary unit is the *leva*. The *leva* is divided into 100 *stotinki*.
[6] Bulgar means "man with the plow."

At once, the Death Merchant sensed that the church was his and Katherini Nocheki's destination and that the vehicles belonged to tourists, the buses to the official Bulgarian tour service. It figured. Bulgaria was a veritable "Red Riviera," particularly during the warm months, to which flocked an ever-growing number of British and American visitors.

"Neat . . . very neat," mumbled Camellion, the wire lying across his tongue irking him. "Who would suspect a safe house in a church?" He turned his head, peered at the woman, and saw that, for a change, she had lost some of her composure. He added, "And don't tell me I'm wrong."

"How you know?" she asked. "I no tell you."

"You didn't have to. A church is a perfect place for a safe-house facility. There was another reason why I knew. A private house would be too conspicuous, too dangerous. Eventually word of people coming and going would reach agents of the DS."

"All true what you say. The church be safe house. There we go."

"How do we play it?"

She frowned. "How we do what?"

"I assume we will mingle with the tourists. How will we manage to slip away from them and do what we have to do in order to get to safety. What about this car? We can't leave it parked in front of the church, not for long. And I suppose you realize there will be DS agents mingling with the tourists!"

"You no worry. Stay with me. A person speak to you, point to your jaw. Prove you no can talk."

She pulled into the square in front of the church and parked the Zaporozhets beside a Balkantourist bus. As they got out of the car, Camellion noticed that she did not leave the key in the ignition.

Together, they walked toward the front steps of the Church of St. Dimitur.

Do we know where we're going? The Death Merchant would have smiled if his jaws had not been wired. *Of course we do. We have led a good Christian life. . . .*

CHAPTER FIVE

Carey Winkler could only stare at the Death Merchant in disbelief. Stephen Traikov, drinking *Mastica*, was clearly astonished. Expressions of amazement dropped over the faces of Zhivko Stoichev and Petur Dzhurov, the two other leaders of the revolutionary National Freedom Council.

Winkler put his hands flat on the table and leaned closer to the Death Merchant, who was standing across from him. "I did hear you correctly? You did say you had a plan to blow up the entire building? Yeah, you did!"

"I did—and we will!" Camellion resumed looking at the map of the Sofia *okrug* spread out on the table.

"It—it can't be done!" exclaimed Petur Dzhurov. "The building is too big. It would require tons of explosives. It would be impossible for us to obtain that much *pjâsaci*!"

"I rather like the idea," mused Traikov. "The entire headquarters building of the DS! The building, Colonel General Shopov, all his directors, and the five Russian 'Uncles'—all with one big bang! What a blow for freedom such an explosion would make!"

Camellion didn't look up from the large map. "Don't ever believe in absolutes," he responded to Petur Dzhurov. "Some dreamer like me will always come along and prove you're wrong. Give me a moment and I'll tell you how we can do it."

Thinking that Dzhurov's voice was as irritating as a fingernail scratching on a blackboard, Camellion gave his full attention to the map. He could see that Sofia extended across the terraces of the Iskur River and its tributaries, the Vladayska,

Perlovska, and Erma. Very close by, to the northeast, were the Lyulin Mountains, with the city practically at the foot of Mt. Vitosha. *The mountains are out. We'll have to land inside Sofia or just outside the city, in some secluded area. It would still be extremely dangerous.*

"Such a plan is insane!" said Zhivko Stoichev in his gruff voice. He almost glared at the Death Merchant. "To destroy DS headquarters on Boulevard Anton Ivanova we'd need several truckloads of explosives. Why the trucks would never be able to get past the front gate! American, whatever your plan might be, it would never succeed. It is too fantastic to be practical."

Camellion pushed back a chair, sat down, and glanced at Stoichev, who was a tall, wiry man with furry brown eyes and hair so thick and curly he might have been wearing an Afro. His appearance was not impressive. His suit, old to begin with, needed pressing. His shoes were very worn. Camellion estimated his age to be around forty-five.

"My plan only seems uncommon," Camellion said with controlled patience, although he was worried that Stoichev and Dzhurov would veto the operation. "It's because the plan is incredible that it will succeed. It will be a strike that no one in the DS or the KGB would ever think of, not even if we gave their imagination free rein for the next ten years."

Petur Dzhurov and Zhivko Stoichev regarded Camellion with even more skepticism.

"Look. Let's assume we did have the necessary explosives," the practical Winkler offered. "We'd have to cart them in trucks, in tractor-trailer jobs. Even if we—"

"We can't assume," interrupted Traikov, who had sat down six feet from the table. "Such vast destruction would require thousands of kilos of explosives. We don't have it and can't possibly get that much. That's all there is to it. Ah . . . *tosvarkish* Camellion, your plan is doomed at the outset."

"I estimate four thousand, eighty-two kilograms," Camellion said matter-of-factly, "or nine thousand English pounds. Four and a half tons, in three large trucks."

Winkler looked away and reached for his cigarettes.

Petur Dzhurov, an ex-psychiatrist, who was ordinarily a quiet, thoughtful man and the senior leader of the *Narodno Gorsiku Rakigladenov*, became angry. "To even discuss this blueprint is to indulge in fantasy. It is first-degree madness!"

he raged in very good English. "Let us suppose we did have the trucks? Further, let—"

"It wouldn't be all that impossible to obtain the trucks," cut in Stephen Traikov. "Our contacts in SOMAT are excellent."

"Suppose the trucks could get close to the SD building?" Dzhurov gave Traikov a dirty look. "How could the drivers escape?" He shook his head violently up and down. "*Ne! Ne! Ne!*[1] I am surprised, American, that you would even suggest such an impossible plan."

Intoned Zhivko Stoichev gravely, "To attempt such an operation would mean failure and possibly that failure would be the beginning of the end of our organization. I am beginning to wonder about the people who work for the American Central Intelligence Agency. The two of you came to Bulgaria to help us. Instead, you put forth a plan that would extinguish the only flame of freedom burning in this nation."

Hellfire flared in Winkler's eyes. "Get something straight, both of you! We didn't come to this damn country to be insulted!" he lashed out at Stoichev and Dzhurov. "And I'd think twice about knocking the CIA—or have you forgotten about all the arms and technical help you've received—and there's more on the way!"

"Even worse is your bad manners," Camellion said, taking another approach. "By that I mean your putting a seal of disapproval on my plan before you have even extended me the courtesy of telling you what it is."

Camellion had managed to keep his temper, but his voice indicated a small measure of his disgust. He couldn't decide which was worse: Stoichev's scratchy voice or the utter lack of imagination exhibited by the two leaders.

Stephen Traikov looked for a second at Petur Dzhurov and Zhivko Stoichev, his eyes sending daggers in their direction. He turned quickly then to Camellion and Winkler. "I apologize for my two comrades," he said sincerely. "There are times when they permit emotion to overcome hospitality."

"Very well. Tell us this plan of yours, Mr. Camellion," scratched out Zhivko Stoichev.

"We will listen to what you have to say," Petur Dzhurov said stiffly.

The Death Merchant began by explaining that there was

[1] "No! No! No!"

plenty of explosive lying around—in storehouses of the state collective farms.

"*Ammonium nitrate!*[2] It's a common enough fertilizer, but when properly primed with a blasting cap and a booster will explode at rates up to almost four thousand three hundred meters per second."[3]

Speaking slowly so that the Bulgarians could absorb each word, the Death Merchant explained that the heart of his scheme involved three large trucks loaded with 9,000 or 10,000 pounds of primed ammonium nitrate. The three trucks would leave the road, crash through the protective barriers, slam into the DS headquarters building, and explode.

"That much explosive will rip apart the bottom girders in the walls and the entire building will come down," Camellion said, sounding as though he were giving a lecture.

He could see that even Winkler was far from convinced of the practicality of the plan, his face a big mask of incredulity. Camellion knew that this was normal enough for Winkler, who considered him the Patron Saint of the Perpetually Strange. Just the same, Camellion felt that Winkler would go along with the plan—*If I can prove it will work*. Winkler was a large plus for Camellion. Winkler survived, with a kind of stoic equanimity, because he knew that caution was a way of life. Even under normal conditions, he was not the kind of man who would sit in a restaurant unless his back faced the wall and he could see the door. Or use a phone booth with his back presented to the public. Or even use a urinal in a public rest room. No way. Winkler would go into a stall and lock the door. If he had to defecate, he would sit down, pull his autoloader, and lay the weapon in his shorts around his legs.

Traikov? The Death Merchant knew he could count on the man, but only up to a certain point. Again—*Only if I can prove the plan will work. I'll need pur-dee luck too—three drivers who are going to die*. At the moment, Camellion was far from a home run. It didn't even look as if he would come up to bat! Traikov's expression was one of extreme doubt. Stoichev and Dzhurov were not even considering the plan. The Death Merchant knew why and couldn't blame them.

---

[2] In the U.S. ammonium nitrate is made by Du Pont and put into fifty-pound bags called "prills." Each bag is marked "Nitramite FR, Nitro-Carbo Nitrate."

[3] 4267.20 meters per second equals 14,000 feet per second.

Petur Dzhurov said coldly, "Mr. Camellion, your plan has merit only for fanatics, for men willing to commit suicide."

"We are not Palestinians who desire to throw away life foolishly," appended Zhivko Stoichev. "The three drivers could not survive the blast. In fact, they would probably be dead from machine-gun slugs before the trucks could even smash into the building."

"Your plan is ridiculous," Dzhurov said bluntly. "I see no reason to discuss it further."

"I wasn't thinking of fanatics, nor of a useless waste of life," persisted the Death Merchant. "What I have in mind are men already dying of some terminal disease, perhaps cancer, men who have only a year, at the most, to live. In a sense, the three would have to be fanatics. Most people fear death and will cling desperately to life, if only for a few minutes. It would depend on how philosophical the three men might be and how much they love their country . . . how much they are willing to give for freedom. . . ."

Traikov broke the short silence, saying seriously to the two other leaders, "His idea is worthy of consideration. Drivers who would be willing to die! That adds a whole new dimension to the plan. Think of it, Comrades. The destruction of the DS headquarters. We have to consider the plan!"

The Death Merchant was quick to see that Stoichev and Dzhurov felt fear and indecision—fear of failure and indecision over what to do. Both men made him think of men who are afraid and uncomfortable in the presence of assertive women.[4]

Dzhurov began to speak rapidly in Bulgarian to Traikov and Stoichev, making a lot of gestures to punctuate his speech.

Camellion leaned back and thought of Katherini Nocheki. She certainly had been assertive and self-confident. Hanging on to Camellion's arm as if she owned him, she had marched into the Church of St. Dimitur where she and Camellion had mingled with tourists, who, at the time, had been absorbed in listening to an elderly Eastern Orthodox priest, dressed in cassock and overcoat (for the inside of the church was as cold as a whore's heart) explain in broken English who had painted

---

[4] Whether a construction worker or a chairman of the board, the average man does not like an aggressive woman—all due to little boys being taught that while they should be nice to little girls, they are superior to the female.

the frescoes. Another priest was standing in the transept to the left of the main altar.

The uncertainty would have given an inexperienced agent a nervous breakdown. The Death Merchant had taken it in stride, his hands in his overcoat pockets, one hand wrapped around the butt of a Bulgarian Bidja autopistol.

Camellion and Katherini Nocheki had stood there, acting as though they were interested in what the priest was saying. There was one flaw: the tourists, many of whom were British and American, were better dressed than Camellion and his companion. However, no one gave them a second glance.

Gradually, the priest and the tourists had moved up the nave toward the opening in the communion railing near the high main altar. Camellion and Nocheki stayed on the fringe, with no one behind them. . . . All the while the priest kept talking about the paintings on the sides of the vaults. Within another ten minutes the priest and the tourists were standing in front of the main altar, the shiny black marble topped with a statue of Jesus Christ with outspread hands. Over this main section of the church was the sixty-foot domed ceiling, and it too was covered with frescoes depicting the Last Judgment, Heaven, and Hell.

As the priest pointed upward and began to explain the paintings, Katherini Nocheki had nudged Camellion and jerked her head to the left. Camellion nodded, that is, he shook his head horizontally, meaning that he understood. He glanced at the tourists. All were looking up at the rounded ceiling. Step by step, he and Nocheki moved to the left, their turtle-crawl pace finally putting them to the end of the altar. The other priest was nowhere in sight.

Katherini Nocheki took one last look at the tourists. No one was watching. "We go quick," she whispered to Camellion. "Go behind altar."

It took only seconds to duck behind the altar to a position that placed them in front of the large apse, which was deserted. The woman had not wasted any time, Camellion reflected while listening to the three leaders of the NFC jabbering back and forth. She had hurried along the rear of the altar, and he could see that she was counting the stones in the floor, from the left end of the altar. After she had come to the eleventh large stone, she looked from left to right to make sure no one was watching. She then turned to the altar and tapped one of the rear stones with the ignition key to the Zaporozhets-968.

A section of the altar swung inward, presenting a dark opening that was very uneven on both sides and at the top, many of the stones of the "door" projecting from six to fifteen inches.

No sooner had the slab of stone moved inward than a priest, a small flashlight in his hand, appeared and beckoned them to step inside. After they had done so, the priest—the same man who had been standing in the left transept—pulled down on a wooden lever. Just as quietly as it had swung inward, the stone "door" swung outward, sealing the jagged opening.

There had been only the small beam from the priest's flashlight. Even so, the Death Merchant had been able to detect that he and his companions were in a very narrow passage that moved toward the right side of the altar. Reaching the end, the priest flashed his light downward, showing Camellion and his companion an opening in the floor, below which were narrow but steep stone steps, a long flight twenty feet long. Wooden handrails were on each side of the steps.

The priest whispered something in Bulgarian.

"He said we be careful," Nocheki translated for Camellion. "Steps very steep."

The priest had descended first, then had shone the beam on the steps so that Camellion and his female escort could come down. At the bottom Camellion saw they were in another corridor whose walls and ceiling and floor were of solid stone, the darkness, pressing in on all sides, reminding him of the escape tunnel from the destroyed safe house to the garage. This passage was much larger than the one above it; the roof was supported by massive stone pillars whose tops and bottoms were decorated with a frieze depicting fierce demons and even uglier gargoyles. The air was musty, the halitosis of age, of a perpetually enclosed place. However, the cold was gone, the temperature at this depth underground in the lower fifties.

Short, thick-set, and with a thick, long beard, the priest started down the passage, which, on a slight downward slant, was seventy-four feet long and had rooms on either side. Finally the trio drew close to the end of the tunnel—a blank wall—and the man of God hurried over to a pillar, reached up, and pulled down on the long neck of a sculpted griffin. Once more, a section of the wall opened, this time swinging outward, light coming from the opening, dim light that drifted upward. The priest, his face expressionless, motioned to

Camellion to move through the opening. He then spoke to Katherini Nocheki in Bulgarian.

"*Blagodarya, zashto. Suhozal-gospi hi ranta,*"[5] she replied. Then she turned to the Death Merchant. "I go. Leave you here. Me and priest we go back. Beyond opening is safe house. Priest he say *tosvarkish* Traikov and other American they wait below for you. We wait to make sure you go down steps okay. God he be with you, American. *Shavisko!*"[6]

He turned, stepped through the opening in the wall, and found that he was on a stone platform half the size of an average room, a platform that was the top of a wide flight of stone steps that slanted to the right. The area below was an enormous room with a vaulted ceiling, round pillars reaching from the floor to the ends of the arches of each vault. Camellion could detect, in the dim light of a few light bulbs, doors to smaller areas. The work of construction must have been tremendous. The entire area gave the impression of great age, of a past that had been misplaced by even God.

Below, standing close to a massive table, were Stephen Traikov, Carey Winkler, and a priest, the three looking up at him.

The Death Merchant started down the steps. He soon learned that the secret compound of rooms had been constructed 470 years earlier as protection against invasion. During those troubled times St. Dimitur's had been much larger and had been served by thirty or more priests of the Eastern Orthodox Church. Now, there were only six priests.

Father Gregori Fodgiv, tall, thin, in his seventies, and as frail as tissue paper, explained that the Communist government of Bulgaria, while it frowned on any belief in God, never bothered the priests in any way.

"It is not out of any human compassion that the government does not interfere with people who worship in any church," said Father Fodgiv, sipping Turkish coffee, thick and black, strong and sweet. "It is a matter of official policy, of propaganda. The government wants tourists to see priests at the churchs and imams at mosques. The government is desperate for trade with the West and does not want the stigma of violating human rights and the freedom of religion."

Father Fodgiv—he was the head priest at St. Dimitur's—

---

[5] "Thank you, Father. I will tell him."
[6] "Good-bye."

gave a tiny chuckle and almost immediately went into a fit of coughing. After his coughing, he explained, with labored breathing, that he suffered from bronchiectasis and that relations between the Bulgarian government and all religions—Eastern Orthodox and Muslim, with a smattering of other denominations—was quite good.

"I find it strange that the government doesn't know about these secret rooms," the Death Merchant said. "This place may not be as safe as you think."

"There isn't any danger," Stephen Traikov said confidently. "There were blueprints of the churches and mosques. They were destroyed when the Americans bombed Sofia during the war and City Hall was destroyed. Many of the churches and mosques have hidden rooms, and the DS is aware of most of them."

Camellion waited for the rest of the explanation.

Winkler was not as patient. "Oh boy! That's just dandy! And here we are!"

"Calm yourself, *tosvarkish* Winkler, and you also, *tosvarkish* Camellion," soothed Father Fodgiv in excellent English. "We men of God have what might be called a coalition whose purpose is to outwit the DS and other branches of the Ministry of the Interior. For example, these rooms were constructed over a period of some thirty years. It took that length of time for the priests to do the work in secret. These rooms were built after the other passage and rooms above were constructed. Let me explain that in those days, when our land was being invaded periodically, from east and west, the priests assumed that it was possible for invaders to discover the first set of hidden rooms. For that reason, these rooms—seventy feet below ground level—were built. So it was with rooms in other churches and mosques." He paused for a moment to get his breath. "The DS knows about the first set of rooms. Years ago, we told them. Officers of the DS inspected the rooms. They felt and still do that everything is in order and that we have nothing to hide."

"The tour you saw upstairs," announced Stephen Traikov. "Those tourists were taken through the passage and the rooms on that level. Here, where we are, is a different matter. These rooms are a total secret. Here we are safe."

"Anyhow, here we are," Camellion mused. "What time will the other two leaders arrive?"

"Tomorrow evening," replied Traikov. "It is not easy for them and they are very cautious."

Too damned cautious! Camellion, feeling like a ten-year-old boy sitting on the edge of his seat during the Saturday afternoon matinee, noticed that Winkler was also disgusted with Petur Dzhurov and Zhivko Stoichev, both of whom were still arguing with Stephen Traikov.

At length, Traikov smiled at Winkler and the Death Merchant. "It is settled. Let us discuss the details of your plan to blow up DS headquarters."

"One thing we must know. How can you be sure that the Soviet advisers will be in the building at the time. It is your job to kill them, is that not so?" Petur Dzhurov said in a conspiratorial growl.

"Making sure the Russian Uncles are in the building is something we must still resolve," Camellion said. "There's a lot more I want to do. I intend to take ten picked men, go inside the building, and kill the Soviet Uncles and Colonel General Grigor Shopov and his aides. This will be done before the three trucks crash into the building."

Petur Dzhurov made a face and shook his head up and down.

Zhivko Stoichev frowned. "Another impossibility," he muttered.

"I've solved more complicated problems," Camellion said, not hiding his irritation. "In my own experience I've found that an opportunity is hidden in every problem."

"We do have militia uniforms and an expert forgery department," Traikov commented. "Forging passes and special papers would not be any problem." He turned his attention fully to the Death Merchant. "It will be a great risk no matter how we do it. We would have to go through the gate in order to get inside the building. That in itself could be very tricky."

Carey Winkler crushed out his cigarette and turned his ruddy face toward Camellion. "I'd like to know if we're going to invade the building on the same day that the trucks make the headquarters go boom? We would have to, and that means we're going to have a devil of a time with the timing— the synchronization of our blowing up the Russian trash and DS 'High Mandarins' on the fifth floor and our escape with the three trucks hitting the sides of the building. How about escape? Don't try to tell me we'll go out the same way we came in! That leaves only the helicopters on the roof.''

"You said it. We leave in two of the choppers." Camellion sighed and cracked the knuckles of his left hand. "Don't ask me about details for any of this, not yet, not now. But aren't we getting ahead of ourselves? If we can't find three men willing to commit suicide—and that's what it amounts to— why bother with the truck part of the operation?''

"We're not certain right now. But we feel we can find the men." Traikov shifted on the box on which he was sitting. "I know of one man who is slowly dying. Whether he would be willing to drive one of the trucks is another matter. He's being closely watched at the present time.''

"Which leaves us where?" Camellion said. "We can go into DS headquarters independently of the trucks. I prefer not to. I want to use the ten-man strike to divert attention from the trucks.''

"So that's how the wind blows!" Winkler gave Camellion a long, searching stare. "You want to tie together the two different operations. We go in, shoot the shit out of everyone and everything, then get to the roof and take off. Right behind us come the three trucks and—blooie!''

"An oversimplification but, essentially, that's it," acknowledged the Death Merchant. "It would only take one slip and we'd all fry in hell.''

Zhivko Stoichev said, "The Moslems hate the *Darzhavna Sigurnost* even worse than we do. They are crazy with hatred. Very possibly some of them would help us. We can trust them.''

"The three trucks are another problem. Getting them will not be easy," Petur Dzhurov said slowly. Broad-shouldered, he had the strong chin, balanced carriage, and quick, light step of a man who knew the world for what it really was: a murderous society of barbarians.

"Is there any chance of our hijacking the trucks?" said Winkler. When he saw that none of the Hungarians understood the meaning of the word, he reiterated, "I mean, stopping the trucks on the highway, then taking them over. We could kill the drivers and put your men in their place. We would need silencers though to do the job. Another flaw is that even if we find three dying men, they have to know how to drive large trucks." His eyes locked with the Death Merchant's. "You know, we have taken on the impossible."

"What you suggest is not possible, Mr. Winkler." Stoichev sounded sad. "The *Jokka* patrol the motorways too efficiently for any American gangster tactics to be effective. And within Sofia . . . even more of an impossibility." He stood, pushed his chair closer to the table, and sat down.

"Even if it could be done, it would be a sheer waste to stop the vehicles on the motorways," explained Petur Dzhurov. For a short moment, he stared over his glass of red wine, then lowered it carefully to his lap, holding the stem as though he were clutching a dagger. "There are nine different SOMAT depots in the Sofia *okrug*. To stop the trucks after they have left their depots and their drivers are on their way to pick up loads would bring us nothing but trouble. When the trucks don't arrive at their destinations, the managers of the places will phone the depots. The managers of the depots will notify the *Jokka*. To stop the trucks after they are loaded would also defeat our purposes. What would we do with the loads? Where could we even take the trucks to be unloaded? We do not have such places of concealment. . . ."

"I have been wondering how we can obtain four and a half tons of ammonium nitrate and get it loaded on the trucks!" Traikov pushed his tongue into the left side of his mouth and looked up at the ceiling.

"Well, I think all of us know the answer," Winkler said. "That means we're still up a creek without a paddle."

The Death Merchant shrugged. "Somehow, we have to obtain three empty trucks at the depots, forge the transfer manifest for the loading, and then drive the vehicles to three different farm collectives."

"The forgery of the papers will be simple enough," Traikov said.

Winkler looked like a burglar caught in the act.

"Why not one farm collective? And come to think of it, why not use only one truck? Ten tons could easily be carried in one truck. I presume the ammonium nitrate is bagged? Hell, it has to be."

"All that fertilizer in one truck would make the vehicle too heavy," Camellion told him. "To scatter it out in three trucks will make each truck lighter. Anyhow, I want the trucks to hit the building at three different angles. Why three different collectives? Three trucks, all getting loads of ammonium nitrate at one collective warehouse might cause someone to become suspicious."

There was a long pause, shattered when the Death Merchant looked at Stoichev and said, "I know you have members in SOMAT. On that basis, is it possible for you to find out the details about truck schedules, routes, the kind of orders we would need, and anything else we might need to know?"

"That kind of information is the least of our worries. We could forge all the necessary forms, but the three drivers—three men willing to kill themselves!—would still have to go to SOMAT depots in the morning and obtain the trucks." Stoichev stood up, walked to the table, picked up a pencil, and motioned to the Death Merchant. "Come here. I will show you—and you also, Mr. Winkler."

Along with Camellion and Winkler, Stephen Traikov and Petur Dzhurov came to the table.

"I'll show you the locations of the SOMAT depots and the collective farms in the Sofia district. There are only three such farms," Stoichev said, studying the Death Merchant. "It will give you a better idea of the complex problems facing us and our enterprise."

Patiently (and impatiently), Camellion (and Winkler) waited as Stoichev circled the nine SOMAT depots, six in Sofia, two in Dragalevtsi, and one in Boyana. He then circled the three state collective farms, one to the north of Sofia, one to the south, and one to the west.

"You two gentlemen will notice that SOMAT station number four is closest to collective number two," Stoichev said, "and that SOMAT three is the one nearest to collective one. SOMAT one is in the same vicinity as collective three."

The Death Merchant surprised Winkler and the three Bulgarians by giving the results of his rapid mental calculations. "Assuming that the trucks have reached the collectives and have been loaded with the fertilizer, the closest truck to the DS headquarters on Anton Ivanova would be the truck leaving collective three. It would be about nine kilometers from the headquarters. The truck from collective two about thirteen kilometers. The vehicles from collective three around sixteen or seventeen klicks. But none of this is important right now."

"Not important!" Stoichev sounded insulted. He tossed the pencil onto the table. "These details have to be worked out. Won't the three trucks have to make some kind of rendezvous? Won't they have to strike the building at more or less the same time?"

Winkler cut in, "I have a question."

"With the trucks headed toward the headquarters building along various routes, how could the ten-man force possibly know when the three drivers were approaching Boulevard Anton Ivanova?" inquired Petur Dzhurov.

The Death Merchant answered Stoichev, his tone extra polite. "Of course each tiny detail must be resolved. As a minister would say, you're not listening to the bleatings of your flock. In this case a flock of one—me! I am saying that for the moment, everything we have discussed is speculation."

"We have to start someplace!" Stoichev said with harsh conviction.

"Sure we do and we have. You three leaders of the NFC have to first find three men—or women for all I care—who are not only willing to die but who can also drive tractor-trailers. Driving those rigs is an art. We couldn't have one of the drivers stopped by the *Jokka* because he doesn't know how to handle such a vehicle. In the meanwhile—"

"I want to know how we're going to detonate that much ammonium nitrate?" demanded Winkler, his resignation at an end. "I know a lot about explosives, but a booster for nine tons of fertilizer! I don't think it's ever been done—and the stuff will be in three different trucks!"

"A good question—and another problem to be solved," Camellion said. "In my estimation it will require the explosive equivalent of a hundred sticks of dynamite to trigger four hundred and fifty-three kilograms of—"

"That's a thousands pounds," Winkler interrupted. "Shit! We'd need the equivalent of nine hundred sticks!"

Stephen Traikov laughed. "It might as well be nine thousand sticks! We couldn't even steal that amount. It would take months!"

"It won't be necessary to steal any dynamite—*pjâsaci,*" said Camellion, who had pulled out a chair and sat down. He leaned back, crossed his legs, and addressed the three Bulgarians. "Before Winkler and I even arrived in Greece, I made arrangements with the CIA to have certain items smuggled into your organization. Included in the shipment are three hundred pounds—a hundred and thirty-six kilograms—of RDX, or cyclonite, the most powerful military explosive in the world. I figured at the time it would come in handy."

As he spoke, Camellion detected recognition in the expressions of the Bulgarians, a signal to him that they knew what he was talking about.

"The shipment was to follow Winkler and me, on the regular route through the Rhodope Mountains. It should have arrived by now, or didn't the shipment get to Sofia?"

Traikov and Stoichev stared at Camellion.

"Is that all you have to say about the shipment?" Dzhurov thrust out his chin, his voice sly. He gazed expectantly at the Death Merchant.

Camellion smiled, then said in Bulgarian, "*Molya vuh tova, razvalite nyakolko nosickka poruh-cham shokolat!*[7] Now that I've given you the proper code, give me some answers."

"Half of the shipment got through," Zhivko Stoichev said in a pleasantly neutral voice. "It arrived in Sofia yesterday and is at another safe house. We were waiting for you, *tosvarkish* Camellion, to mention it."

Quick to notice Stoichev's use of the trusted *tosvarkish*, the Death Merchant felt a stab of concern. "Half the shipment? How can you be sure that half got through—or did you have advance information on the items coming in? what happened?"

Traikov explained, "The mountain people were ambushed by the DS *Subranie-Kozivcho*, the border guards. If the firing of weapons had not caused an avalanche that buried most of the border guards, we would have lost the entire shipment. Our estimation of half is based on the information that was given us by the men who brought the shipment into Sofia."

An angry expression bloomed on Dzhurov's face. "Those damned mountain people should have been more cautious. But what can one expect from those stupid Bulgars?[8] They are a disgrace to this land of ours." He gave the Death Merchant and Winkler a knowing look. "The Bulgars are our curse."

Camellion remained silent, thinking that racism, along with gambling, prostitution, and wife beating, had been with the human race since the beginning of history. *We Americans don't have a monopoly on racial discrimination.*

"As yet we have not had the time to check the boxes," Zhivko Stoichev said. He had sat down on the edge of the table and was swinging his legs back and forth. "Perhaps your explosives are there, perhaps they are not. . . ."

---

[7] "The Eagle will always fly high and to the left."
[8] The Bulgars are a Turko-Tartar race that originated in the steppes of southern Russia. They are the "hillbillies" of Bulgaria and looked down on by the Slavs.

Not to mention weapons, grenades, my makeup kit, and the radio!

"This evening we'll check the crates and get the stuff over here tomorrow morning," Petur Dzhurov said. "You will know then what is missing. You know what was due to be shipped?"

Before the Death Merchant could say anything, Winkler cut in. "When do we make contact with the agent from the U.S. Embassy? By now the three of you have had time to set up a meeting."

Camellion jumped in right behind him. "That's another reason why we can't make any hard decisions about blowing up the DS building. Much will depend on the information I receive from the Agency station at the embassy."

"Tomorrow night at eight o'clock," Traikov said promptly. "Please do not ask where, not at this time. The two of you will know tomorrow night. There is much to be done before then."

Winkler nodded in the Western manner—head up and down. The expression on his face was not one of peace and contentment.

The Death Merchant didn't feel like tap dancing. As far as he was concerned, Satan was going wild in the sanctuary . . .

And we're fresh out of holy water. . . .

CHAPTER SIX

Should Richard Camellion have permitted his mind to wander, it would not have been difficult for him to have convinced himself that he was in a hotel bar in Houston, Texas. The day before, he had wondered where and how he and Winkler would meet the special emissary from the CIA station at the United States Embassy in Sofia. It wasn't until the afternoon of the next day—today—that he had found out, a revelation that had rocked him and Winkler on their heels, for neither had suspected that the meet would take place in the Slavyanska Hotel on Lenska Square, a first-class hostelry favored by American and British tourists. As proof, the Buffalo Bill Room was now packed with Americans and the queen's subjects.

Sitting with his back not far from a wall plastered with posters of the American Old West—and not liking it—the Death Merchant studied the laughing men and women at the tables and at the bar, behind which, on the center wall, were the enormous horns of a Texas longhorn. On both sides of the horns were large toy pistols—six-shooters—and reproductions of ancient dageurreotypes of Billy the Kid, Jesse and Frank James, the Dalton Gang, and other bad men of the Old West.

At Camellion's table, to his right, was "Myrna Beckworth." Next to her was her "husband," "Charles Beckworth." To his right, and directly across from Camellion, was the man who carried the name "James Walter Kline" on his United States passport. Dressed in a black Monet blazer, trousers to match, a silk black and white geometric tie, pin collar white shirt, and European styled black and white dress shoes, "Kline" was Carey Winkler.

Leonard Bundy and his party of three had been in the Buffalo Bill Room only fifteen minutes and were still working on their first drink—Scotch on the rocks (but only *Manastirska Izba*, a sweet, white wine, for Mrs. Beckworth) —when Bundy, whose passport listed him as being born and still living in Blue Island, Illinois, spotted a tall, fortyish man moving through the tables with a slow measured stride, a cocktail glass in his hands. Appearing to be slightly drunk, the man had a magnificent mane of gray hair, cut short, a small, precise mustache, and was dressed in a sportcoat of subtle pastel tones, flannel burgundy slacks, and black Nettleton loafers.

Winkler, who had half turned his chair from the table and was sitting so that he could partially look over the crowd, also noticed the man moving through the tables. He took a sip from his glass, turned subtly to Bundy, and said in a low voice, "You've seen him too. Notice how his eyes keep looking downward?"

"If he's our man, he won't have any trouble seeing our pins," Camellion replied, his lips barely moving.

Charles Beckworth and Myrna Beckworth, knowing better than to turn around, sat quietly. A moment later, Charles Beckworth said in perfect American English, with a Bostonian accent "Looking downward you say. Perhaps the guy's a tit man. I'm a leg man myself."

"Tch, tch, tch!" mocked Myrna Beckworth. "Such language. You'll embarrass me." She spoke with a southern accent, the deep South at that!

"It was just an idea," Charles said.

The Death Merchant—admiring the acting ability of the "Beckworths," who were as Bulgarian as Colonel General Grigor Shopov—thought of the chain events that had placed him and Winkler and Grisha Dyuni and Julia Mirokeb in the Slavyanska Hotel, in an extremely dangerous position if everything didn't go as planned.

By nine o'clock that morning, eleven wooden boxes of various sizes had arrived at the Church of St. Dimitur, delivered by the same truck that had brought candles and other church supplies. By 9:29 the boxes were in the secret passage within the large middle altar and were being carried to the truly secret complex of rooms that were the safe house—carried by Winkler, Camellion, the three Bulgarian leaders of the NFC, and three priests. Father Korzo was carrying the last box onto the platform of the wide steps when the first Balkantourist tour arrived at the church.

The boxes were quickly opened. There was only 100 pounds of RDX. The other 200 pounds had been lost in the ice and snow of the Rhodope Mountains. The makeup kit had not been lost; neither had the radio, a Gould Manpack PCS-2001 transceiver. But only a third of the weapons and ammo had arrived, and not a single frag grenade. Two-thirds of the firepower had been lost and all of the grenades.

"We'll have to make our own grenades," Camellion said.

"Uh huh—how?" Doubt was written all over Winkler's face.

"Dynamite sticks with short fuses."

"How in hell can we take time out to strike matches!"

"We don't. We light cigars. all except me. I'm allergic to tobacco. It gives me double vision at times."

"I'll be damned!"

"I would be too if I smoked."

One box contained eight Viking submachine guns. A cross in size and in looks between an Uzi and a MAC SMG, the Viking could get off thirty-six rounds of 9mm. Parabellum projectiles, or could be set to fire three-round bursts. Manufactured by WSI,[1] the Viking came equipped with Sionics suppressor, electronic Aimpoint sight, and grenade launcher. The "silencers" and the grenade launchers were not on the eight Viking SMGs. Two other boxes were filled with magazines and boxes of cartridges for the eight choppers.

Other crates contained Walther P-88 fifteenshot 9mm. autopistols, the hard-to-get Czech CZ-75[2] pistol, three Beretta M92SB autoloaders with Larand suppressors attached, and four .22 Ruger MK-1: counterinsurgency pistols. The Rugers were the best of all silenced assassination pistols, as the

---

[1] This is not fiction. W.S.I. means Viking Submachine Gun System. W.S.I. is a small company operating out of Malden, Massachusetts. I've test-fired the Viking; it's a fine, efficient weapon.

[2] Very difficult to get because of BATF import restrictions. The weapon is expensive—$900—and is easy to field-strip. But it's a nightmare to *detail-strip* because of its many small parts. Readers who are interested might write to International Gun Co., P.O. Box 3551, Tucson, Arizona 85740.

silencers were built directly into the weapons, around the barrels, and the barrels were modified by the addition of gas vent holes for the gases to escape into the expansion chambers around the barrels.[3]

Winkler continued to examine one of the Ruger Mk-1 CIPs. "Tell me, Camellion. Do you think we'll be able to pull off this whole deal? I think we have enough weapons. But with only a hundred pounds of RDX—any ideas?"

"We'll have to improvise," Camellion said, and looked at Petur Dzhurov, who was closest to him. "Right now, I'd like to know where we're going to meet our man from the embassy."

"Later," Dzhurov said.

"Later" came about two in the afternoon, as the group was eating a lunch of *Gyuvech* (a hotpot of a variety of vegetables) and drinking coffee. It was during lunch that the three Hungarian leaders told the Death Merchant and Carey Winkler that they would meet their contact in the Slavyanska Hotel, specifically in the Buffalo Bill Room.

"The Buffalo Bill Room?" Winkler pretended to laugh. "You have to be kidding—and I know you're not!"

Stephen Traikov quickly added that it was not he nor Dzhurov nor Stoichev who had made the arrangements. "It was a week before the two of you arrived in Sofia and your embassy sent this information. We have not had any contact with the CIA since then."

Zhivko Stoichev put down his fork. "We have had our people in place at designated meeting points, but no one from your embassy has shown up."

"It was the last agent we had contact with who explained that the needed essentials would be delivered four days later," Petur Dzhurov said while chewing his food.

"You must mean the proper clothing?" Camellion said brusquely. There was only a single electric light burning in the large stone room, and due to where Camellion was sitting, his face was deeply shadowed but not so much that the others couldn't see the hostile look under arched eyebrows and the firm, angry set of his lean jaw. "Whoever thought of a hotel as a meeting place has to be a double idiot! Now about

---

[3] This type of silencer is suitable for automatics that have fixed, *exposed* barrels. Because of the silencer built around the barrel, the Ruger MK-1 CIP looks as if it has a bull barrel.

the clothes. It wouldn't surprise me if the Agency didn't send mechanics' coveralls!''

Winkler snorted and made a peremptory gesture with his hand. ''I've been in all the rooms down here and I haven't seen any clothes fit to wear to a fancy commie dump like the Slavyanska! The 'Buffalo Bill Room'! That's got to be the joke of the year!''

''The proper attire is at a private home, a kilometer from here, the home of one of our members,'' Traikov said. He then dropped another verbal bombshell by saying that two members of the revolutionary National Freedom Council would accompany Camellion and Winkler to the hotel. ''A man and a woman. He's an actor; she's an actress. We felt, and so did your CIA, that the deception could be better achieved if the two of you were seen with another couple, with two other tourists.''

''But the NFC and the Company didn't cook up the scheme together?''

Traikov frowned at the Death Merchant, his own tone petulant. ''We of the NFC didn't plan anything with the CIA. It was the CIA's idea. We only happen to agree with the idea. Do you understand?''

Camellion wasn't concerned about Traikov's own mini-anger--let the Bulgarian thicken his skin. ''I could ask about passports, but if the same ant brain who decided on our meeting the contact in a hotel had a hand in total identification, we might have to pose as Indians or Japanese!''

Winkler let out a low ho-ho-ho. ''We could darken our skin or maybe put a slant to our eyes with Scotch tape. You do have your makeup kit. Shit, we could even go as Eskimos!''

Camellion let him have a double icepick stare. ''You're so happy about all this, you could be a Mormon!''

Winkler laughed again. ''Okay, old buddy. Pardon me for breathing.''

''The four of you will pose as American tourists,'' Dzhurov said earnestly. ''The passports—and they are genuine United States passports—and other papers you will carry, your billfolds, cards, and photographs that will be in your billfolds—it is all with the clothing at the house.''

''Photographs for the passports?'' Camellion wanted to cover all available ground. ''We don't have time today. That must mean that you took our photographs surreptitiously?''

Dzhurov nodded yes, moving his head from side to side.

"Two days after the two of you arrived in Sofia. Do not worry, *tosvarkish* Camellion. You and *tosvarkish* Winkler will see, when you get to the house, that we have made all the necessary arrangements."

Stephen Traikov finished pouring *Mastica* into his coffee. "I will be going with you to the house. At four, a truck from collective two will bring a load of potatoes to the rectory. We will ride in the back of the truck to the private house on Ruginkav Ulitsa. We should be there no later than five-thirty."

More likely by six-thirty! Damn it!

Camellion was wrong. It was five-twenty by the time he and Winkler and Traikov were actually in the living room of the house, a shabby, five-room affair in the extreme southeast section of the city. The house was chilly, almost cold. Not only was meat scarce for the common people of Sofia but fuel oil and coal as well.

"We're damned lucky we shaved before we left the church," Winkler said, taking off his *chivva* and looking around the dimly lighted combination living room and parlor. Old were the sofa and the two overstuffed chairs that were from another period. Well worn and paper thin was the rug, but clean. And the red flowered wallpaper was new, so much so that one could still detect the faint odor of wallpaper paste. The large oil heater, in the center of the room, was also very modern.

Traikov had locked the front door and had checked to make sure the shades were all the way down. Now he hurried across the room.

"The bedroom is this way," he said, moving into a tiny hallway. "The clothes are in a wardrobe. Your passports, billfolds, money, and other forms of identification are under the wardrobe."

"Where are the three who live here?" Camellion walked into the bedroom behind Traikov, his right hand wrapped around a Walther P-88 pistol in the pocket of his *chivva*. He glanced at the old-fashioned bed and large wooden wardrobe with mirrored double doors. "On the way over here, you mentioned that a man and his wife and her brother lived here."

Traikov pushed back his fur trooper hat and sat down on the bed. "They didn't want you and Winkler to see their faces. That way you couldn't identify them in case you're captured."

Camellion pulled off his heavy outer coat and opened the wardrobe.

"I'd like to know where we're going to put our guns," Winkler said. "We can't carry them in shoulder holsters. A blind man would see the bulges. . . ."

"Here's your answer," Camellion said cheerfully. "Below the overcoats, by the shoes." He reached into the wardrobe and pulled out a chocolate nylon shoulder tote and a "continental" maroon naugahyde camera bag. Camellion held them up for Winkler to inspect. "Could it be that some planner in the Agency was farsighted enough to know we'd have a problem of where to stash our weapons?"

"Do rhinoceroses fly?" Winkler said. "Or is it rhinoceri? No, rhinoceroses." He started to inspect the clothes in the wardrobe. "Is there a camera in the camera bag?"

"It's empty." Camellion put the shoulder tote and the camera bag on the floor and reached for the brown tweed suit hanging next to the Churchill trenchcoat. "Wellll, this looks like my size."

Carey Winkler began pulling off his sweater.

While Camellion and Winkler changed clothes, Traikov smoked a Russian cigarette and told them about Point B7, a motion picture theater whose manager was a member of the NFC. "The Tsar Kaloyan Theater on Kaloyan Ulitsa will be your closest place of refuge should you have trouble at the hotel and have to flee. Once you reach the theater, simply buy a ticket, go inside and sit in the last row. I will contact you."

Camellion paused in zipping up the brown tweed trousers and glanced at Traikov. "Then you'll have to be watching the front of the hotel—or else you must have a NFC member who works at the Slavyanska. It's got to be one or the other—and I don't suppose you'll tell me which!" He went back to zipping his pants.

"I will know if there is trouble at the hotel," Traikov said. "Do not concern yourselves about my finding out. Should there be difficulty, I will go at once to the Kaloyan Theater. Buying tickets would not be a problem. You will have plenty of money, and you, *tosvarkish* Winkler, speak our language."

"And write it," Winkler said, buttoning his pin collar white shirt. "But I speak Bulgarian with an accent. If it comes to that, we'll have to risk it. We've come this far. We might as well play out the hand."

The Death Merchant began tying his brown silk pin-dot tie. "Trouble inside the hotel could mean that the DS will carry us out stone dead." He almost sneered at Stephen Traikov. "How could we find the theater on Kalyan Street? We're not familiar with Sofia. I can picture certain streets in my mind. That's about it. You might as well ask us to find the head of a pin in a haystack during a tornado."

"Grisha Dyuni and Julia Mirakeb know how to get to the theater," Traikov said, all the while wondering what a "tornado" was. A heavy snowstorm?

"Well! I like this!" Winkler said, and pulled a navy, wool duffel coat from the wardrobe. "Of course, I wouldn't wear it to a Puerto Rican wedding."

"I'll tell you one thing, Traikov," Camellion said, and lipped his arm into the right sleeve of the brown tweed suit coat. "Those two had better be what you said they are— damned good."

Grisha Dyuni and Julia Mirokeb arrived fifteen and twenty minutes later, both driving Soviet Ladas,[4] the woman being the first to knock on the front door. Looking much younger than her twenty-seven years, Julia Mirokeb was fashionably thin, her features delicate, making the Death Merchant think of a fine painting on Dresden china. Her hair was dyed blond and fell to her shoulders; she stood five-feet-five and wore a gray Merion wool, double-breasted polo coat, gray leather snow boots, wool gloves, and a Stremel hat with a dark fleecy trim. When she removed her coat, they could see her long-sleeved bronze evening dress, the long V-neck shirred softly from the shoulders and glimmering above the whirl of a circle skirt.

Stephen Traikov had finished introducing Julia Mirokeb to "James Walter Kline" and "Leonard Bundy" and she was explaining that she had traveled widely, including the United States, with the Bulgarian State Drama Company when Grisha Dyuni arrived. He hurriedly removed his British tan walker, looked at Traikov, and got right down to business. "Okay. Who am I supposed to be and where's the passport and other junk?" He sounded as American as Winkler and Camellion— and Mirokeb, who could "play" her voice the way one stretched a rubber band.

---

[4] The Soviet Lada is a chunky, no-frills automobile that looks like a cheesebox on wheels. The Lada guzzles gas and breaks down frequently. But the four-door station wagon appeals to Europeans because of its low price: $3,600.

Carey Winkler, who had always been against going "public," gave Camellion a long look and subtly shook his head, his eyes conveying a silent message: *We're talking bent noodle here. All this is right out of a cracker factory, straight out of the funny farm. . . .*

Dyuni's hair was dark and straight, his lips full, his eyes heavily wrinkled at the corners. He might have been thirty-five and could have lost ten to fifteen pounds. He had on a suit-type denim coat, a bright red American Old West shirt, and bell-bottomed Levi's. His wide leather belt was hand-tooled and had a huge silver buckle that displayed a pair of spurs and was emblazoned with the legend: "Texas, the Lonestar State."

The remainder of his outfit didn't match: tan calfksin boots with cushion crepe soles, a gray English wool tweed cap, and brown leather gloves. To Camellion, the man could have been American. But he still didn't look right.

Dyuni took a long look at the name on the passport, put the slim green book inside his denim coat, and smiled like a shy barracuda. "So I'm Charles Beckworth. I suggest we get the show on the road. We can't end up with less than getting our butts shot off."

Traikov left in one car. The other four drove off in the second Lada, Grisha Dyuni behind the wheel, explaining that the Soviet Lada "is an insult to the automobile world. Eight kilometers to the gallon is all you get and the damn thing won't go over sixty miles an hour."

It was on the way to the Slavyanska Hotel that Camellion and Winkler, in the rear seat, learned that both Dyuni and Mirokeb had been forced to leave the acting profession because of "antisocial" remarks they had made.

"In a democratic country, a remark such as 'We're slaves of socialism' would be ignored. Not in the 'People's Democratic Republic' of Bulgaria! That made me a political unreliable. That ended my career as an actress."

"And mine," Dyuni said bitterly. "I said that the DS was worse than Hitler's Gestapo. The remark was heard by the wrong ears. I went from actor to janitor. I've been a janitor for the past six years."

Mirokeb sighed deeply. "I'm a maid in the Grand Hotel Balkan."

The night was very cold, a pale sliver of moon dismally pushed to the surface of the sky. The dark, frigid night triggered in the Death Merchant a remembrance of the few weeks he had once spent in Moscow. Yet a Bulgarian winter could not be compared to a *Russkaya zima*. The Russian winter involved a much crueler span of time than that which annually slowed the nations of Europe and the United States. The Russian winter was a life sentence of hardship, an adversity that haunted the Russian mind even during the summer months. It was the long, ruthless winter that molded the Russian attitude toward life, that gave the pig farmers a pessimism possessed by no other people.

Ruthless and impatient, winter always came early, snow often falling in late August. By the end of September the trees would be naked. For seven months, the only foliage, apart from beloved house plants, would be the dark mantle of the fir. For seven months, the ever-vicious *Russkaya zima* would eat away precious food and fuel and freeze away energy, patience, and imagination. The harsh Russian winter was only one reason why the Russian people perceived other nations as hostile and felt that "we are not like other people in the world."

Grisha Dyuni had just turned onto Najco Pozitano and the car was passing prefabricated apartment buildings that looked like cell blocks against the black sky when he said, "We are only four blocks from the hotel. Any special instructions from you good men in the back?"

Winkler, slumped down in the seat, snickered. "Think before you speak and be on guard at all times—or Burger King won't make us honorary waffles!"

"Make sure your weapons are handy," Camellion answered Grisha Dyuni. "What kind do you have, or don't you have any?"

"I have a German Mauser in my belt," Grisha Dyuni said. "It's seven-sixty-five caliber and is in excellent condition."

"An Italian gun is in my handbag," Julia Mirokeb said, "and please don't ask us if we know how to shoot. At age eighteen, all Bulgarians, men and women, are drafted into the army, men for two years, women for six months. I can shoot and shoot well."

Carey Winkler smiled unkindly. "Just hope you don't have to prove it tonight." No longer joking, he had meant every word.

The circumstances of the meet are in our favor," Camellion said. "As for the factors of X, there are so many of them that almost anything could happen, including an asteroid's hitting the Earth. The bottom line is that everyone dies. All life is but a slow and steady march toward death. If something goes wrong, we have to be prepared to shoot our way out—or die trying. Hell is not a myth on earth—it's a commie prison. . . ."

"Bullshit!" Winkler, having flipped out his cigarette, rolled up the window. "Who in his right mind wants to die in this damned city. You take Miami Beach. It's twenty miles of sand looking for a city. Sofia is twenty miles of snow looking for a nation."

"We'll be pulling into the parking lot of the Slavyanska in a short while," announced Grisha Dyuni.

The Death Merchant unzipped the shoulder tote on his lap and took out the Walther P-88 pistol. A superb army and police weapon, the P-88 had a fifteen-round magazine, good trigger cocking, and, due to Walther's internal safety, no external safety lever. He checked the pistol. Perfect. One 9mm. jacketed hollow point in the firing chamber.

"I just hope the guy knows how to ID us," Winkler said, taking his own P-88 from the continental camera bag.

Camellion didn't comment, his thoughts on "Mr. and Mrs. Charles Beckworth." So true. Politics did make strange bed-fellows out of different people. But assassination plots made even stranger marriages. . . .

The tall man, moving around the tables, a cocktail glass in his right hand, drew closer to the table where the Death Merchant, Winkler, and the "Beckworths" were sitting.

Back at the safe house of the Church of St. Dimitur, Traikov and the other two leaders had said that they didn't have the slightest idea how the CIA contact would recognize Camellion and Winkler.

"Why should we have such need to know information?" Petur Dzhurov had said. "We supposed you two and the contact have certain identification code phrases."

"We have, but the contact has to find us first, or vice versa," Camellion had told him.

Now, watching the tall man weaving closer to his table, Camellion strongly suspected that the tipoff to the contact—if the man were the contact—was the clothes he and Winkler were wearing, or maybe only the Knights of Columbus buttons in their left lapels. Probably both, since there was always a chance that another tourist could be wearing a Knights of Columbus button.

"Here he comes," Winkler said in a low voice, then glanced down at the camera bag on the floor between his feet.

"What do you want us to do?" asked Grisha Dyuni.

"Nothing. Sit tight," Camellion said.

The tall man with the shock of gray hair and the small mustache was soon at the table, standing between "James Kline"—Winkler—and "Charles Beckworth"—Grisha Dyuni— swaying slightly as if drunk. Before he said a word, his eyes went downward, first to Camellion, then to Winkler, his gaze fastening momentarily on the Knights of Columbus pins in their lapels. Camellion and Winkler looked up at him. So did the Beckworths.

"It is sure nice to see you folks again," the man said in a loud voice. " You remember me, don't you? Sure you do. We met the other day on a tour of the National Archaeological Museum. Besides, how could you forget good old Harry Cross? You don't mind if I join you? Of course you don't."

Without waiting for an invitation, Cross put his glass on the table—Camellion noticed that it was almost full—then turned and half stumbled to a table to his right. There was only a man and a woman at the table where there were also two empty chairs.

"You won't mind if I borrow a chair?" Cross said good-naturedly. In another few moments, he had pulled the chair to the Death Merchant's table and was sitting down between Winkler and Dyuni, the former of whom was trying to decide whether Cross was The Man or just another pesty tourist who couldn't hold his liquor.

Camellion had no such doubts. Listening to his intuition, he was convinced that Cross was either the CIA contact or a DS agent. As Cross was getting the chair from the other table, the Death Merchant had seen something at the bar that was the same as a knife being twisted in his back. One of the men seated at the bar, ordinary looking and dressed in a neat blue suit, was engaged in conversation with a woman who was obviously as American as Mom's apple pie. For only an instant, the man had started to nod yes in agreement with something the woman had said. Only he had started to nod in the Bulgarian manner, by shaking his head from side to side. Very quickly the man had caught himself and had nodded *yes* in the Western manner, by nodding up and down. The side-to-side motion had lasted only a microsecond, so short it had not really gotten off the ground. On that basis, Camellion could not be positive. The side movement of the man's head might have been an innocent motion, or . . . *Could I have been mistaken? Or is the man a DS agent?*

Cross didn't give Camellion or anyone else a chance to speak.

"I came to Bulgaria a week ago," he said heartily. "Caravan Tours. They operate out of Chicago. I think about a hundred of us flew over from the good old U.S.A." He looked around at the drinks that were barely touched. "Come on, come on. Drink up and I'll buy us a round."

He turned in his chair, looked toward the bar, and began snapping his fingers, trying to get the attention of one of the white-coated waiters. There were a dozen waiters in the Buffalo Bill Room, and one soon came to the table, all smiles and politeness.

"Give 'em the same, whatever they're drinking, and bring me another martini, light on the vermouth, no olive, no lemon," Cross said.

After the waiter had left, Cross grinned first at Winkler, then at Camellion. "Before I came to Bulgaria, I was in Mexico. Took myself on a tour that showed me all the Aztec ruins. Have you ever seen the four large temple pyramids at Tenayuca, Mr.—what did you say your name was?"

"I didn't. It's Bundy. Leonard Bundy," Camellion said, positive now that Cross was the contact. The "Have you seen the four large temple pyramids at Tenayuca?" was the opening sentence of the identification exchange. Clever, since there was only one temple pyramid at Tenayuca.

Grisha Dyuni and Julia Mirokeb slowly sipped their drinks.

Winkler, studying the man who called himself Harry Cross, reached down, picked up the camera bag, and slipped the strap over his right shoulder.

"I have seen the four temple pyramids at Tenayuca," Camellion answered in a low voice. "I have also seen the hilltop temple at Tepoztlan, honoring Hemotipec, the god of drunkenness." *Your turn!*

Cross reached into his multicolored coat and took out a gold cigarette case. All the while looking at Camellion, he opened the case and removed a cigarette. "I think you have also seen the statue of Chicomecoatl, the maize goddess. She holds a staff to symbolize fertility."

"I have seen Chicomecoatl. What did you see at Zócalo?"

"The Stone of Tizoc. Can you tell me who Nezahualcoyotl was?"

"Certainly," Camellion said. "He was the Aztec poet-king. He ruled over Toxcoco for forty years. Can you tell me what Chapultepec means."

"Grasshopper Hill," Cross answered promptly, completing the identification code. Now, knowing that Leonard Bundy was the man he was supposed to contact, Cross said in a firm voice, without any trace of intoxication, "You haven't introduced me to your three friends."

Watching three men and a woman in the middle of the dimly lighted room, the Death Merchant jerked his head toward Winkler. "He's Kline. He came into the country with me. The Beckworths are cover. They're actually Bulgarians and members of the National Freedom Council."

"We can't talk here," Cross said, taking a cigarette lighter out of his coat pocket. "We'll finish the drinks I've ordered, then leave. I have a Kalota out in the hotel lot. It will be crowded with five of us, but we'll have to make do. I have much to tell you."

"I have a lot to ask you."

"Mr. Bundy, I think we might have a slight problem," Winkler said softly. He looked down at the table and lowered his voice. "I could be wrong, but for what it's worth . . . there are two men behind you. Both are sitting by the wall. They're not together, but both of them seem to have an intense interest in us. I'm certain. I've been in this game too long not to know a setup. I think we're right in the middle of it."

"You're not wrong," Camellion said easily, all the while smiling for the benefit of any enemy who might be watching. "Behind you and the Beckworths are three men and a woman. They're at one table. They didn't start taking an interest in us until Cross sat down. There's also a joker at the bar. I think he's DS."

Julia Mirokeb paled and slowly reached for her large handbag.

"If you're right, the slip-up didn't come from my end," said Cross, smoke curling from his nostrils. "I couldn't have been made by the DS or the KGB. I did come into the country as a tourist."

"It's irrelevant for now. Are you armed?" Camellion said, pleased that Cross's voice had not contained any trace of panic. It could be that, like Winkler, he performed best under pressure.

"No, but I wish I were. I hope you four are. What are we going to do? What do you suggest?"

His eyes everywhere, Camellion leaned to the left, picked up the chocolate nylon shoulder tote, and slipped the strap over his left shoulder, his mental circuits clicking. The bar was full of foreigners. The DS could not want any unpleasantness in front of people—most of whom were American and British tourists—who would return to the West with horror stories about Bulgaria. There were several conclusions to the problem. Possibly the DS was in the bar only to observe and watch to see where Cross and the others would go. *Which means they've already put a bumper beeper on his Kalota—or else the secret police are here to make an arrest, to take the five of us into custody. If it's to arrest us, the DS has to be desperate. Is it possible the DS knows about the entire plan?*

"There's only one thing we can do," Camellion said calmly, and placed the tote bag in his lap. "We get up and leave— and shoot if we have to."

"And go to where—and in what?" demanded Winkler in a whisper. "We can forget the parking lot. They'll have it covered, and there will be *Nersko-Tsopska* out in front in their damned jeeps."

"Precisely. And those jeeps can get up to eighty miles an hour." Camellion actually smiled. "And think of the pretty flashing red lights and the loud sirens those jeeps have!"

Winkler caught on at once. "A jeep to Point B7," he mused. "I like that. . . ."

"You're both crazy," hissed Grisha Dyuni. "We would never be able to get near one of the militia vehicles!"

"The Lord will provide," Camellion said, and glanced toward the long bar. Confident that DS eyes were watching his every movement, he had not been able to keep a constant check on the waiter who had taken Cross's order. He had seen the man go to the bar and give the order to one of the bartenders. The same waiter was still at the bar, and although Camellion could not be positive, it appeared that the order had been filled and the drinks placed on the tray. Why then was the waiter stalling?

Carey Winkler, who had also glanced toward the bar,

intuited what the Death Merchant was thinking. "I've been wondering the same thing. What's he waiting for? But why should we wait? The drinks could be drugged. Let's ease out of here."

"I think he's right," whispered Cross.

"Sit tight. Cross ordered drinks. It might look suspicious if we left before the drinks were served—and we need every second we can get."

Camellion and Winkler soon saw the reason for the waiter's procrastination. A well-dressed burly man, carrying an overcoat over his right arm, came into the bar through the wide door to the west, the doorway that opened to the main desk area of the hotel, to the north, and to the kitchen section and other rooms, to the south.

Damn it! They intend to arrest us, right here in this stupid Buffalo Bill Room!

It was the way the man carried the overcoat that tipped off the Death Merchant—and Winkler too. The coat not only covered the man's right forearm but his hand as well—so obvious to pros that he was also carrying a piece in his right hand, the weapon pointed downward.

The man paused and looked around, as if searching for friends. He walked leisurely forward and stopped when he was only six to eight feet from the waiter, who, seeing him, picked up the tray of drinks and started toward the Death Merchant's table. At no time had the man with the overcoat even glanced at the waiter who was visibly nervous. Still acting as though he were looking for friends, the DS agent followed the waiter.

"I could ask why you think that son of a bug didn't check his coat like everyone else," Winkler said dryly. "How do you want to play it?"

"I didn't think it would come to this!" muttered Julia Mirokeb.

Harry Cross, his expression frozen, looked fearfully at the Death Merchant. "What did he mean—how do you want to play it?"

Camellion didn't have the time to explain. The waiter was only twenty feet away—"Mr. Overcoat" thirty. . . .

"I'll take him out," Camellion said to Winkler. "You get the jokers behind me. The rest of you drop to the floor when I fire."

The waiter was only seven feet from the table when

Camellion pulled the Walther P-88 pistol from the tote bag, swung it toward the waiter, and began to tilt his chair backward.

Winkler's right hand dove into the camera bag.

The waiter, seeing the big muzzle of the P-88 pointed in his direction, fell apart. He let out a strangled cry, dropped the tray, tried to jump to his left, stumbled, and fell against a man at one of the tables.

Gheorghe Dunajan, the DS agent with the overcoat, was very fast. Instantly realizing that the silent approach had failed, he jerked the overcoat aside with his left hand, raised his right arm, snap-aimed, and twice pulled the trigger of the Vitmorkin machine pistol in his right hand—all with amazing speed, but he was still too slow. That half-second lag time was on the side of the Death Merchant.

Because Camellion was falling backward the two 9mm. projectiles burned air eight inches from his chest and buried themselves in the wall, in a large poster of a buffalo with fierce red eyes.

Your arse is glass and I'm a big bad hammer! Camellion fired twice when his chair was halfway to the floor, the first 9mm. JHPT stabbing into Gheorghe Dunajan's chest, the second also cutting into his chest just above the top of the sternum. The bullet zipped through his trachea and esophagus, smashed several cervical vertebrae, and tore its way through his neck. Only by a miracle did the slug miss another human being. It was a marvelous way to die, Dunajan feeling only a millisecond of agony, the kind of pain that can never really be recorded by the dying brain, the kind that is experienced by a victim during that last blink of a micromoment as the falling guillotine blade slices keenly and quickly through skin, muscle, and bone, half an eyeblink before the blade hits the block and the head—eyes fluttering—drops into the bloody basket.

A jet of blood jumping from his throat, Dunajan dropped the Vitmorkin, did a half spin, and fell sideways, his head hitting the side of a table and causing even more shrieks from one of the two women sitting there, both of whom had been switched into hysterics by the loud roaring of the Vitmorkin and the Walther P-88. They were not alone in their high-pitched arias of terror. All over the Buffalo Bill Room, women were screaming and diving to the floor. Their escorts and the bartenders also hit the deck. But not all of the waiters. Four were SD agents.

While the Death Merchant threw himself backward, Carey

Winkler pulled his P-88 pistol from the camera bag, moved from the chair, dropped to one knee, and brought up the West German weapon, supporting his right wrist with his left hand. Simultaneously, Cross, Dyuni, and Mirokeb—Julia hanging on to her handbag—dropped to the rug with such speed that two of the chairs were overturned. Dyuni reached for his Mauser. Julia Mirokeb pulled a 9mm. Sile-Benelli B-76 DA autopistol from her handbag.

Ivan Liskovik and Krustiu Goincheva, the two DS agents at a table behind the Death Merchant, had not been caught unaware. However, they had not anticipated the quick, electrifying action of Camellion and his people. Quicker than Liskovik but only half as intelligent, Goincheva half rose from his chair and was jerking a Bidja pistol from a shoulder holster as Winkler's JHPT projectile nailed him in the center of the nose, stabbed through the brain stem, and went bye-bye via the back of his head. The impact of the slug knocked back Goincheva's head and pushed him back onto the chair. There he sat, head hanging backward, his right arm and the Bidja on the table, his other arm dangling at his side.

Ivan Liskovik had thrown himself to the rug and had pulled his own Bidja autoloader, intending to fire from the floor. He was dead and didn't know it. He knew he didn't have time to even halfway aim. The instant the Bidja was free of its shoulder holster, he pointed it in the direction of Winkler and began pulling the trigger.

A pro never remains in one position for any length of time. After blowing up Goincheva, Winkler flung his body to the left and fired at Liskovik while on his back, his P-88 barking at the same time that the Bulgarian secret police agent's first bullet passed sixteen inches over his stomach. Winkler had moved and fired with such speed that even his "sense" aim was off. For this reason, his 9mm. slug cut through Liskovik's coat, tore through the trapezius muscle, and barely clipped the top of the right clavicle bone. Ivan Liskovik howled like a cat caught with its tail in a meat grinder, the pain and shock jerking him to the right, forcing his gun arm to drop and making his finger contract against the trigger. This time the Bidja's 9mm. flat-point projectile came uncomfortably close to Winkler, cutting horizontally, at a steep angle, across the left front of his Monet blazer. It dug a slight ditch in the black material and buried itself in the red rug. Pulling the trigger the second time had been the last act in the life of Ivan Strvo

Liskovik. Winkler's next slug struck him sideways in the left temple. There was no way that life could last. Like a guitar picker running away from his past, the dead Liskovik fell to the right, his right leg doubled up underneath him. His eyes were tightly closed, his mouth wide open in an earsplitting scream that only the dead could hear.

Within that very short span of time, the Death Merchant and his chair had hit the floor. Camellion had gotten to his knees and was preparing to ice the three men and a woman at another table, twenty feet to the east. There were two other tables between Camellion's table and the table at which the four DS agents had been sitting. At the next table, three young women had been sitting. The three women at this table and the two men and two women at the table next to Camellion's were hugging the floor, all of them terrified. Now, one man, overcome with curiosity, pushed himself up on his hands and gaped at Winkler who promptly snarled in broken English, "Get back down or I'll blow your capitalist head off! Almost fainting, the man dropped flat and buried his face in the thick red rug.

The four DS agents, although prepared, in theory, for any eventuality, had not expected the sudden death facing them. Because the action of the enemy had been so very sudden, the four forgot to think clearly—the very first rule of any gun battle. Even Captain Peturi Riskilin was rattled and indecisive. To redeem himself from the failure on Kirili, from his inability to kill or capture the NFC rebels in the old mansion, he had insisted that he should be one of the agents in the Buffalo Bill Room in the Slavyanska Hotel, a decision that would cost him his life.

Instead of dropping down and throwing themselves prone, Riskilin, the two other men, and the woman stood up and attempted to waste the Death Merchant and the four persons with him. That was their first mistake—standing up. Their second mistake was that they had not considered the possibility that Camellion and his people had spotted them. That is why Riskilin and the other three had stood in the first place—he and they hoped to blow up Camellion and Company before the Death Merchant and his crew could realize what was happening.

The Death Merchant was more than prepared. He said in a loud, calm voice, "The waiters. To my right. Kill 'em! They're DS!"—and automatically used his natural-born talents of being able to analyze a dangerous situation within a microsecond. Seeing that both Peturi Riskilin and Nikolai Yakvol were throwing down on him with Soviet Vitmorkin machine pistols, he jerked mightily to the left and headed for the rug, firing the Walther P-88 simultaneously with the movement and in conjunction with Carey Winkler's sending a bullet at Dimitri Vidin, almost at the same instant that Vidin fired his Helwan pistol.[5]

Julia Mirokeb had scooted around and was drawing a bead on Irina Zulisev. With a Bulgarian B13-D pistol in her left hand, Zulisev was about to open fire, her right hand holding firm her left wrist.

To the south and the southeast, DS agents, disguised as waiters, reached under their short, white jackets and pulled B13-D pistols, the Bulgarian version of the 9mm. Soviet Makarov. Ducking and weaving, at times going into a half crouch, the waiters started to close in, ignoring the screaming women and now and then stepping over a patron on the floor.

Gunfire exploded in the northwest section of the long, wide room, a few seconds of blasting sounds that caused more pandemonium among the patrons. Some were even brave enough—or frightened enough, only God would ever know which!—to get up and dash through the west door and the north side door, which opened into the dining room which was named the Lode Star.

While Dimitri Vidin's 9mm. slug passed within an inch of striking Winkler in the right side of the forehead, Carey's slug popped the Bulgarian between the lapels of his suit, right through his pink tie and cream shirt and into his chest. With a short, quick cry, Dimitri Vidin fell back and started to go down next to Nikolai Yakvol, whose Vitmorkin, on full automatic, was making a loud *brlbrlbrlbrlbrl* sound, the muzzle spitting out fourteen clugs, all of them cutting to the right of the Death Merchant, only inches from his body. Yakvol's machine pistol was still vomiting projectiles—and Riskilin's too—when the Death Merchant's first 9mm. projectile punched Yakvol in the stomach and started to double him over. The bullet had cut through an artery and he was only minutes away from his new home in hell.

The wild-eyed Riskilin's stream of hot metal had missed

---

[5] An updated version of the Beretta Model 1951. Made by the Maadi Co. for Engineering Industries of Egypt.

Camellion by an even greater margin than Yakvol's, some of them exploding two of the glasses of Scotch and the glass of *Manastirska Izba*. The Death Merchant's next bullet missed the bull's-eye because, almost prone on the floor, he did not have any balance and because Riskilin was weaving, horizontally, from side to side. Instead of the slug striking Riskilin in the chest, the 9mm. bullet tore off the lower part of the right earlobe. The Bulgarian DS agent cried out in pain and fear and, in a spray of blood, half turned to his right, the sudden stab of agony forcing his right arm to swing down and his finger to contract against the trigger of the Vitmorkin. The Soviet machine pistol roared out its last six rounds. Three almost whacked out Harry Cross, who was flat on his face underneath a table, his legs in the direction of Peturi Riskilin. One of the Vitmorkin's projectiles stabbed through Cross's flannel slacks into his left thigh. Another slug cut through his pants by his left knee.

Camellion fired three more times in rapid succession, the roaring of the big P-88 autoloader drowning out the cracks of Julia Mirokeb's Sile-Benelli B-76 pistol and Grisha Dyuni's M-1914 Mauser.

The Death Merchant's first projectile stabbed into Peturi Riskilin's right hip, shattered the pelvic bone, and crashed into the descending colon. The second and third slugs slammed into Riskilin's right rib cage, breaking several ribs and tearing through his lungs. A tremendous roaring in his head, a terrible blackness closing in on his consciousness, Riskilin crashed to the floor only a second ahead of Irini Zulisev and Pekiv Rodiudji. Julia Mirokeb had put a 9mm. JFP slug into Zulisev's chest and Grisha Dyuni had used his M-1914 Mauser to take out Rodiudji, one of the DS agents disguised as a waiter. Two of the Mauser's 7.65mm.[6] slugs caught the Bulgarian in the chest, a third hit him in the groin.

A Bidja bullet passed over Camellion's head, coming in from the southeast. Another slug, aimed at Winkler, thudded into the top of the table, shaking the fragments of glass already on the tablecloth.

The last three DS "waiters" tried to close in, all three in the position of a man who, determined to commit suicide, has

---

[6] This is .32 caliber. Many .32 autos rank among the best-built pistols in all history, reflecting the heyday of the "baby" blowback, during the first three decades of this century.

jumped from the roof of a building and no longer can change his mind. The three agents couldn't retreat without Camellion and his people shooting them to pieces. To drop to the floor with the tourists from Great Britain and the United States was out of the question, absolutely unthinkable! Such cowardice would be a reflection on the DS and on Bulgarian manhood.

More afraid of disgrace than death, all the brainwashed boobs could do was move forward. Stepping over and between men and women on the floor, keeping as low as possible, the three agents kept tossing random slugs, hoping to keep the enemy down and bottled up in the northwest section of the tap room.

The difficulty for Camellion and Winkler was that, from their respective positions on the floor, they could not see clearly the approach of the three DS men. Tables were in the way. Hearing two more slugs thud into the table at which he had been sitting, Camellion crawled to the other side and dropped flat between Grisha Dyuni and Julia Mirokeb.

"We should save the last bullet for ourselves," Dyuni said calmly. "We cannot escape from this hotel."

Camellion knew the reason for Dyuni's placid attitude. People who have fully accepted death are usually undisturbed.

Winkler had also crawled to the east side of the table, so that now he was only a few feet from the man he had ordered to drop down and quit rubbernecking.

One of the women, sensing Winkler's presence, whispered, "P-please d-don't k-kill us. Please!" She did not look up.

Winkler continued to give the impression that he and the others were neither American nor British by replying in broken English, "We Russian revolutionaries. We only fight Communists. No kill innocent people."

Speaking in Russian, the Death Merchant said to Winkler, "Watch your side, chum. They'll try to outflank us."

Winkler replied in Russian. "What do we do when the militia arrives? The militia was probably very close to this dump since we walked into this trap with all the gullibility of country boys going into a big-city whorehouse the first time!"

The Death Merchant was too intent on watching the area to the south to make a reply that wasn't even necessary. Winkler was right.

The militia should be coming through the lobby about now! His left leg crossed over his right leg for balance, Camellion reached out toward Julia Mirokeb, who was lying flat beside him. He didn't trust being in the proximity of inexperienced personnel when slugs were flying and the Cosmic Lord of Death was working overtime.

"Give me your piece," he whispered.

She reared up slightly. "My—'piece'?"

"Your weapon."

Harry Cross sounded angry. "Damn it! Don't you people have a spare weapon?"

"If we had, you'd already have it," Camellion said, and accepted the Sile-Benelli autopistol from Julia Mirokeb. No sooner was the weapon in his left hand than he saw two of the DS agents, just as one of them saw him and snapped off a shot. The bullet thudded into the rug to his left, missing him more than it missed Julia Mirokeb. The slug had bored into the rug only inches from her face; she jerked back and began spitting out fragments of red polyester-nylon as Camellion fired both the Sile-Benelli and the Walther P-88. The slug from the P-88 cut upward and streaked into Parza Turatsa's stomach, giving him the last big hurt of his life. The 9mm. bullet from the Sile-Benelli only grazed Vlad Lovech's left rib cage, just enough to sting and draw a blood line and make him jerk reflexively to his left. For only a second he paused, but that "1001" was enough. Again Camellion fired. This time the bullet trapped Lovech an inch below his left ear, the blob of metal boring through his throat. He jerked, flopped his arms, and started to sag, a bubbling volcano of blood starting to explode in his throat.

Mikhaili Kareliv, the last DS agent, was trying to come in from the east. He had not been too enthusiastic about rushing in to begin with. Now, seeing Parza Turatsa and Vlad Lovech blown away into eternity, his training-engendered bravery vanished like smoke in a high wind. He caught only a glimpse of winkler's grim face as he attempted to turn around and retreat. But he had come too far with too little. He was still on the turn when Winkler fired twice, both slugs catching Kareliv in the right side of the back and kicking him forward to fall across a fat middle-aged Rumanian tourist who began to scream at the top of her lungs.

The Death Merchant eased himself to his feet and looked first toward the west door, then toward the archway to the north, the one that opened into the Lode Star. Winkler, Cross, and the two Bulgarian "Beckworths" also got up, their expressions one of frustration, all except Winkler who looked angry.

"Cross." Camellion looked from him to Grisha Dyuni and Julia Mirokeb. "You three pick up the weapons dropped by those four agents by the other table and get any spare magazines they might be carrying. Carey, get the spare mags for eighty-eights out of the tote and the camera bag. I'll cover us."

As Cross and the two Bulgarians hurried over to the corpses to the east and Winkler reached for the camera bag, Camellion fired a shot into the ceiling and yelled, "All of you on the floor! Stay put! We'll kill the first person who raises his head!"

It required only a small amount of time for Winkler to pull out the spare P-88 clips from the bags and for Cross, Dyuni, and Mirokeb to pick up the two Vitmorkin machine pistols, pull the B13-D from the stiff hand of Irina Zulisev, and grab the Helwan auto that Dimitri Vidin had used. In addition to the four pistols, they found four spare Vitmorkin magazines and an extra mag for the Bulgarian B13-D autoloader.

Winkler, his forehead dotted with sweat, cast a skeptical eye in the direction of Camellion. "All right, which way now?"

"The west door," Camellion said, noticing that Cross had a Vitmorkin machine pistol in his right hand and that, from the way he carried it, he knew how to use it. "Cross, you and Dyuni watch the north-side doorway, the entrance to the dining room. Julia, keep an eye on the bar. If a bartender raises his head, kill him. Let's move."

Camellion turned and Winkler, right behind him, whispered, "I suppose you know we have as much chance of getting out of here as we have of building a roof over the Grand Canyon?"

"Yeah . . . a roof with a zipper," Camellion said.

As a group, they moved toward the west doorway.

The Death Merchant thought of Point B7.

We have got to get our overcoats and hats. . . .

CHAPTER SEVEN

A great believer in luck, the Death Merchant found that the harder he worked, the more work he had to do. He "worked" like an expert to get to the west archway that opened to the wide space that would take him and the others to the main desk and then to the lobby—or, if they went due south, down the hallway past the kitchen to the rear of the hotel and to the alley. Just before reaching the archway, he paused and whispered to Winkler, "You take the left; I'll take the right."

"And we'll both be snuffed together," said Winkler, who had lit a cigarette on the way.

The paradox facing the Death Merchant and him was that there were so many different approaches that had to be watched simultaneously. Using tunnel vision—focusing only on one danger point ahead of you—was the easiest way to get killed, especially on the street, even more within the confined space of a building. Even with Cross and the two Bulgarians watching the rear, it was impossible for Camellion and Winkler to see everywhere in front of them at once. All they could do was their best—chance it—confident that the *Nersko-Tsopska* would not be subtle. Now that shots had been fired, the militia boys would come in like gang busters. The only reason they hadn't put in an appearance was that eleven DS agents had been in the Buffalo Bill Room, and they hadn't had time. The gun battle had not lasted longer than four and a half minutes.

With Winkler watching the area to the south, Camellion eased to the north side of the archway, the P-88 in his right hand, the Egyptian Helwan in his left hand. There was only one way to do it—lean back and look. That's exactly what he did—and just in time. Not ten feet away, six militiamen, in greatcoats, combat helmets with plastic face shields raised, were crossing the area from the main desk section to the open space that could take them to the Buffalo Bill Room. Four were carrying Zeff assault rifles; two were armed with RKZ submachine guns.

"North of me!" Camellion yelled at Winkler, and jumped from the doorway and began firing both semiautomatic pistols from hip level. Three of the militiamen died before they even had time to realize that they would never again see a sunset or make love to a woman—or ever again have to worry about hemorrhoids.

The Death Merchant had a few seconds of lag time and he made good use of that very short time. Before the three militiamen could swing their two Zeffs and RKZ toward him, both his P-88 and the Helwan roared four times and slugs ripped into the surprised militiamen—four slugs because one man had almost succeeded in lifting his assault rifle. A bullet from the Helwan hit the man low in the throat, made his head jerk as if on a swivel, and knocked him down to join his comrades—all six lying in a heap on the floor, two of the bodies still twitching. Camellion fired again, once, twice. The bodies lay still.

"Cover me!" he said savagely. "We can use those subguns."

Convinced that Richard Camellion was a madman courting death, Winkler didn't argue. He didn't have time. The Death Merchant was already racing ahead, his eyes watching the corner where the Buffalo Bill Room partially merged with the main desk section. He was only a few feet from the first corpse when he saw four more militiamen halfway between the main desk and the six doors to the forward part of the long lobby. To add to his problems, he heard the resounding chattering of assault rifles and RKZs from the north side of the Buffalo Bill Room and Vitmorkins and other handguns answering in reply. The automatic weapons remained silent, indicating that either the militia had aced Cross and the two Bulgarians—*And maybe even Carey; damn it!*—or vice versa.

Camellion didn't have time to go back and look. He fired at the same moment that one of the militiamen saw him and began to raise his Zeff AR. Two 9mm. projectiles from the Egyptian Helwan pistol turned him into dead meat and knocked him back, almost into one of his companions. A 9mm. from the P-88 stole another man's thunder; he went down with the bullet, having gone through his stomach, lodged against his spine. A third Helwan 180-grain slug rained on the parade of the third enemy, going in just above the buckle of his equipment belt over his greatcoat. The fourth *Nersko-Tsopska* crud, who had stepped back to prevent the first victim from falling into him, was clever. He threw himself to one side and fired the Zeff as he did so, the Bulgarian AKM belching out a stream of 7.62 X 39mm. (Russian short) projectiles that would have butchered Camellion navel to neck if he hadn't sensed what the man was about to do and ducked to the left. Two 9mm. slugs, one from the Helwan and one from the P-88, struck the unlucky Bulgarian in the lower chest and the upper part of his stomach and smashed him straight into the land where time was a stranger. Camellion was about to put another bullet into the man with the Helwan, but the firing pin clicked on an empty firing chamber. The weapon was empty. He tossed aside the useless pistol, turned, saw that Winkle was by the north side of the archway, and rushed over to the first six militiamen he had snuffed. He picked up one of the RKZ submachine guns, made sure the safety was on, then tossed the SMG to the south, the weapon landing on the rug only several feet from Winkler, who remained in his position, watching the area to the north of the Death Merchant. Camellion repeated the procedure with the second RKZ chatterbox, first pulling it from under the torso of a corpse. After he tossed the weapon toward Winkler, he unbuckled the leather pouches of spare RKZ magazines from the two dead men—two mags to a pouch—ran back to Winkler, and picked up the two submachine guns. He handed one of the RKZs to Winkler, stepped beneath the arch into the bar, and turned his attention to Harry Cross and Grisha Dyuni, both of whom had their eyes glued to the archway on the north side of the Buffalo Bill Room. Camellion glanced down at Julia Mirokeb sprawled facedown on the floor.

Cross explained how she had died. ''Three of the militiamen appeared at the door to the north. We got them before they could get us . . . well, all of us. She caught a blast in the chest.''

The Death Merchant finished reloading his P-88 pistol, shoved the weapon into his right hip pocket, and accepted the

RKZ that Winkler handed him, then the two spare magazines which he shoved into his belt, as Winkler had done.

"I'll cover the door for you," Camellion said to Cross. "Get her U.S. passport out of her handbag. We can't have the DS finding that kind of evidence on her."

"We have got to get out of here," said Grisha Dyuni, his voice on the edge of panic. "It's only because of the tourists that they haven't attacked in force."

On one knee, Carey Winkler was doing his best to watch the area to the north and the south, first turning in one direction and then the other, ready to trigger off bursts with the RKZ.

Once Cross had taken the passport from Mirokeb's handbag and put it into his coat pocket, the Death Merchant yelled at the patrons on the floor, "You people on the floor! Get up and go into the dining room. From there you can get to the lobby and out of the hotel. This entire hotel is going to blow up in ten minutes RUN! GET THE HELL OUT OF HERE!"

The men and women didn't need further encouragement. With shouts and yells of terror, almost 116 men and women scrambled to their feet and made a wild dash to the wide archway between the Buffalo Bill Room and the Lode Star dining room.

Cross and Dyuni glanced uncomprehendingly at the Death Merchant. At once, the more perceptive Winkler understood. "We can't follow them through the dining room," he said in a low voice, "and the militia might be out in force in front. Have you thought of that?"

"Yeah, the militia will be in the front of the hotel," Camellion said, watching the patrons stampede through the door to the dining room and thinking of a herd of wild horses out of control. "As many, if not more, will be waiting in the alley. Since I knocked off those ten militiamen, the others will assume there's too many waiting for us to the north. They'll conclude we're trying to escape through the rear and get lost down the alley."

"We'll have to go by the main desk to get to the lobby," Winkler said, cocking his head to one side. "It should work. By then the lobby will be crawling with tourists. Let's get it over with."

The Death Merchant grabbed Grisha Dyuni with his gaze. "On the way out, go into the cloakroom and grab four overcoats and four hats. You'll have to judge sizes and hope you get lucky. Just so you do it fast.''

Dyuni's heavily wrinkled eyes opened wider in surprise. Cross was more than slightly astonished.

"Coats? Hats?'' exclaimed Dyuni. ''At a time like this?''

The words jumped from the Death Merchant's mouth. "Once we park the jeep—whatever vehicle we have—say a few blocks from the Tsar Kaloyan Theater, how—''

"A theater!'' Cross was confused. ''What in hell does a theater have to do with the fix we're in?''

"We can't walk down the street without hats and topcoats, not in subzero weather. We'd look half 'undressed.' That alone would call attention to us.''

"Look, Bundy,'' began Cross.

"Later. Cross, you and Grisha keep a sharp eye on our rear when we move out toward the lobby. The militia might come in at us from the back.''

"If they do, we're dead,'' Winkler growled.

"Don't sweat it.'' Camellion smiled. ''Life isn't all that great. It's nothing more than one long coffee break between two deaths.''

By then, almost half of the patrons had fled the bar. Those that remained were doing their very best to squeeze through the archway into the Lode Star as the Death Merchant and Carey Winkler, followed by Cross and Dyuni, moved from the archway toward the main desk. Ahead were scores of customers who had been not only in the bar, but had also been in the Lode Star Room, peacefully eating dinner. Rushing out, they yelled and shoved each other in a frenzied attempt to reach the swinging doors to the front lobby, some of the terrified people even stepping on the corpses of the four militiamen. When the first wave of patrons reached the lobby, the several dozen militiamen, guarding the doors to the sidewalk, were helpless to prevent them from reaching the street. The concern of the militiamen and the four DS agents with them was that the terrorists would mingle with the innocent patrons and escape; yet the militiamen and the DS agents were powerless. There weren't enough of them to hold back the crowd, and they didn't dare shoot.

The Death Merchant and his three men moved forward, Cross and Dyuni pausing long enough to pick up several Zeff assault rifles dropped by the first group of militiamen Camellion had terminated. Many of the tourists shouted and moved with greater speed when they saw the weapons in the hands of Camellion and the other three men.

Close in now, Camellion and his men could see that the desk clerks and the elevator operators had abandoned their posts. Had the DS been clever enough to position men behind the long desk, which was enclosed at both ends? Camellion found out by firing a short blast of 7.62mm. RKZ slugs through one end of the desk. Nothing happened. Not a single enemy reared up to return the fire.

At the corner where the bar area merged with the front desk, Camellion glanced at Grisha Dyuni and jerked a thumb toward the cloakroom. Dyuni ran over to the open section of the check room, vaulted over the counter, paused, and inspected the coats on racks and the hats on shelves.

Camellion, Cross, and Winkler waited, watching all avenues of approach. Camellion's concern was that sooner or later the militia would wise up and send in men from the rear of the hotel. Soon Dyuni had returned, wearing the same hat and British tan walker he had worn to the hotel, thereby proving his sharp eye. His outstretched arms were loaded with Camellion and Winkler's own coats and hats, plus a Zeff assault rifle and a hat and coat for Harry Cross.

After they had put on their coats and hats—Cross's coat was slightly too small and his hat was almost useless, being too large—Camellion and the three men waited for the last of the patrons to leave the dining room. The Death Merchant's blast of gunfire into the registration desk had increased both the panic and the speed of the departing crowd and out in the lobby was sheer confusion, people knocking each other down in their rush to reach the street. Keeping themselves and their weapons low, the Death Merchant and his tiny group moved in behind the last men and women heading toward the doors that would take them into the lobby.

"We're not going to be able to reach the sidewalk," Cross whispered nervously, "not with these guns in our hands." He had his too-large hat pushed back on his head.

Winkler cut in. "What the hell will we do if there aren't any jeeps parked by the curb?"

"We have to play it as we see it," Camellion said. "There are still plenty of people in the lobby and I don't want any of them hurt if it can be avoided. Another thing, if there are jeeps by the curb—"

"There had damn well better be." Winkler sounded vicious.

"If you have to fire at the jeeps, don't hit the engines and the tires. We'll need at least one to escape in—and watch the east and the west ends of the lobby. There's a flower shop on the east end and a souvenir shop on the west side. Militiamen could be hiding behind the counters."

By then they were in the lobby and could feel the cold air coming in through the open doors, hear the babble of excited voices, and see that men and women were squeezing through the doors to the street. There were still terrified patrons—some with children in their arms—coming out of the Lode Star doors on the east end, yet the flow of frightened traffic from the dining room's west-side door had ended, with Camellion and his crew being right behind these last men and women as they edged toward the street. There were plenty of people between them and the flower shop, but not between them and the souvenir shop. There were three militiamen and a DS agent waiting behind the counter of the souvenir shop. The militiamen were down on the floor and completely out of sight; however, Sanker Chevjiz, the DS agent, was looking over the top of the counter now and then. Chevjiz quickly spotted the SMG and assault rifles in the hands of Camellion and his men. He dropped down and nervously ordered the militiamen to fire, but to be very careful and not hit any innocent bystanders.

Fortunately, Harry Cross had detected Chevjiz's ducking down and sounded a warning. "The souvenir shop! I saw them!"

Cross fired immediately, raking the front of the counter with a hail of Zeff AKM 7.62mm. projectiles. Dyuni also spun and triggered off a short burst, his slugs following Cross's, which had ripped through the fiberboard and massacred two of the militiamen who were getting to their feet. Dyuni's burst ripped into the third trooper, the slugs ripping open his lower chest. He fell back with a choked cry, unlike Sanker Chevjiz, who died so quickly he did not even have time to know eternity was upon him. One of Dyuni's bullets had hit him high in the right arm and broken the bone. The second slug tore off his nose before boring through his head and speeding out through the high part of his neck.

Since the enemy was in the souvenir shop, it was reasonable to assume they were in the flower shop—a decision Camellion made in a split second.

"Carey, watch the front! Shoot when you have to."

Camellion moved ahead of the other three and, in a crouch, swung to the east. His hunch had been on target. Bull's-eye! Two troopers and two men in ordinary street clothes were moving from behind the counter of the flower shop. Unable to fire through the people in front of them, they were soon doing the next best thing: brutally shoving men and women out of the way.

Outside, on the sidewalk, the *Nersko-Tsopska* troopers began to engage in the same tactics. The explosive gunfire was a clear indication that the terrorists were still inside, and the militiamen, following the orders of DS superiors, began to prod tourists to one side with the barrels of their Zeff AKMs. The Bulgarians had only one goal: to reach the doors before the terrorists did.

For the moment, neither the Death Merchant nor the Bulgarians could fire because of the men and women between them. For that reason the two DS agents and the two NT troopers were desperately shoving men and women away in a determined effort to clear the area and have an unobstructed field of fire.

The Death Merchant didn't intend to let them acquire the advantage.

"Hit the deck!" he yelled, dropped prone to the floor, and, hoping his timing was right, fired a short burst through the moving legs of a woman. The two militiamen yelled and went down, slugs practically tearing off their lower legs. With a high shriek of pain and terror, the woman crashed to the floor. One of Camellion's slugs had ripped through her shoe and torn off her right heel, taking most of the heel bone with it.

Grisha Dyuni twisted around on the tiled floor to face the south, on the possibility that the enemy might come in behind them. Cary Winkler and Harry Cross, also lying flat on the floor, cut loose with their automatic weapons, having decided to be more daring and practical than the enemy milling around on the sidewalk. Winkler and Cross sent projectiles steeply upward at six militiamen about to open four of the outside doors, the loud snarling of their Zeff and RKZ mingling with the chattering of the Death Merchant's submachine gun as he blew apart the two DS agents frantically trying to flatten themselves on the floor, one man triggering his Vitmorkin machine pistol as he started to drop. All eighteen of the 9mm. slugs missed, finally coming to rest in carved wooden figures resting on shelves in the souvenir shop. The two DS agents dropped—stone dead, shot to pieces. The two troopers, squirming around on the floor and bleeding to death, were the next to die, the Death Merchant holding the RKZ at floor level and blowing them into that far country with the remainder of the cartridges in the magazines of the SMG.

The six militiamen on the sidewalk had even less of a chance than their comrades inside the hotel. A tidal wave of splintered glass and steel-cored projectiles washed all over them and sent them crashing to the sidewalk.

The Death Merchant rolled over on his left side, reached through his open overcoat and tweed suit coat, pulled a full magazine of 7.62mm. cartridges from his waistband, thrust it into the submachine gun, and sent a shell into the firing chamber. Getting to his feet and satisfied that his companions had reloaded, he took a deep breath and gave the only order he could give: "Run for it! It's the only chance we have."

Most of the tourists had fled from the front of the Slavyanska Hotel. Nonetheless traffic was still moving on this side of Lenin Square, mostly small Volgas and Bulgarian Kalotas, with a sprinkling of Ladas. And a lot of enraged militia gunmen were moving, although some of the dummies, in their ankle-length light blue greatcoats, were crouched down to fire. The ones with good sense were rushing to get behind three Soviet Chor-7 vehicles parked at the curb.

Carey Winkler, ducking and dodging, was the first to leap through one of the shot-out street doors, his speed catching the militia off guard for a single moment. It was that brief blink of time that saved his life and took the lives of many of the enemy. His RKZ moving from left to right, the muzzle spitting out slugs, Winkler fired at anything that moved. The Death Merchant, Harry Cross, and Grisha Dyuni stormed through the shot-out doors a microsecond later, their weapons spewing out slugs that struck the militiamen and killed them with the quickness of an electric light being turned off. Yet many of the troopers and the DS men got off rounds that certainly didn't increase the longevity of the Death Merchant and his trio of "terrorists."

Semyon Budyovevik, a DS man, managed to get off a burst with his Vitmorkin machine pistol, and a half-dozen troopers, who had succeeded in finding refuge on the left side of the first Chor-7 jeep, triggered off quick bursts with Zeff AKMS. A hot stream of 9mm. round-nosed projectiles, fired by Denko Yulikok, a captain in the DS, tore along Carey Winkler's right side, the deadly metal cutting through his navy duffel coat and black blazer, but not even touching his shirt. More slugs almost stopped Camellion. One knocked off his hat, the bullet almost parting his hair—if his hair had been long enough to part. Another four 7.62mm. projectiles pierced his trenchcoat and passed only inches below his left armpit. During that microsecond another bullet burned through the wide collar of his trenchcoat and missed the right side of his neck by only an inch. Other enemy projectiles came very close to Harry Cross and Grisha Dyuni. In contrast, the slugs of the Death Merchant and his men did what they were supposed to do.

Denko Yulikok, who had fired from the rear of a jeep, was knocked back, then onto the pavement by a burst of Zeff steel that exploded his face and head and scattered most of his brain over his shoulders, the rear of the jeep, and the paving stones. The Death Merchant used the last seven rounds in his RKZ to blow away a trooper firing from a jeep.

Positioned in the middle of the sidewalk, Camellion couldn't take time to reload the SMG, nor could he reach the Walther P-88 pistol in his hip pocket. He placed the SMG on the sidewalk, took a dozen long steps to the right, and picked up a Zeff assault rifle that had belonged to one of the dead troopers. He jerked himself to the left in time to avoid another burst of slugs from the militiamen firing from the first jeep. They didn't know it at the moment, but their time had run out. It had because Winkler and Dyuni had also ducked down and picked up assault rifles dropped by dead troopers. They now opened fire on the jeep. Camellion's finger was about to squeeze the trigger when he saw another jeep and a Soviet ZIL drive from the west side of the hotel. Harry Cross, who had also picked up a Zeff and was getting ready to fire on the jeep by the curb, also saw the two vehicles which had been parked in the alley.

Winkler and Dyuni fired only a fraction of a second before Cross and the Death Merchant sent streams of steel-cored 7.62mm projectiles at the jeep and the Zil, the hail of slugs punching holes in the sides of the two vehicles and exploding the glass. Most of the occupants were killed instantly, including the drivers. Out of control, the jeep shot out onto the pavement and crashed into the rear end of a Lada, the smash sounding like a grenade going off. A Soviet Lada has a lot of deficiencies, one of which is a gas tank prone to explode. Instantly the gas tank of the Lada exploded, inundating the Lada and the jeep in a sea of fire and black oily smoke. In the meanwhile, the riddled Zil with its cargo of corpses passed through the flames and headed out onto Lenin Square, the drivers of other cars swerving in a frantic effort to keep from running into the "mindless" vehicle.

The troopers, using the first jeep by the curb for cover, were butchered by the hurricane of slugs from Winkler and Dyuni, the storm of steel dissolving the glass in the windows and cutting through the four doors. Somehow, though, one trooper—Pazlik Wokoguj—escaped injury—until he tried to dash to the second jeep. He was ducking down behind the engine of the jeep when some of Winkler's slugs stabbed not only into the engine but also stung Wokoguj in both legs, the savage impact half ripping off the limbs and making him fall to the ground as though his legs had been cut off, which, in a sense they had. With a hollow-throated yell, he squirmed on the cold, snow-packed stones, his long exhalation turning into a small cloud of steam in the cold. An ex-medical student too dumb to make the grade, he realized with a numbing horror that the slugs had cut through his femoral veins and arteries and that he was bleeding to death. He was determined to take as many of the enemy with him as he could, but wasn't even able to swivel himself around and fire from underneath the jeep. It was Winkler who fired—from the sidewalk. His last four 7.62mm. slugs sliced into Wokoguj's abdominal section, one breaking his back and tearing apart his spinal cord. Mouth open, eyes closed, Wokoguj fell to his left side. He didn't slip out of life lonely, only surprised.

The jeep and the Lada were giving off more smoke than the jeep, the fire consuming the two vehicles much larger. The stink was also greater, a miasma of burning metal, paint, cloth, and roasting corpse flesh. The popping sounds of cartridges, exploding like firecrackers from the heat, came from inside the jeep.

The Death Merchant tossed away the empty Zeff assault rifle and shouted to the other men, "Get in the third jeep and we'll go sight-seeing."

He ran over to where he had dropped the RKZ submachine gun, picked it up, and saw that Winkler had picked up his chatterbox and Harry Cross and Grisha Dyuni were pulling Zeff magazine pouches from the dead militiamen sprawled out on the sidewalk. "Grisha, you drive; you know the way," he said as they headed toward the jeep, his eyes going from left to right. *All we need now is for more militia morons to show up!*

"There had better be a key in the ignition. I'll be damned if I'm going to walk to point—what is it again? No matter," Winkler said, yanking open the right front door of the Chor-7 jeep.

"There'll be a key in the ignition," Camellion said, his hand on the door handle. "The militia boys didn't expect us to attack."

The key was in the ignition. Dyuni was soon moving the jeep onto Lenin Square, increasing speed steadily with each vital second. In the backseat, Camellion and Harry Cross turned and saw through the rear window that the Zil had come to a halt against the base of the gigantic statue of Lenin in the center of the square, and that a dozen militiamen had run out of the front of the hotel. By then the jeep was weaving in and out of traffic and the troopers were unable to fire.

"We're lucky they waited out in the alley until the last minute," Cross said, sounding relieved.

"It would appear that our good fortune just left us," Camellion said with a slight smirk as two jeeps and a Kalota, red strobe lights revolving on the roofs, streaked out from the west side of the hotel and, tires screaming, pulled out onto the square.

"Not even half a block away from us," Winkler said. "We won't be able to lose them." Sitting in the front seat, next to Dyuni, he had looked into the rearview mirror and seen the three vehicles pulling out. For once he sounded genuinely worried, yet he retained his usual briskness.

Dyuni turned on the red lights on the roof and pressed down on the gas pedal, his eyes going nervously to the rearview mirror.

Unexpectedly a voice, speaking Bulgarian, jumped from the police transceiver centered below the dash.

Winkler translated. "This is scout car number sixteen. The dispatcher wants to know what our location is."

"That joker is behind the times," Cross said. "He will soon know we've taken over when the other cars behind us report in." He glanced with annoyance at the Death Merchant, who was pushing against Cross in an effort to reach his back pocket. "Kline is right," Cross went on. "There isn't any way we can outdistance them, and we can be expecting other militia jeeps to try to cut us off. What are we going to do?''

"His name isn't Kline," Camellion said, and pulled the Walther P-88 from his back pocket. "It's Carey Winkler, and I'm Richard Camellion. You're right. We can't lose them. The thing to do is let them catch up with us when they don't expect it.''

"Give it to me straight," Cross said sarcastically, disliking the incongruity of Camellion's remark.

Camellion leaned forward on the hard seat, his cobalt-blue eyes calculating. "Grisha, how far are we from the Tsar Kaloyan Theater?''

"Several kilometers. But the jeeps in pursuit can equal our speed. I could put us on Aleksandar Stambolijski. If we went that way, the militia could cut us off too easily; and by now the *Jokka* have been notified," Grisha Dyuni said. He pulled out of Lenin Square onto Georgi Dimitrov Street, swerved around a slow-moving Piaka, and increased the speed of the jeep to seventy-five mph.

"How well do you know Sofia?" asked Camellion. He glanced sideways at Cross. The CIA man had not only picked up two AKMs, but had also taken two 9mm. Bidja autos from several dead militiamen on the sidewalk and was now inspecting one pistol. He was proving he was familiar with handguns. Always he kept the muzzle pointed downward.

"I was born in the Bizokja district," answered Dyuni. "I know this city—how would you say it? Yes, like you know the back of your hand. Why do you ask?''

Winkler swung around and looked at Camellion. He held his subgun so that the muzzle was pointed toward the roof. "Why not let them catch up with us? We can take them out by firing through the rear window. Oh hell! That's as long as it's wide or something like that. The militia could do the same to us once they got close enough.''

"Grisha, do you think you can find a fairly long alley to turn into?" asked the Death Merchant.

"Two or three if you want. But what good will an alley do us. Their vehicles will only follow.''

"Damn it, spell it out!" Winkler said impatiently.

Camellion spelled out his plan, finishing with, "It's all a matter of timing.''

"I only hope we're not trying to sleep double in a single bed," Winkler said thoughtfully. "If they don't fall for it . . .''

Cross said, "I'm more concerned with our commandeering another car."

"One step at a time," Camellion said. "There isn't any other way to play it."

"Yeah, one step at a time . . . like Alcoholics Anonymous." But he sounded as sober as God Almighty when he saw the vehicles of the militia. "They're gaining, Grisha."

"Yes, but they'll have to slow down when they reach this traffic," Dyuni said. "Not all the cars pull over at the same time."

At seventy mph the jeep roared down Georgi Dimitrov Street, three red lights flashing, the screaming siren more than enough to make other drivers ahead slow down and pull over to one side. Half a block behind came the two jeeps and the Kalota of the militia, all four vehicles filling the night with the wailing of their sirens.

An open stretch of road appeared and Dyuni slammed down on the accelerator until the jeep was almost leaping through the cold, black night, a night so tenebrous that the sky was a stranger to sun and moon and stars.

Dyuni did not slow down when, several hundred feet later, he shot between a dozen cars that were pulling off to the left and a bus going in the opposite direction. He did, however, decrease speed when he turned onto Dimitar Blagonev and roared south. Dimitar Blagonev was a short street and Dyuni had soon turned east and was moving at high speed on Majco Canov, the four men inside the Chor-7 jeep bracing themselves as the not-too-comfortable vehicle rocked from side to side on its shocks.

"Get set in the back," called out Dyuni, his voice, an octave higher, filled with tension. "There's an alley ahead, to the left. It's wide and there are apartment houses on each side. It should serve our purpose well."

"I think I'm getting car sick." Winkler turned around in the front seat and stuck out an arm toward Cross. "Let me have one of the automatic rifles. I might not have time to reload my machine gun, or it could jam."

"You might have to take out two jeeps," Camellion said as Cross handed Winkler one of the Zeff AKMs. "It depends on how close the three vehicles are to each other. I suspect there will be plenty of room between the three of them. Either way, don't fire until the first jeep is almost in front of you.

We have to get all three cars." His hand on the handle of the door on the right-hand side, Camellion leaned against Cross, his body pulled by the momentum of the swinging car—almost on two wheels! Almost as quickly, Dyuni began applying the brakes, the jeep skidding six feet before it came to a stop thirty feet inside the alley. The Death Merchant and Harry Cross scrambled out, almost falling over each other in their haste, Camellion carrying the RKZ submachine gun with a full magazine, Cross armed with an automatic AKM. Both men were filled to the brim with desperation tempered with a lot of hope.

No sooner had Cross slammed the door than Dyuni shot the jeep down the alley, lights still flashing, siren going full blast.

Even though the alley was almost as dark as the bottom of a grave, Camellion and Cross saw that on either side were eight-story buildings, tall piles of bleak concrete that, without frills and decoration, were apartment houses for workers in this "people's paradise." The rear of the apartment houses—they stretched the length of the alley—were dotted with lights, their distance conveying to Cross and the Death Merchant that there was ample space behind the buildings where they could take cover, but only if they had the time. Even now the first militia jeep must be preparing to turn down the alley.

At the other end of the alley, Grisha Dyuni again slowed long enough for Carey Winkler to jump out. Moments later, Dyuni started up, moved through the mouth of the alley, turned, and drove east.

"Over by those trash dumpsters; I take one side," Camellion said. The snow, much of it over their shoes, crunching beneath their feet, was not piled up near the large dumpsters and soon Camellion and Cross were in position by the middle dumpster.

The wait was less than ten seconds. The first militia jeep pulled into the alley, then increased speed and headed south. It was halfway down the alley when the second Chor-7 appeared.

Damn! The two jeeps were too far apart from each other. By the time the first one closed on the south end of the alley and was close enough to Winkler for him to take it out, the second jeep would be too far to the right of Camellion and Cross for them to fire, yet still too far north of Winkler—and how far behind the second jeep was the Zil?

And instant decision had to be made. On the assumption that the Zil would be closer to the second jeep than the second vehicle was to the first one, the Death Merchant stepped from the side of the dumpster and fired a medium burst, the muzzle of the RKZ submachine gun flashing red tongues of flame and spitting out projectiles that exploded the glass of the jeep's doors and knocked the four militiamen into the Absolute Elsewhere.[1] The 7.62mm. projectiles had torn into the heads and the necks of the two troopers in the rear seat and had come very close to decapitating the driver and the man next to him. The driver's foot relaxed on the gas and he slumped against the other man who had sagged against the right-side door, his head caught on a shard of glass protruding upward. The jeep began to lose speed, the two dead men in the rear wobbling from side to side, their eyes wide open, the blood oozing from their heads and necks beginning to congeal.

It was also too late for the four troopers in the first jeep. Winkler, also to one side of a dumpster, raked the first Chor-7 jeep with a full magazine of 7.62mm. slugs, then completed the hit by exploding the right-front tire. He didn't want the vehicle to continue out into traffic on Hargiz-gat Brog Street. It didn't. Predictably, the jeep swerved to the right. Its three red lights continued to revolve; its siren continued to wail.

Winkler pulled the empty magazine from the RKZ SMG, pulled a full one from his belt, and glanced toward the north. He had seen the flashes of what he knew to be either Cross or Camellion's machine gun and felt that something had gone wrong. And now, another chatterbox was playing its deadly muzzle music.

What had taken place was that the Zil had not been as close behind the second jeep as the Death Merchant had expected, nor had it been as far behind the second jeep as the second vehicle had been behind the first Chor-7 that Winkler had blasted and that was now stopped against a dumpster.

The driver of the Zil was turning the long black automobile into the alley as Camellion massacred the four troopers in the second jeep. The driver of the Zil stopped, reversed gears, and with Lieutenant Aleksei Borakov yelling, "It's an ambush!

[1] This is actually a term used by mathematicians in the doctrine of elementary particles, to show that nothing can be known on either side of the "arrow" of Time that points only forward, to the future.

It's an ambush!'', tried to back out. He had moved the Zil ten feet and might have succeeded if it had not been for the quick-thinking Harry Cross, who had first detected the Zil by the twin beams of its headlights, its siren, and the roof lights tinging the black shadows with a flickering red glow.

Cross stepped out from the dumpster and fired on instinct— half blinded by the headlights but mentally measuring the target by the flashing lights on the roof. The vehicle was gaining speed and a mere thirty feet from Cross when he fired a raking burst across the windshield. The first three round-nosed 7.62mm. slugs wrecked the windshield and scattered parts of the driver's face all over the dash, the back of the seat, and the inside glass of the left front door. Lieutenant Borakov died as quickly, projectiles tearing off his lower jaw and knocking his peaked cap on the back of Sergeant Lenko Hizobychiev, who had ducked down in the rear seat and was frantically trying to open the door at the same time that a single bullet went through the cheek of Alexandr Velchev and cut through the back of his neck. Blood pouring out of his mouth, Velchev slumped against the right rear door. More slugs blew apart the rear window, stabbed into the corpse of Aleksei Borakov and into the front seat. Many of the projectiles were stopped by the thick padding and the framework, but several slugs did bore all the way through and skimmed across Lenko Hizobychiev, who had opened the door and was halfway out of the doomed vehicle, on his way toward falling to the alley.

The front bumper of the Zil was only six feet from Cross when he jumped to his left, tripped, and fell into the snow. Losing speed, the long Soviet automobile continued on its way, moving straight down the alley. Hizobychiev fell half on his face and his right shoulder. He hadn't, however, managed to take his assault rifle with him. He rolled over and, his heart thumping within his chest, tried to pull his holstered Bidja.

Equally as fearful, Harry Cross also reached into his overcoat pocket for his own Bidja auto. He was also too slow.

The Death Merchant's P-88 roared twice. An ''Uhhhhhh'' skidded out of Hizobychiev's mouth. He flopped to the snow, rolled over, and lay still.

During the brief interim, the second jeep had turned to the right and rammed into a concrete block fence. Its engine idling, the jeep sat there, strobe lights flashing, siren still screaming out its useless warning.

"Thanks," Cross said, brushing snow from his clothes. "If it hadn't been for you, I'd be a dead man."

"You'd be dead, but not a man. Dead is dead," mused Camellion.

The two men ran south, and when Camellion passed the Zil, moving at only five mph, he paused and put a 9mm. bullet into the left front tire. But the vehicle did not veer to the left; it continued to move slowly ahead, the wheel and the flat tire making a fub-abub-abub sound.

Carey Winkler, who had reloaded his submachine gun with the last magazine in his belt, was soon running with Cross and Camellion from the mouth of the alley. The three turned left and raced east on Hargiz-gat Brog Street, tearing by frightened pedestrians who had heard the gunfire in the alley and were huddled down in doorways, their backs turned to the sidewalk.

In only minutes, Camellion, Cross, and Winkler were in the jeep and Grisha Dyuni was moving the vehicle into traffic. The red lights were still revolving, but Dyuni had turned off the siren.

"Stop four blocks from here," Camellion ordered Dyuni. "We have to get rid of this jeep and get another car as quickly as we can. By now the whole militia in Sofia, including the *Jokka* traffic boys, is looking for us."

"Four blocks!" exclaimed Dyuni. "That's cutting it close. The militia will be crawling all over the alley back there in a very short time—and four blocks!"

"I'm counting on the militia converging on the alley," Camellion said. "By the time they wise up what has really happened, we'll have ditched this baby and be in another one."

Cross had turned and was looking out the rear window. "This whole business is like looking for the missing link," he remarked to no one in particular. "And so far, it's been as productive."

"How do you mean?" Somehow, Winkler had the feeling that Cross was putting them all down.

"Scientists have been looking for the missing link for only God knows how long. The idea is more like a lot of links lying around looking for a chain with the necessary connectors. No one can find the chain. It seems to me we're in the same kind of situation. We're running around all over the place and getting nowhere. All I know is that all of it is connected with KINTEX. Damn it all! I was supposed to give you certain information. Instead, I end up getting involved in a cowboys-and-Indians shoot-out in the middle of Bulgaria. I didn't expect that!''

"We didn't either . . . if that's any consolation," Winkler said with a slightly bitter laugh.

"I don't even know what we're doing." Cross turned from the window. "But I wasn't supposed to be part of the operation."

"We know what we're doing," Camellion said resolutely. "However, now is not the time to get into the nuts and bolts of it. It is somewhat complicated."

"Complicated—hell!" mocked Winkler merrily, looking straight ahead. "All we have to do is kill Colonel General Grigor Shopov, the boss of the DS, and the main Soviet Uncles from Kremlinsville. Oh yes, one more thing: blow up DS headquarters."

Harry Cross turned incredulously to the Death Merchant. "I can understand terminating 'Bulldog' Shopov and the Ruskies. But not even the home office would dream up a scheme to blow up DS headquarters. What weirdo concocted that nutty idea?"

Smiling, the Death Merchant shoved his right hand in Cross's direction.

"I'm delighted to meet you. I'm 'Mr. Weirdo'. . . .''

CHAPTER EIGHT

"It was a disaster that will have repercussions in Moscow," said Colonel General Grigor Shopov. "That son of a bitch Chernenko is probably raging right now. We of course will get the blame."

The cafeteria, on the second floor of the DS building at 66 Boulevard Anton Ivanova, hummed with the subdued voices of personnel eating lunch. Colonel General Grigor Shopov and Colonel Georgi Kraisin sat at their personal table in one corner of the area. The table might have been contagious. It was not surrounded by other tables, and it was square and bolted to the floor, unlike the other tables, which were round and unfastened to the floor.

Neither Shopov nor any of the bosses of the DS Directorates ever ate at this table until they had personally checked it for hidden transmitters with a pocket detector.

Today, nine days after the massacre at the Slavyanska Hotel, Shopov and Kraisin had much to discuss and wanted to make certain that their conversation did not reach the KGB. For over a week, they had discussed ways and means to strengthen their positions within the *Komitet Darzhavna Sigurnost*—and had not resolved anything. . . .

Kraisin finished chewing a mouthful of *agneshki drebuliiki*,[1] paused, and glanced over at the dour-faced Shopov who was toying with his food. "Comrade, at least we were wise in not

---

[1] This is grilled liver, kidneys, and other "offal" of lamb, and it tastes far better than it sounds. It is, however, beyond the purchasing power of the average Bulgarian, who earns the equivalent of $125 American.

trying to minimize the loss to the Soviets. Fourteen dead DS agents and thirty-six dead troopers can't be dismissed lightly. The real tragedy was that the bloody business had to take place in the Slavyanska and could not be concealed from the West. We were even trapped in the press releases we gave to the West."

Sensing that Shopov was not going to reply, Kraisin resumed eating. Why permit any problem—even one as serious as this one—to interfere with good food or good music?

His expression grave, Grigor Shopov began to cut his *sarmi*. Georgi was only repeating himself, saying what they had both said a hundred times. The DS had not had any choice but to tell reporters from the West that the murders of government troops had been committed by a "well-organized group of anti-Communist terrorists determined to overthrow the existing social order." The truth had been followed with the big lie that "authorities would soon arrest the terrorists." The government spokesman had been careful not to mention the American CIA. Western dollars were too important.

Shopov bit more viciously into the piece of *sarmi*[2] when he thought of Lieutenant General Cherfesky, the senior Soviet adviser. The two-faced hypocrite! He had readily accepted the explanation that the entire plan of entrapment had fallen apart. Cherfesky had then gone straight to Boris Chubenko, the secretary of the Bulgarian Central Committee. It had been an enraged Chubenko who had met with Shopov and had demanded a detailed report. Shopov could only again recite facts. The trap had failed. The hares had escaped the snare. . . .

The flat-nosed Boris Chubenko had not been concerned with the loss of life. Why should he have been? In Bulgaria, computers were worth more than human beings. Chubenko's rage had been turned white hot by the unfavorable publicity the nation would receive. Why should people from the West—for that matter, from the Communist nations—want to vacation in Bulgaria and risk being killed by terrorists? Twenty-six tourists had been injured in the Slavyanska. That most of them had been trampled by other tourists was of no consequence. They had been injured, all due to the shoot-out. That in itself was enough.

Comrade Boris Chubenko's parting remark had not filled

---

[2] Cabbage leaves stuffed with meat; various other leaves or vegetables, such as peppers or aubergines, come in for similar treatment with various tasty results.

Grigor Shopov with confidence. "Comrade Shopov, if you can't operate the state security apparatus efficiently, the Central Committee will find someone who can. The rebel National Freedom Council must be smashed completely. I ask you: when can we of the Central Committee expect results, expect arrests?"

"Within a few weeks," Shopov had told him with a straight face.

Shopov had not lied to Chubenko. Arrests did not present a problem. The DS would arrest a dozen suspected members of the National Freedom Council and turn them over to Russian medical technicians at Darvo. Drugs and Colonel Dr. Josef Gavva's method of hypnotic suggestion would soon have the "terrorists" confessing to everything but the death of Joe Stalin!

Using his spoon with all the expertise of a dilettante, Colonel Georgi Kraisin began eating his desert—*banitsa*, a sweet, sticky pudding. "Comrade, we can be certain that the Death Merchant is one of the agents we're after," he said at length. "It took a lot more than 'good luck' to do what those four did. It was more than nerve and desperation. It took a lot of experience to kill those agents and all those troopers. That ambush"—his spoon paused several inches from his mouth—"revealed very quick thinking. At least we have proof it was the National Freedom Council. Julia Mirokeb was well known for her antisocial ideas, although we have no actual proof that she was a member of the NFC."

"The four were very expert," Shopov grudgingly admitted. He looked up from his plate at Georgi Kraisin. "Especially the way they escaped after they fled the hotel in a jeep. Yet it doesn't require any nerve to force a car to pull over, not when you're in a militia jeep. But making Javik Stivokisk and his wife lie on the floor and letting them overhear conversation about a 'safe house' in Metooi—nonsense! Parking the Lada in an alley and knocking out Javik Stivokisk and his wife fooled no one. The Stivokisks were supposed to tell us about the safe house. It was a gamble on the part of the Death Merchant. He is too intelligent and too experienced to think we would actually believe such a story."

With a precise movement, Kraisin pushed his spoon into the dish of *banitsa*. "Comrade, the real question is where the Death Merchant and the other three went after they left the

Lada in the alley. Part of what the Stivokisks told us could have been the truth: that an escape car was waiting on Sofijski Praga. Sofijski Praga is only a block from the alley where the militia found the Lada."

A look of distaste worked its way across Grigor Shopov's face.

"Georgi, at the moment we have three main problems. The first is Secretary Chubenko. Not only do he and Lieutenant General Cherfesky eat from the same bowl, but Chubenko would like nothing better than to make Major Divuncha director of the DS. Those damned Turko-Tartars stick together."

Colonel Kraisin's owllike face knotted with concern, and rightfully so. His own position, as chief of the First Directorate, depended on Shopov remaining director of the DS. He knew that Shopov was being very confidential since he had dropped the formal "Comrade" and had addressed him by his first name. His next thought was what Shopov might have in mind for the troublesome Chubenko. An in-fighter, Shopov was not a man to let anything or anyone stand in his way.

Kraisin leaned forward slightly and said almost in a whisper, "What do you suggest, Grigor? There isn't any way we can neutralize Chubenko, unless . . ." He let his voice trail off, knowing that the implication had not been lost on Shopov.

Shopov placed his fork on the table, put his right hand in front of his mouth, and began to rub his upper lip. A lip reader, reporting to the KGB, might be in the cafeteria.

"We don't have the time to arrange an 'accident' for that damned Chubenko," he said in a rush. "The only thing we can do is to make certain that he doesn't get the opportunity to question our efficiency again. Do I have to tell you what I am talking about?" He awaited Kraisin's answer with an anticipatory smile.

Finished with patting his mouth, Kraisin placed the napkin on the table; it was difficult to imagine him accidentally spilling a glass of water or dropping any food on his lap. "You said it yourself, Grigor. The Death Merchant is not a fool, and he is only one man," he said conversationally. "Even with the help of the revolutionaries, he wouldn't dare try to kill Colonel Gavva and Comrade Oleg Skarbovenko when they land at the airport." He shrugged. "Even so, how could the *Cempt Tobtocpam* and the rebel scum even know when Gavva and Sharbovenko will land? How could they even know that Gavva is in Moscova? By the way, when you met with Comrade Chubenko, did he mention the KGB mole who supplied the information about the American Cross?''

"He didn't mention the mole. Why should he? He doesn't know the identity of the mole any more than we do." Shopov's expression of cold distaste did not change. "After all, it's obvious that the mole is high within the American Central Intelligence Agency. The puzzle is why the mole didn't warn the KGB about the Death Merchant and the other agent? Why didn't the mole know when they would be sneaking into our country—and why?''

"The mole has to be in the same CIA department—either operations or counterintelligence—or he wouldn't have known about Cross. He even knew that Cross would make contact with the Slavyanska Hotel.''

"Exactly," said Shopov with savage courtesy. "It is even stranger that our Russian 'friends' have never discussed this paradoxical discrepancy with us. Logically, we can only assume that the Death Merchant and his assistant have targeted KINTEX.''

Colonel Kraisin said with calculated restraint, "Grigor, I hardly think that the Death Merchant, the other agent, and a handful of rabble plan to attack the KINTEX building. It would be suicide. They would be cut to pieces before they could leave the building.''

"I agree," Shopov said blandly. "Nonetheless, we can't afford to overlook any possibilities—because of Chubenko. I intend to increase the guard at the KINTEX building. And I'm not going to discount entirely that the targets might be Colonel Gavva and Commissar Skarbovenko. We'll increase the guards at the airport. With every five militia troopers, we'll have one of our own people.''

Colonel Kraisin stopped scraping his tongue with the end of the knife.[3] "There won't be a problem once we fly the two of them here, to headquarters. Taking Sharbovenko to see the sights is a different matter. I don't suppose there's a way we could cancel taking him to Alexander Nevsky Church and other points of interest?''

"Not without admitting we can't maintain kill-proof security. If something should go wrong, the damn Soviets might

---

[3] A common practice in Bulgaria. The custom is not considered gross or impolite at table.

send in a unit of *reydoviki*.[4] That's the last thing we want."

"It will be a risk," sighed Kraisin.

"Not as much as one might think. We'll send our own people to the buildings in advance. We can station snipers at various points along the routes and surround him with guards. There really isn't any problem in protecting Sharbovenko. We still have thirteen more days to make the necessary preparations." Shopov paused, then asked in an agreeable manner. "The plans have been made for tonight?"

"We'll strike at three in the morning." Colonel Kraisin smiled pleasantly. "We'll net nineteen suspects. They'll be taken straight to Darvo. We'll have confessions within ten days—a nice welcome for Comrade Commissar Sharbovenko, wouldn't you say?"

Colonel General Shopov finished his coffee and once more tried to reassure himself. The feeling that fate was about to spit in his face persisted, warning him that his own private cup of catastrophe was filled to the brim. . . .

---

[4] The word means "raiders." Actually, Shopov was referring to the *spetsnaz* ("to strike"), the Soviet Union's very special forces whose members are extremely mobile and specially trained in sabotage, infiltration, and assassination. *Spetsnaz* would hit targets behind NATO's front lines during the first few days of a war.

Under the direct control of the GRU—Soviet Military Intelligence—*Spetsnaz* has 32,000 men (and women) and the membership is rapidly increasing. Senior and staff officers are trained at the Third Faculty of the GRU academy. Line officers receive training at the Ryazan higher airborne school and at the reconnaissance section of the Kiev higher arms school.

The Soviet commanders of the Western, Southern, and Far Eastern theaters each have *Spetsnaz* regiments under their command. A central *Spetsnaz* intelligence center coordinates all operations. The main body of *Spetsnaz* is made up of independent companies, consisting of approximately 120 men and 12 officers. These are subdivided into sabotage and assassination teams of 12–15 men each.

The real danger is the hardcore men and women who are trained killers. Their mission is to track down and assassinate Western and political military leaders on their home territory, in competition with similar KGB "hit squads." Western nations actually invite these killers to visit the potential target areas in peacetime, since they are among the best athletes in the Soviet Union.

This information supplied by Colonel George Ellis.

CHAPTER NINE

The safe house at the Church of Saint Dimitur
Twelves days after the escape from the Slavyanska Hotel
02.00 hours

Carefully assessing the words of Stephen Traikov, the Death
Merchant felt that Thucydides and Marx had been wrong in
their belief that human passions and economics could explain
the overall social adventure and human condition. *The sum
total of causes that determine the sum total of effects are
beyond understanding. My risking my neck for a mere hundred grand! That's beyond even my understanding. . . .*

Radio contact had been made with the United States Embassy in Sofia, under conditions that had been extremely
dangerous. The Gould PCS-20001 transceiver was a first-
class radio, providing 280,000 channels spaced 100 Hz apart.
NiCad (7AH) battery life was fifteen hours minimum. Range:
2000 miles (with sky wave propagation). Receiver sensitivity:
0.25 V. (SSB); 0.079 V (CW). And while one could transmit
by frequency hopping—enemy receivers would pick up only a
babble of static—the transmission could not be made in split
microseconds, not without a "black box." This meant that an
hour's transmission would give Bulgarian secret-police radio-
tracking trucks an hour to do a compute and triangulate the
source of the static—almost impossible to do in an hour, but
still time enough to give the DS clues to a fix. But only if
transmission was made from a fixed point.

The Death Merchant had transmitted from a Kalota that had
moved through the traffic of Sofia at high noon. Fedor Rykov,

who had arrived at the secret St. Dimitur station, had done the driving. Stephen Traikov had ridden shotgun. Rykov, looking so ill-tempered he might have been chewing nails, had driven along Ruski Boulevard and other main streets. He had moved onto Aleksandar Stambolijski, after which he had cut south and had found Septemvri General Totleben. Up one avenue and down the other, but always in a jigsaw pattern. The Kalota was passing Georgi Dimitrov Mausoleum on September 9 Square when Camellion broke off contact with the CIA station in the U.S. Embassy.

One thing was certain: even if Camellion had not been able to hop from frequency to frequency, the Bulgarian secret police would never have been able to break the code that Camellion had arranged with Courtland Grojean, who had sent a copy by special diplomatic courier to the Sofia station.

The "Sixfix" code had been the language of the Hopi Indians (with some changes), a language better adapted than English when applied to the exact sciences. The Hopi language contained words representing not verbs or nouns, but events. The event-word had three moods: certitude, probability, and imagination. Instead of saying, "A man crossed the river in a boat," the Hopi would employ the group "man-river-boat" in three different combinations, according to whether the event was observed by the narrator, reported by a third party, or dreamed.

With his photographic memory, Camellion had not had any difficulty in the messages he had received from the embassy; instantly he had known the meaning of the word combinations. It was a different matter for the radio operator at the station. He had been forced to use a computer to translate Camellion's transmissions.

All of it had been a waste of time, in Camellion's opinion.

"Leapfrog" had explained why the contact—Harry Cross—had come as a tourist: because personnel, leaving the American Embassy, were being so closely watched by the DS—trailed everywhere the moment they left the embassy grounds—that it had not been possible to send a contact from the Sofia station.

The station had wanted to know if Harry Cross had given his report.

What a dumb question! Naturally he had, Camellion had replied, a personal message from the home office that there was a distinct probability that the KGB had obtained information about the operation, something the Death Merchant had assumed while still in Rome.

So what else is new?

We cannot give you any assistance, the station had said. *Should the operation be successful, it will be up to the NFC to smuggle you back into Greece. However, we do have information that could be of value to you. . . .*

The information was that Josef Gavva, a colonel in the KGB and one of the Soviet Uncles stationed in Bulgaria, had flown to Moscow and would soon be returning to Sofia—landing on the fourteenth. With him would be Commissar Oleg Skarbovenko the third minister in the Soviet Central Committee.

"There is always danger in sending men with forged credentials," Traikov was saying. "Yet we know it isn't likely that any employee of a SOMAT depot is going to pick up a phone and call the secret police for verification. He couldn't. That's why DS men go in person—to avoid use of the phone and radio."

He looked at the various faces, as if unsure of himself, as if expecting one of the eight to disagree with him.

"Tell me," urged Camellion, "is the NFC absolutely certain that it's common practice for DS messengers to hand-carry special orders to various SOMAT depots? Should the odds not be heavily on our side, why risk your people? There are other questions that have to be answered."

"Such as how expert will the forged orders be?" the skeptical Winkler said, a look of anxious concentration on his determined face. "The forgers would have to have the right paper and seals. They would have to have a sample of the handwriting of the proper authority at DS headquarters, wouldn't they? I'm under the impression that you fellows aren't too concerned about forging DS IDs and special word orders for the three trucks. Correct me if I'm wrong. . . ."

"You're right—and wrong," began Traikov. "We're not concerned, but you're—"

"Let me explain, *tosvarkish* Winkler," interrupted Petur Dzhurov. He relaxed his large shoulders and placed his hamlike hands on his legs, just above the knees. "We are very familiar with how the DS conducts much of its hellish business. For one reason, during the past four years, six DS agents have told us—let's say under conditions that could be called 'friendly persuasion'—what we demanded to know, down to the last detail.''

Harry Cross, who was wearing work pants and shirt, sat up straighter on the box in the small room that was one of the stone chambers off the main underground area.

"You mean you kidnapped them?"

"And extracted the necessary information," admitted Dzhurov.

"Okay. So six DS boys vanish," Winkler said, frowning. "It seems to me that for that reason alone, the DS would automatically change their operational methods, say on a weekly or monthly basis."

"Who said those DS agents vanished?" Dzhurov's thick lips formed a smile. "They were found, every one of them—killed 'accidentally.' Automobile crashes, and other kinds of accidents. Some were very ingenious. One agent died within six hours of—the Bulgarian word is 'deklarirane.' ''

"Botulism,"[1] translated Winkler, looking at Camellion. "Or *clostridium botulinum*, if you want to be technical."

"I'm familiar with that poison," Camellion replied. "Mexican guerrillas used botulism very effectively and the American OSS[2] tried it during WW II, or were going to use it against German troops. Their experiments failed. What I'd like to know is how the NFC made the cultures?"

"We didn't," said Stephen Traikov. "Your CIA smuggled a gallon of the poison to us. It was in liquid form."

The Death Merchant's eyes went up. A gallon! One ounce could kill one million people!

Zhivo Stoichev said dryly, "Naturally the agents we kidnapped didn't know they would be departing this life . . . not when they told us what they knew." He turned his attention to the Death Merchant.

Knowing that Stoichev wanted him to speak, Camellion said, "We can't use as drivers the same three NFC members who pose as DS messengers." He then gave his reasons. It was a matter of security that the three DS "messengers" not

---

[1] Botulin is the poison that results from *clostridium botulinum*, these bacteria occupying every inch of fertile soil on Earth. But conditions must be just right for botulism to occur from *cooked* or *canned food*. It is very easy to make the cultures, but we are not going to tell how, for obvious reasons.

[2] The OSS goofed. They made enough botulin to kill the whole German army—then tried it out on a mule. Nothing happened because *mules are immune to botulism*!

know anything of the master plan. Men could not reveal what they did not know—in case something went wrong. On that basis, six men would be needed: three to pose as DS agents and three drivers to report to three different SOMAT depots.

"I suppose it's superfluous to even mention it," Camellion said. "The three drivers wouldn't even be in the same age range as the messengers"—he looked at Stephen Traikov for confirmation—"going on what you said a few days ago."

Asparuch Meszaros said incredulously, "The drivers will have to know the plan. When you ask a man to blow himself to bits, you have to tell him where and why, especially why!"

"Well . . ." Harry Cross tugged at his shirt collar uncomfortably.

"That leads to another question," Winkler said, rubbing the end of his chin. He realized what Camellion was doing—employing a time-tested technique: doing his own scheming and at the same time playing the devil's advocate . . . ingesting all the various bits and pieces and churning them in his mental computer. "I mean the drivers." His gaze skipped to Stephen Traikov. "A few days ago, you said that you and Zhivko and Petur were making progress. What about it?"

Concern flashed over Traikov's long face. "We are going to have to put together some kind of alternate plan." He sounded apologetic. "We did find a sixty-one-year-old woman who has less than a year to live. She has chronic lymphocytic leukemia. She is willing but she can't drive one of those rigs. Any driver will have to be very good to drive one of those big SOMAT jobs through traffic."

Peter Dzhurov continued in a voice that made Camellion think of a very scratchy record being played over and over. "We already knew of one man who was dying, with less than a year to live. He was the attendant at the garage of the state apartment house on Kuskiko Street, remember? He was more than willing. Unfortunately, he was arrested by the DS three days ago."

"Let me explain, Petur," Traikov said. "We found two other persons. One man is seventy-two and only a week ago learned that he has inoperable cancer of the liver. The other man is only forty-one. He's dying of some kind of rare blood disorder. But the old man can't even drive a car. The other man can't drive a large tractor-trailor job." He spread his hands in a gesture of helplessness. "Time seems to be running out on us. In ten more days, Colonel Gavva and the Russian pig will land in Sofia."

"Who gives a damn," Winkler said, his tone cutting. "We're not going to hit 'em at the airport. We can't even go for broke the day the plane lands. We don't know what time it gets in. Gavva and that big-shot Russian son of a bitch might not be at DS headquarters until the next day."

"What's the difference?" Grisha Dyuni was unemotional. "Without drivers, we can forget blowing up DS headquarters."

All that time, Fedor Rykov had been using his pocket knife to work carefully on the nose of a four-inch figurine he had carved. "It's not surprising. It takes a lot of practice and experience to drive one of those outfits."

Tilting back his chair slightly, the Death Merchant surveyed the three commanders of the National Freedom Council, the NFC. "I assume you would have worked out a plan to transfer the three persons to the trucks, if they could drive the SOMAT rigs?"

Stephen Traikov regarded the Death Merchant with a second's speculation. "The only thing we were able to plan is where the trucks would stop after they had picked up their loads of ammonium nitrate. They would have to stop in order for the detonators to be placed in the fertilizer."

"It's not too much of a problem to find places where the trucks could stop for ten minutes, but not any longer," Zhivko Stoichev said slowly. "There would be some problems."

"*Tosvarkish* Camellion, you are apparently confused," Dzhurov said, a heavy frown on his brow. "In the first place, the three people, willing to crash the trucks, couldn't possibly get to the depots, not even if they were capable of taking those big machines through traffic. A seventy-two-year-old could hardly pose as a driver! I ask you, what's the point of discussing any method to get the three aboard? Let me warn you, we can't stop the regular drivers of any trucks. It would be too dangerous. Where the trucks would stop for the detonators is off regular routes. Only men working with us could drive the trucks to these locations, and we don't have those men. And by 'transfer,' I presume you mean after the trucks have picked up the fertilizer?"

"It's somewhat ironic," sighed Zhivko Stoichev. "We have more than a dozen members who can drive SOMAT rigs, but they're in excellent health. As Petur said, you're mixed up about something.''

A hint of a smile appeared around the corners of the Death Merchant's mouth. *Not mixed up or confused. I'm only finding out how well you jokers have thought this thing through.*

''Spill it, buddy. What have you in mind?'' Way ahead of the others, Winkler was positive that the Patron Saint of the Strange had already cooked up some wild scheme.

Camellion moved his right hand over his hair. ''All we have to do is change the orders. The first three false DS agents will carry orders that direct each SOMAT manager to have three trucks and three drivers available the next day for a special job. Since—''

''Don't forget. Each tractor and trailer will have to leave the depot in accordance with the amount of time it will take it to reach the farm collective, make a stop for the detonators, and then drive to the DS building,'' Winkler interjected. ''The three trucks have to crash more or less at the same time. Or they should!''

''Wait a minute!'' Harry Cross, greatly surprised, almost stood up in his excitement. ''Didn't you two hear what Mr. Stoichev said? He said he has more than a dozen men in the organization who can drive those big trucks. What's the problem. Use three of them for drivers.''

''They're too old,'' Stephen Traikov said gently. ''SOMAT drivers go all over Europe. Very seldom are they ever over forty. The men we have are in their fifties. Let's permit Camellion to finish. I think he's about to suggest that the next day we send three more of our people to pose as DS special agents. They will leave the stations in trucks driven by genuine SOMAT drivers. Please continue with your scenario, *tosvarkish* Camellion.''

''The SOMAT drivers will believe the three NFC are DS agents,'' said the Death Merchant. ''They'll naturally do what they're told to do. They'll drive to the collective farms and pick up the tons of ammonium nitrate. Later, when they're ordered to drive to the intercept points, they'll do it without any questions.''

Grisha Dyuni flashed an ear-to-ear grin. ''And that's where the SOMAT drivers will be disposed of, carted off in the same cars that will bring the suicide drivers to the trucks. But''—his enthusiasm vanished—''there's something wrong! The three who are dying can't drive rigs!''

"A point! A point! He's got a point!" Winkler smirked, all the while confident that Camellion had an answer. He didn't really care who Richard Camellion might be. He did know that wherever the tall, lean man walked, he left only dust and brought only death.

Asparuch Meszaros, the electronics specialist, gave Camellion an up-and-under look with his inky eyes, his stare intense. "Even if we put NFC drivers into the trucks, what good would they be? They wouldn't commit suicide!"

"They wouldn't have to," Camellion told Meszaros, who was tall, had a brush mustache, usually wore a preoccupied expression, and was around the Death Merchant's own age, a year or two either way from forty. "At the transfer points, the three DS agents would leave the trucks and the NFC drivers, and the three men who would crash the trucks into the building would get aboard."

"Damn it! You're saying what I just said!" Meszaros said in exasperation, waving his arms. "American, you are not making sense!"

"I would if you would let me finish—Bulgarian!" snapped the Death Merchant. "The NFC drivers would drive as close to the DS building as possible. For the moment, for the sake of conversation, let's say they'd jump from the tractors just before the trucks smashed into the barriers. The drivers would be picked up by NFC cars following close behind."

The three commanders and Dyuni and Meszaros stared at Camellion. Even the phlegmatic Fedor Rykov stopped carving long enough to look up, disbelievingly, at the Death Merchant. He was convinced that this strange American with the odd blue eyes would get them all killed. . . .

"Well! Hell and great gobs of goose grease!" Winkler exclaimed huskily, breaking the strained silence. "If the real drivers are going to get that close to the headquarters building, why bother with the three poor guys about to 'go west'? We wouldn't need them. The NFC drivers could turn the trucks toward the barriers and then jump at the last moment. They'd have to stay with the trucks long enough to turn them toward the barriers. They'd have to do the shifting."

"I thought about that," admitted Camellion. "It wouldn't work. The rigs have to be guided to the building. The front wheel could hit a bump or something and cause the vehicle to deviate from its course. We can rig a metal wedge that would reach from the front of the seat to the gas pedal. The drivers can put the wedges in place just before they leap out. From the road to the barriers is roughly forty feet. But the steering wheels must be held. That will be the job of the three NFC drivers."

Harry Cross wiped his face with a handkerchief. "This is weird," he said nervously. "In my opinion every one of you is going to get killed!"

Acting as if he hadn't heard Cross's remark, Camellion cocked his head toward Stephen Traikov. "The three you have in mind, the three already tapping at death's black door, they can steer, can't they? I know they're not bedridden or you wouldn't have thought of them. And you did say that the trucks have power steering."

"The diseases killing the three are doing it very slowly," Traikov said hesitantly. "It will be months before they would lack the strength to guide a vehicle. *Dai*, they will be able to steer. You know that you are asking our own drivers to run the race against suicide. And I am curious. I like your suggestion for holding down the gas pedal. But why should it be necessary? It doesn't require much knowledge or driving skill to keep one's foot on the gas. . . ."

Camellion told the truth. "It's a gamble. If all goes as planned—and it had better—we should be in the building half an hour before the trucks arrive and—"

"And going bye-bye in one or two of the choppers when the first truck hits!" Winkler said grimly. "Or we'll be dusting ourselves off!"

"We'll have created enough fireworks and confusion inside to divert attention from the outside," went on Camellion. "Who really knows? The half-dead drivers could be machine-gunned by the time the trucks are halfway to the building. Should that happen, so what? The trucks will keep going because of the bars wedged against the gas pedals, and they will be close enough to the building to hit, even if they aren't being steered. Once they're halfway to the target, they won't be able to miss."

Petur Dzhurov's low voice was hard. "You're expecting a lot from our drivers. Their chances for survival will be very slim, if for no other reason than the reinforcements that would be arriving. Let's assume there is a lot of gunfire from within the building. By the time the three trucks arrive, someone will have called the militia. Their arriving on the scene will depreciate the longevity of our drivers."

The Death Merchant spread his arms, palms outward. "Look at it this way, the drivers who jump and the people who pick them up won't be taking any more of a risk than the strike force that goes into the building—eight NFC men and Winkler and I."

"Don't even think of including me!" Harry Cross paled. "I'm strictly a high-class messenger boy. This gung-ho commando business is not for me—no way!"

"For a 'messenger boy' you did a good job back at the hotel," Winkler said with a half laugh.

"Maybe he was only lucky," Camellion said. He knew better. *There's far more to Harry Cross than meets the eye. You're either experienced—and lucky—or you're dead!*

Cross pulled a face and squeezed his hands together. "I didn't have a choice! They were shooting at me! At us! I had to shoot back!"

"*Tosvarkish* Camellion, you forgot to include us," Traikov said, his voice urgent, impatient. "Zhivko, Petur, and myself. We too want to see General Shopov and the Soviet advisers—face-to-face before they die."

"It is our show, as well as yours," Grisha Dyuni said stiffly.

Fedor Rykov folded his knife, dropped it into his pocket, and looked at the Death Merchant. "Without the NFC, it would not be possible for you Americans to get within two blocks of the secret policy building!"

Carey Winkler cleared his throat. Highly intelligent, in spite of his offhand remarks, he knew when to keep his mouth shut. He remained silent.

"To use any kind of strong poison against cockroaches is useless," Camellion said equably. "The strongest insect poison in the world will kill no more than the smallest percentage of a roach horde that leaves its nest to forage at any given time. You see, cockroaches leave their nests in relays, only a few at a time." The Death Merchant let his voice trail off when he saw that Petur Dzhurov was straining at the leash to speak. Stoichen and Traikov were also curious.

"This cockroach," Dzhurov said, frowning. "What is it?"

Grisha Dyuni spoke rapidly in Bulgarian.

Dzhurov's face lit up with understanding. "Ah . . . I see." With narrowed eyes, he looked at Camellion. "We call the little fellows *rapeztista*. But what do they have to do with the attack on the headquarters of the *Darzhavna Sigurnost?*"

Winkler opened his mouth . . . thought better of what he wanted to say, and closed his mouth.

"Like I said, the roaches go out a few at a time. After the first two come back, the second pair go out for food, knowing that it is safe to move about. Roaches—or *rapeztista*—are equipped by nature to *know* when they've been contaminated with poison, and a contaminated roach will not return to its nest. This means that in order to eliminate roaches their *nests* must be contaminated. You have to destroy all the baby roaches, and by so doing destroy all future generations. The best chemical to use for this purpose is boric acid. Adult roaches are immune to boric acid and don't consider the chemical a poison. This is ideal because baby roaches die very quickly from boric acid. What happens is that the adults become covered with boric acid powder and take it back to the nest, not realizing it is deadly to their young. The off-spring are killed very quickly by the boric acid."

"Goddamm it, get to the point!" Winkler could no longer contain himself. "What the fiddler's fuck do cockroaches have to do with the subject under discussion—or do you expect us to throw boric acid at the DS?"

"The point of comparison is that we have to outwit the DS in much the same manner that one destroys a nest of cockroaches," Camellion said. A moment earlier his voice had been summer dew. Now it was mid-winter in Siberia. "And we're not going to get the job done without losing lives."

Winkler chuckled. "I think it's rather to the point to compare cockroaches to the DS and the Russians. There isn't much difference between the three."

"Yes there is," chimed in Harry Cross. "Roaches are more clean. The truth is that they are among the cleanest, in their habits, among all insects."

"By outsmarting the DS, I do mean the manner in which we'll get past the guards at the gate and into the main building," Camellion went on, his steady gaze drifting to Stoichev, who was moving a forefinger slowly over his lower lip. "It's all contingent on your drivers doing their part with the SOMAT rigs."

Silence. . . .

Finally broken by Dzhurov. "In regard to the three trucks, I think your plan will work, but only on condition that three of the drivers are willing to put their lives in such danger. I—we—will not order them to steer the trucks toward the wooden barrier."

"Fair enough," Camellion found himself saying. He was forced to. He had done all the shoving he could do. Now the Bulgarians were pushing and it would be wise on his part to take it.

He said, "Zhivko, a little while ago you said there would be problems. What are they?"

"They are no longer important," Stoichev replied. "Our own drivers—should they decide to do the job—will have answered all the questions I had."

"We should discuss why I'm here." Asparuch Meszaros hunched forward in Camellion's direction. "My sole concern is the detonators for the fertilizer. We have five hundred and seventy-six sticks of—'dynamite' is the English term. At minimum it will require seventy-two sticks to detonate one English ton, or four hundred and fifty-three kilograms of ammonium nitrate. On that basis, we can explode only eight tons or seven thousand two hundred and fifty-seven kilograms of ammonium nitrate."

Winkler locked his hands on top of his head. "A bit more than a hundred and fourteen sticks of dynamite per rig. A large package, if you ask me—to get inside each trailer. I suppose we could use trunks. Sacks would be better, I think . . ."

"We need remote-control detonators," Camellion said bluntly to Meszaros. "I have neither the equipment nor the technical knowledge to build them. I understand you have the ability and can get necessary parts."

Meszaros nodded in the Bulgarian manner. "I'm an instructor at the Rigkivog Electrical Engineering Center in Sofia. There isn't any problem in building the three detonators. The problem is in getting all the parts. Every solenoid, every pulse relay flexode . . . everything required to make a RC detonator is checked off in inventory. I will have difficulty in obtaining all the necessary components. I'm sure I can get them and do what needs to be done."

"Each control unit must have a time-delay circuit with a three-minute delay capacity," Camellion said. "We need the space of three minutes from the time the trucks head toward the barriers until they explode."

"A minor technicality," Meszaros said without hesitation. "I'll use a time-interval selector hooked to function with a pulse distributor and time quadature."

"Three minutes . . ." mused Winkler, blinking at Camellion. "I get it. You're going to have the NFC boys trigger the RCs before they jump, before the trucks crash through the fences. Not a bad idea, not bad at all."

"There are flaws in the truck scheme." Zhivko Stoichev was very good at lifting his eyebrows. "One glaring flaw has not been mentioned."

"I admit we are counting on a mobius strip of fortuitous circumstances to assist us," Camellion said. "Plus a lot of nerve. After all, no guts, no glory—and no success."

"The drivers who remain with the vehicles will be machine-gunned before the cabs are able to crash into the building," continued Stoichev in an even voice. "Should the drivers be killed, the braces against the gas pedals will keep the vehicles moving. But what assurance do you have that bullets won't hit the engine?"

"We don't have any assurances," Camellion said. "Slugs will rip into the engines. It won't make that much difference. The momentum of the trucks will keep them moving forward. All they have to be is close to the buildings when they explode."

"None of which has any bearing on our getting past the guards and into the building, not to mention snuffing General Shopov and the five Uncles, then getting to the choppers on the roof," Winkler said, his expression sinister.

"Don't be so pessimistic," Camellion chided him. "I know what Shopov and the five pig farmers look like." When he saw Stoichev's eyebrows raise and the other men frown, he added, "I've studied photographs of the six, and I have a very very good memory."

"Screw your memory! We still have to get past the guards at the gate." Winkler persisted with the tenacity of a starving leech. "We have to get inside the building and all the way to the fifth floor. After we make the hits, we have to get to the roof. And that leads to another problem: suppose there aren't any choppers on the roof? Assuming there are, where do we take off to? Where do we land. One of the eight NFC men was in the Bulgarian air force and can fly an eggbeater. If he buys the business, that leaves you and me to pilot the birds. We're not that good. Anyhow, where in hell do we land?''

Camellion told him point-blank, ''At the moment, I haven't the slightest idea. . . .''

CHAPTER TEN

One jagged tooth is all that is needed to strip a gear. Only one tiny mistake was needed to wreck the Death Merchant's daring scheme to assassinate Colonel General Grigor Shopov, his aides, and the five Soviet advisers and to demolish the headquarters building of the secret police.

As the days flew by, the various complex problems were resolved, one by one. For example, each of the three trucks would have to leave their individual SOMAT depots at different times, the time of departure of each vehicle contingent not only on the distance from the depot to the collective farm, but also the distance from the collective to the DS building on Boulevard Anton Ivanova. Included in the tricky schedule would be an hour for loading the sacks of ammonium nitrate, plus fifteen minutes for each truck to stop, when the remote-control detonators and the suicide drivers were transferred and the real SOMAT drivers spirited away in NFC vehicles. There was only one logical way to synchronize the arrival of the three trucks at the DS headquarters building: make a test run and do a time study . . . first, from the general vicinity of the selected SOMAT depots in the Sofia *okrug* to the three different collectives, then from the farms to the DS building— and add an hour and fifteen minutes to each schedule.

No matter how meticulous the planning, Camellion and all the others knew that there were any number of factors beyond their control. Suppose one of the trucks developed engine trouble, or DS agents happened to be passing when one of the transfers was being made? Or if there were a slip-up at one of the three SOMAT depots, or at one of the collectives, or . . . ?

It was the plain-speaking Carey Winkler who put into words what everyone—except Camellion—was thinking: "The whole scheme will work, provided there's a God who'll drop miracles all over us!"

"I've seen operations worse than this one pulled off successfully," Camellion said nonchalantly, wishing Carey would keep his big mouth shut. "We have the timing of the trucks down pat. We've figured out a way to get past the guards at the gate and into the building." He smiled broadly and motioned indifferently with his left hand. "Once inside, we hit the targets, go to the roof, fly away, land in the woods south of Dragalevtsi, transfer to the vehicles, and head for the new safe house being set up."

Petur Dzhurov spoke up quickly. "After we take off from the roof, it will take less than fifteen minutes for us to reach the woods. We'll be in the tourist buses and on our way before the DS and the militia realize what has happened."

"Exactly," Camellion was quick to agree. He had noticed the note of uncertainly in the Bulgarian's voice and felt that Dzhurov was trying to reassure himself more than anyone else.

"Oh yeah, sure! As easy as a stroll in the park!" Winkler tilted back his chair and put his feet on the table. "The trouble is that it sounds easy. But when you get to where the rubber meets the road, it's a different deal. Stealing a personnel carrier is crazy enough, but stationing NFC men at the militia post to make sure the radio operator minds his P's and Q's is more than enough to make us candidates for a rubber room. And if the guards at the gate become suspicious? Hell! We're all nuts!"

One day before S-Day, before Strike Day. There was a final conference on the plan and reports from the three leaders of the revolutionary National Freedom Council, the NFC. Every man and woman who would take part in the operation was ready and knew the part he or she would play.

Another part of the time schedule was very carefully checked: the Death Merchant, Winkler, and the eight Bulgarian NFC men who would accompany them had to mesh their movements with the three tractor-trailer jobs that would converge on the DS headquarters building at roughly 14.30 hours, give or take ten minutes. Therefore, Camellion, Winkler, and the other eight would have to be moving through the front gates of the DS headquarters building at two P.M. or 14.00 hours.

Fedor Rykov said in his low, husky voice, "We should get to the other safe house on Slivnica Spipka on schedule. Katherini Nocheki knows the city well and is a careful driver."

Sipping coffee laced with *Mastica*, Winkler hunched forward and hooked a thumb over the shoulder holster strap crossing his chest. "It seems to me that we could save time if the seven came here. I suppose, though that—"

"Out of the question. The fewer people who know about our headquarters here at St. Dimitur's, the more security we'll have," insisted Zhivko Stoichev, who appeared rather comical in the hat he was wearing. It wasn't the hat itself but Stoichev's thick, wire-brush hair, protruding from underneath the short brim—like a giant Brillo pad—that seemed farcical.

"I was going to say that I suppose it doesn't make any difference," Winkler resumed, toying with the coffee cup. "Even if the seven came here, we'd still have to go across town to the safe house."

Richard Camellion considered Petur Dzhurov with icy blue eyes. "*Tosvarkish* Dzhurov, I want some assurance that the four NFC men we leave at the militia station have the right time fixed in their minds, even if they don't know about the overall operation or why they will be doing what they do. If they goof on the schedule, we could go down the drain."

Dzhurov placed his cigarette in an ashtray and consulted the sheet of paper lying in front of him on the table. "Once the militia station is secure, it will take approximately forty-five minutes for the personnel carrier to reach the target on Boulevard Anton Ivanova. Our four men will kill the radio operator one hour after the carrier leaves the station."

"They will kill the operator immediately after he makes his two o'clock report." Stephen Traikov helped the explanation along. "This means that unless something unforeseen happens, it will be three o'clock before militia headquarters realizes that something is wrong at the Paisji-Botev Street station." His mouth twisted into a self-satisfied smirk. "Only by three o'clock there won't be any militia central, since the DS building will have become a pile of rubble."

"I have a question," Asparuch Meszaros said hesitantly. He glanced first at Camellion, then blinked at Petur Dzhurov and Fedor Rykov. "Are you sure the seven militiamen at the

Paisji-Botev station won't be suspicious when a car full of other militiamen pulls in during the middle of the afternoon?''

"The militiamen won't be at all suspicious." Dzhurov was as brusque as usual, yet there was relish in his voice. "Why should they be?"

"Not the way we'll be dressed," Fedor Rykov growled in triumph. "I'll be wearing the uniform of a captain in the *Nersko-Tsopska*. Another man will be in the uniform of a lieutenant in the militia. The two Americans will be in civilian clothes. The militiamen at the station will think it's some kind of special inspection and that Mr. Camellion and Mr. Winkler are DS agents. Once we're inside the building, the militiamen will be dead before they realize how they've been tricked."

"Our next step will then be to phone the safe house," Camellion said. "In turn, the safe house will contact the men in the other two cars. Each car will carry five men. Six of the men will go with us in the carrier. The six that go with us can change their clothes in the station before we leave in the carrier. Winkler and I will also change in the station. We'll be ordinary privates."

"What will you do if the carrier isn't there?" asked Harry Cross who was not at all happy over being stranded in Bulgaria in the safe house until the revolutionaries could smuggle him and Camellion and Winkler across the border into northern Greece. He didn't know it—for that matter neither did Winkler—but the Death Merchant had no intention of being cooped up in trucks, in boxes and crates, and spending weeks in getting out of Bulgaria. He had a better plan! It was a plan so simple as to be laughable!

"The personnel carrier is always there." Camellion looked across at Stephen Traikov. "I don't suppose your information could be inaccurate?"

"It could be but it isn't." Traikov regarded Camellion with slight amusement, yet he was still serious. "It isn't that the militia need personnel carriers. They have them for only one reason: to impress the people, to instill fear in the people."

Winkler commented: "We'll have to hit the militia station no later than twelve-thirty, considering the length of time it will take the two other cars to get there, after we phone." He was suddenly gruff, his voice uncertain. "Damn it, there's so many intangibles! If the boys in either of those cars are stopped for some reason, either by the *Jokka* or the DS, or if we're stopped . . .''

The Death Merchant laughed in an attempt to inject some jocularity into the discussion. ''Well, my boy, Mom never said the road would be paved with honeysuckle.''

''Piss on a paper moon!'' Winkler snapped out. ''You'll be telling me next to pray for help from on high!''

''Well, it couldn't hurt.'' Camellion, drinking his coffee barefoot, without cream or sugar, raised the cup. ''Emotional adrenaline is always of value. If you believe it, you can do it!''

''Piss on a poltergeist! Prayers are for the weak who are supposed to inherit the earth!''

''Don't you mean 'meek'?'' interjected Harry Cross.

''I mean 'weak'!'' Winkler stared at Asparuch Meszaros, as if uncertain. ''Another thing. Those remote-control detonators you put together. How in hell do you know they will work?''

A shadow of anger fell across Meszaros's full face. He jabbed a finger at the Walther P-88 autopistol in Winkler's left-sided shoulder holster. ''How sure are you that your pistol will fire?'' he asked. ''I saw you take it apart, clean it, check it, reassemble it, and load it. But are you sure the gun will fire?''

Too intelligent to say 100 percent, Winkler snapped, ''I'm ninety-nine point ninety-nine percent positive. But I didn't make the weapon; I didn't manufacture it. Therein, my friend, lies the difference.''

''Now did I personally manufacture the parts I used in the detonators,'' Meszaros said politely. He continued in a frigid and emphatic voice. ''Even if the detonators do not work— and I am telling you that they will—the failure would not have a bearing on the heart of your mission, yours and Mr. Camellion's. Your capitalist government is more interested in killing the five Russians than in blowing up DS headquarters.''

This could get out of hand! Trying to make Carey keep a zipper on his mouth is the same as trying to figure out how many days are in an eternity!

Camellion said very quickly, ''Your hammer has hit the nail on the head, *tosvarkish* Meszaros. My government does want the Russians dead. Demolishing the building is my little idea.'' His voice became cutting, almost insulting. ''It's the same capitalist government that so generously is supplying the NFC with weapons. . . .''

"For its own ends!" pointed out Meszaros. "I'm sure your government isn't going to all this trouble because it loves the Bulgarian people!"

"Gentlemen, let us stop this nonsense," Zhivko Stoichev put in soothingly. "The fact that we are being helped by the Americans in our fight is enough. Let's not argue political philosophies among ourselves."

"*Dai*, you are right," said Stephen Traikov. He swung his head and looked harshly at Meszaros who was a rabid Socialist and was convinced that capitalism was an iron collar around the neck of any person, unless he or she was very wealthy. "There are too many things of importance to discuss at this late time," Traikov gently prompted Meszaros. "Why should we waste time with subjects that have different meanings to different people?"[3]

Wanting to avoid an argument, the Death Merchant shrugged. "A very good suggestion. This is not the place—and we don't have the time—for puzzles in semantics. Any discussion of political mechanisms is as silly as trying to pick one's nose with his elbow." He was happy to see that Meszaros also looked relieved and was relaxing.

"Yeah," murmured Winkler. "In any society, by the time you take the saints from the sinners, you'll be lucky to end up with one Abe Lincoln." He grinned at the confusion pictured on the faces of the Bulgarians. "Lincoln, the American president during the American Civil War," he explained. "But let's discuss getting past the guards at the gate of the headquarters building."

"We'll have to carry Zeff AKMs and Bidjas," began Camellion, "if for no other reason than . . ."

And all the while, off to one side in his mind, the Death Merchant couldn't help but feel that he was only going through

[3] Socialism, in its generic sense, is a term of neutral force under which to group a lot of philosophies. Politically, socialism has a specific use quite different from its generic meaning. This applies to the politico-economic systems of such countries as Great Britain, Sweden, Denmark, Mexico, etc., in which democratic elective processes are combined with governmental welfare programs and government control or ownership of selected industries. We have strong elements of Socialism in our own USA. People can own property—real estate—under Socialism but not under Communism. But it should be understood that the Soviet Union does not have communism. The Soviet Union is a total military-police state.

the motions, that all this was unreal and that he was only one of the actors in the frames in the world picture show. *And, according to the doctrine of elementary particles, I just might be! So is everyone else! Time is thinking! Time is consciousness! Time is a continuous now! All of it a vast illusion in this time continuum.*[4]

This also means that failure is never fatal any more than success is final. . . .

---

[4] The reality might be—according to elementary particle theorists—that Time and Space come in "bits" and "pieces"—called *Kronons*.

CHAPTER ELEVEN

13.15 hours
Ruski Boulevard (ten minutes after leaving the militia station on Paisji-Botev Street)

A Soviet BTR-60PK armored personnel carrier, although not "pretty" with sleek lines, is a very efficient vehicle. The large hull is boat-shaped for good movement through water and to deflect hostile fire. Top land speed is 80 km/h (50mph); water: 10 km/h (6¼ mph). The BTRO6-PK is widely used by Warsaw Pact forces and has been exported to at least ten other countries. Powered by two GAZ-49B six-in-line water-cooled gasoline engines, 90 hp each, the troop carrier moves along on eight land wheels, all powered and with power steering on the front four. At all times, tire pressures are centrally controlled by the driver; and should the vehicle have to cross a river, the two engines can be switched to drive water jets. Other than a driver and a co-driver, there is room for sixteen troops.

There were only ten men in this particular BTR, one of whom, Tsola Nekliv, was doing the driving. Next to him was the co-driver, Pekko Vardikiv. To their rear were Richard Camellion, Carey Winkler, and six other men. Camellion, Winkler, and Belad Freidliv were in civilian clothes, in heavy overcoats, caps with large ear flaps, workingmen's shirts and pants, and imitation leather boots. They were the "prisoners." In contrast, Fedor Rykov was wearing the greatcoat, peaked cap, and uniform of a captain in the *Nersko-Tsopska*. Aleksei Izogyi was wearing the shoulder bars of a lieutenant in the

143

militia. The other five wore the uniforms of ordinary *zhelali* (privates).

The "privates" carried Zeff AKM assault rifles and holstered Bidja pistols. Underneath his *chivva,* Camellion carried one of the .22 Ruger counterinsurgency assassination pistols and one of the Beretta M92SB autoloaders, minus its Larand suppressor, which he had removed in the militia station. Winkler was armed with a Walther P-88, Belad Freidliv with a Beretta.

In two fiberboard suitcases were three Viking submachine guns, nine magazines for the SMGs, and another Beretta, this with the Larand "silencer" attached. These two suitcases were "evidence" that would be carried down the halls of the DS building by two of the *zhelali.*

It had begun to snow when the BTR was leaving the militia station on Paisji-Botev and the windshield wipers kept up their steady zuup-zuup, zuup-zuup across the small, slanted windshields of the personnel carriers.

The weather report could not have been more unfavorable. "Heavy snow, with possible sleet," was predicted from "late afternoon until midnight." It was now fifteen minutes after one in the afternoon and already an inch and a half had fallen. Should the snow fall in greater volume, how much would fall in forty-five minutes, in an hour and fifteen minutes, in an hour and forty-five minutes.

In exactly an hour and forty-five minutes, we have to be within a stone's throw of the safe house in Dragalevtsi. And Dragalevtsi is thirty miles away. Mercy mercy, Mother Percy! A blizzard could be dropping on the road that leads from the woods to Dragalevtsi! As for the three tractor-and-trailer jobs . . . All we know is that everything went well at the SOMAT depots—so it would seem!

"If I were religious or superstitious, I'd say that even God was against us. The truck that left SOMAT station one is going to farm collective three," Winkler said, half putting into words what Camellion had been thinking. "Collective three is outside of Histendil. That's forty miles from northern Sofia. Who knows how it might be snowing there?"

"Ah, my American friend, you are forgetting that particular truck is in the city by now," corrected Grisha Dyuni, who had the gift of remembering complicated schedules. At the very last moment, one of the eight men scheduled to go with Camellion and Winkler had slipped on the ice and had broken his right arm. Both Harry Cross and Grisha Dyuni had offered to go in his place. Camellion had chosen Dyuni. It wasn't that Camellion didn't trust Harry Cross. Yet there was something not quite right about the man.

There could be something wrong with Grisha Dyuni as well. In spite of the danger facing him, Dyuni did not appear to be nervous. Camellion suspected that Dyuni, knowing his acting career was finished, simply didn't give a damn if he stopped a bullet.

Winkler looked across the narrow aisle at Dyuni, his eyes hard, his voice soft. "What I meant was that we have no idea when the snow started falling in the Histendil region, if it ever started falling. If it started falling heavily this morning, then it's possible that the truck from SOMAT one will be delayed either before it reaches farm collective three or after it leaves collective three. The same can be said for the truck that left SOMAT eight to go to collective two. I still maintain we should have used a truck from SOMAT four. That station was only several kilometers from collective two."

Fedor Rykov, sitting next to the driver's seat, called out, his tone as surly as ever, "It was explained by *tosvarkish* Dzhurov why the truck had to go to collective two. SOMAT station four is too close to collective two. The truck would have been loaded very quickly, and the driver—our driver— would not have any way of spending those extra thirty-five minutes. We all know that the schedules of the three trucks had to be tied in as closely as possible."

Winkler didn't even bother to reply to Rykov. His mouth merely twisted in contempt—no surprise to the Death Merchant, who knew that Carey considered any Bulgarian a mental midget, "slaves who enjoy living on their knees," in Winkler's words. Winkler did have a valid point, at least in regard to Asparuch Meszaros. Even Camellion found it absurd that an intelligent man like Meszaros could sincerely believe that social-collectivism was better than capitalism. Only a fool could fail to see that under the system of socialized collectivism one worked for the state—and the hell with individual rights.

The take-over of the militia station on Paisji-Botev Street had gone off as planned, the six militiamen inside the low, square building not being the least bit suspicious. Predictably, the militiamen had thought that Fedor Rykov and Aleksei Izogyi were officers in the *Nersko-Tsopska* and that Camellion and Winkler were either plainclothes officials in the militia or

else members of the secret police DS. Only for the short space
of ten seconds did the doomed men realize their mistake,
when the Death Merchant pulled the Beretta from underneath
his overcoat and began firing, the sound of the pistol and its
Larand noise suppressor no louder than a BB gun. Only the
telephone and radio operator was spared—a thin, middle-aged
man who shook with fear when Rykov told him to obey each
order instantly or else he would be shot.

Aleksei Izogyi had hurried to the Kalota to get two suitcases as Camellion and Winkler had dragged the five corpses
of the militiamen into a tiny storage room and Rykov, having
phoned the safe house on Slivnica Spipka, had kept the
terrified radio operator covered.

As soon as Izogyi had returned, Camellion and Winkler
had opened the two suitcases and taken out the contents, two
chivvas, boots, caps, and work clothes. It would not do for
them to play the role of "arrested men" dressed in overcoats
and suits that average Bulgarians couldn't afford.

There were the X factors. There wasn't anything that the
Death Merchant and the other men could do about the dangers
confronting them, about what could happen while they were
at the station. Suppose, for some reason, another squad of
militiamen dropped in, or some kind of unexpected official
showed up? There were any number of disasters that could
explode in their faces while they waited for the ten NFC men
to arrive. But nothing had gone wrong. The ten did get to the
station and had changed into the uniforms of militia *zhelali*.
The transfer had been made to the BTR-60PK parked to one
side of the green station building. The strike force was on its
way.

Four NFC men had remained behind at the station. It was
really they who were sticking their necks into a noose and
gambling that fate wouldn't tighten the rope. The four would
have to remain at the station until after two o'clock, until
after the radio operator had made his two o'clock routine
report, which would be the last report of his life.

A youthful-looking Pekko Vardikiv, one of the NFC men
decked out in the uniform of a militia private, spoke up, his
English heavily accented. "The way I look at what we're
doing, I think that once we are past the guards at the main
gate, that will be half of the battle."

"The guards will admit us," said Vard Kurdzhali. "It's
normal enough for the damned militia to haul prisoners to DS

headquarters. It happens a dozen times a day. Sometimes the militia brings the poor devils in cars, sometimes in carriers, like this one.''

Aleksei Izogyi said something short and to the point in Bulgarian. Sitting across from Vardikiv, he then dropped his cigarette to the metal floor and crushed it with the heel of his boot.

"He said we shouldn't become overconfident," Winkler translated to Camellion. "I couldn't agree with him more."

The Death Merchant nodded and glanced at Izogyi, who was a heavily muscled man with a beak of a nose and ears as large as trunk handles. Camellion didn't like him. It was Izogyi's eyes. You could always feel his eyes but never catch him looking at you. "He's right," Camellion said mildly. "In this business overconfidence is one of the seven deadly sins."

Ivan Baev smiled faintly at Camellion. Only twenty-two years old, he was the youngest of the Bulgarians in the personnel carrier. He then turned to Vard Kurdzhali. "Over-confidence doesn't have anything to do with some of the dangers we will face. It won't do us any good to kill the Russians if we can't get away. The two Americans are the only ones who can fly the helicopters. Their destiny is our destiny. Should they get killed, we too will be as good as dead."

"We don't plan on getting killed," Camellion said, cool amusement in his voice. "I can't deny that the possibility does exist. The truth is that all of us are taking a great risk. All of us could die. That's the reality of it."

Winkler surveyed Camellion in slow speculation, his expression facetious. "One thing is certain. If we're caught, we won't have the good old ACLU to come to our aid in court. Now that is something to think about!"

The Death Merchant acknowledged with a twisted smile. Winkler could be the world's worst pest at times, but Camellion admired him for his cold-blooded realism—expressed in witty cynicisms—in the face of death. If Winkler had an abundance of any quality, it was sheer nerve. *When he drops into hell, no doubt he will ask Lucifer who keeps his horns trimmed!*

"This ACLU," said Tsola Nekliv. "Some kind of American freedom organization?"

Winkler's little laugh was lewd. "Oh yes, the ACLU is an organization that fights for freedom—of criminals! Should you rape half a dozen women and cut their throats, the ACLU will be by your side, fighting for 'justice'!''

Gleaning that Winkler was in reality mocking the ACLU, Nekliv frowned for a moment. His only comment was, ''Your United States is an odd country, *tosvarkish* Winkler . . . a strange nation,''

''In more ways than a dozen . . .''

Camellion remained silent. In private he agreed with Winkler. He consulted his wrist watch: 13.34 hours.

CHAPTER TWELVE

Dogs bark and the winds carry it away . . . is an old Bulgarian proverb, one that Colonel General Grigor Shopov now applied to the rebel NFC. They had made a lot of threats; yet nothing had happened. The Soviet Antonov-24 transport had landed at the airport on schedule. A Mi-4[1] helicopter had then whisked Commissar Oleg Skarbovenko and other members of the party to the DS headquarters building, the Mi-4 landing on the roof between two Mi-1[2] choppers. From the headquarters building, the party had been driven to the Grand Hotel Sofia on Narodno Sobraniye Square. Included in the party were Colonel General Shopov, Colonel Georgi Kraisin, the four KGB guards of Commissar Sharbovenko, and the five Soviet advisers. Accompanying the four cars to the Grand Hotel Sofia were six BTR carriers filled with special DS troops and five BT-4 armored cars, three of the BT-4s to the rear, two out in front.

There had not been any incidents. The NFC had not appeared.

"Those filthy traitors would not dare attack us, not in the open," Major Stanko Divuncha, the director of the DS's Third Directorate had said. "And that includes the damned Death Merchant, if one of the Americans who escaped is the Death Merchant. Frankly, I don't think so."

---

[1] Mi-4. NATO designation: *Hound*. The Mi-4 has been built in larger quantities than any other Soviet chopper to date. There is a commercial as well as a military version.

[2] Mi-1. NATO designation: *Hare*. Smaller than the Mi-4, the Mi-1 carries only eight troops.

The reception at the Grand Hotel Sofia, given by Boris Cholev, chairman of the Council of Ministers, had been perfect. This afternoon would go equally well. To Colonel General Shopov the meeting was far far more important than the reception, for it would involve even closer cooperation between the *Kah Gay Beh* and the *Komitet Darzhavna Sigurnost.*

First glancing at his watch—1:51—Shopov finished his drink and looked out one of the windows. The snow coming down was heavier. He was wondering why this year's winter was so severe and reflecting that a full blown blizzard might delay the departure of Commissar Skarbovenko—the Russian son of a bitch was scheduled to remain three more days— when the low buzzer sounded and the tiny red light on his desk began flashing. Shopov pressed the button to the left of the middle drawer. A click from the electric lock; the office door opened and Colonel Josef Gavva and Colonel Ivan Mikolov walked in.

"Grigor, the convoy just pulled through the gates," Gavva said. "Commissar Sharbovenko and his people have arrived."

A spare, truculent man with a small nose, very deepset eyes and a yellowish complexion, Gavva had very black hair for a man in his sixties. Even his eyebrows—two fat caterpillars pasted to his forehead—were very thick and black.

Colonel General Shopov stood up and reached for his uniform cap. "Of course, Cherfesky and the other advisers are with Commissar Sharbovenko?"

"Naturally," replied Colonel Mikolov. "I doubt if any of them will have news we'll enjoy hearing. We'll have to be very careful with all of them. We already know that the Soviets want more direct control, and I don't see any way we can prevent them from getting it."

"I do know from talking with Sharbovenko in Moscova that the *Kah Gay Beh* is going to put more of its agents into KINTEX," Gavva said in his high, thin voice. "The KGB is none too happy at our failure to smash the National Freedom Council revolutionaries. And that incident at the Slavyanska Hotel, involving foreign tourists, has made even the politburo furious. Stories that have appeared in Western newspapers would have the world believe that the Bulgarian government is about to be overthrown and that the Soviet Union is powerless to prevent it."

"The Kremlin is afraid the situation here will give the

Poles and the Czechs and the East Germans ideas, especially those Catholic Poles," Mikolov said worriedly.

Colonel General Shopov placed his cap snugly on his head and moved toward the door. "Let's get to the meeting," he said grimly, "and let me do most of the talking."

"We're only five blocks from the corner of Dimitar Bue Avenue and Boulevard Anton Ivanova," Tsola Nekliv called out from the driver's position. "And the snow is coming down harder."

"That's the trouble with riding in these carriers," muttered Aleksei Izogyi, turning down the wide collar of his lieutenant's greatcoat. "Only the driver can see out. It's like riding in a metal coffin."

"This has become a nightmare turned inside out," Winkler said matter-of-factly. "Now if I were boss, I'd take a cab and go home."

Earlier, right after the BTR-60PK had pulled out of the Paisji-Botev militia station, the Death Merchant had used cosmetics to give his face and Winkler's and Freidliv's a beat-up appearance . . . a "bruise" on this cheek, a "bruise" on that chin; and Winkler looked a bit ridiculous with the large blue-black mark under his left eye.

Wanting to hit Winkler full in the mouth, the Death Merchant looked across at Fedor Rykov, who was sitting on the forward end of the bench, directly behind Nekliv. "*Tosvarkish* Rykov, you have the proper identification ready. We don't want any hesitation at the gate."

Rykov patted one breast side of his dark brown greatcoat. "*Dai*, I have everything ready to show to the guard." He sounded as though he were sneering, which was his normal tone of voice. "The passes and my personal identification are perfect forgeries. So is Aleksei's ID. I'm more concerned with the inside, after we're in the garage underground and get out of this vehicle."

"You're referring to the two suitcases?" said Camellion.

"The danger is that we'll bump into some high-ranking DS officer on our way to Militia Center. We couldn't refuse to open the suitcases if he ordered us to do so."

"You're right. But it's a risk we'll have to take." Camellion was casual. "The way my group will play it will be to take an elevator to—"

"You know what happens when you're bottled up in an

elevator!'' cut in Winkler savagely. "I know! It wouldn't look right if we took the stairs. You don't have to explain to me, Mother."

"We'll take an elevator to the Militia Center on the third floor. From the third, we'll use the stairs to the fifth floor. Should we be challenged on the third, we'll have to shoot our way up to the fifth. Our best weapons will be speed and surprise."

"And my group," Rykov said. "We also take the elevator on the third floor. Is that not correct?"

"You know damn good and well it's correct—all the way to the roof," Camellion said. "We went over the plan often enough at the safe house. If you and your three guys are lucky, you'll have terminated the guards on the roof before we get to the meeting room."

Grisha Dyuni interposed, "It's amazing how we're doing all this on assumption only, on the assumption that the Soviet advisers and their guest will even be in the building, much less with Colonel General Shopov and other high officials in the DS!"

"An assumption, yes," Camellion replied, ignoring the irony in Dyuni's voice. "But a supposition based on logic. Yesterday, NFC watchers saw the plane land at the airport. They saw the Soviet big shot convoyed from DS headquarters to the Grand Hotel Sofia. Yesterday was time for wining and dining and all the phony praising. It's only reasonable to assume that today the Russians and the Bulgarians will get down to serious business. We know that the official from Moscow is Commissar Sharbovenko, whose realm of expertise is security. He didn't come to Sofia to discuss how to grow a better strain of wheat. Sharbovenko came to discuss *police methods,* and that means the big sitdown will take place at the DS headquarters building." He shrugged. "If I'm wrong, I'll move to Athens and open a tatoo parlor!"

"Either way, we're all as good as dead!" said Winkler with a big smile.

"And take this big mouth with me!" Camellion nodded toward Winkler.

"One more block to go," called out Tsola Nekliv.

"Everyone check his weapons," Camellion ordered, then glanced briefly at "Captain" Fedor Rykov, who had gotten up and, unsteadily, within the cramped confines of the personnel carrier, was exchanging places with Pekko Vardikiv. As the senior officer of the group, Rykov would have to be sitting next to the driver when the BTR pulled up to the gates.

Once Rykov was seated next to Nekliv, he took a good look through the slanted window in front of him and said in a loud voice, "The snow is so heavy the plows are already at work. The weather people must be expecting a blizzard."

The Death Merchant warned Winkler with his eyes, his stare clearly stating: *If you open your big mouth and bring up snow falling in Dragalevtsi, I'll break your neck twice over!*

Winkler only made a tight mouth and smiled with his eyes.

Tsola Nekliv turned the steering wheel and took the personnel carrier around the corner of Dimitar Bue Avenue and Boulevard Anton Ivanova, the Death Merchant and the others hearing the loud, grinding noise of the snowplow vehicle as it passed. The BTR carrier headed north on Boulevard Anton Ivanova, its eight wide tires leaving tracks in the snow.

Rykov half turned after a few minutes. "Get set back there. We're going in."

Nekliv slowed the vehicle and turned the steering wheel to his left. The personnel carrier moved west and entered the wide concrete drive that led straight to the double gates that, made of sheet steel welded to a metal framework, were painted white and electrically controlled from one of the twin watchtowers on either side.

During the warm months the area was quite pleasant. White birch trees lined the narrow parkway by the sidewalk, their leaves furnishing an unbroken canopy of shade during the summer months; and when the sun shone in full hot glory, it sparkled off the white sandstone of the DS building whose square, clean-cut lines gave it the appearance of a modern office building. Even the tall wooden barrier, painted white, and trimmed in dark green, made a pleasant appearance.

There wasn't anything warm and cheerful about the area now. The bone-bare branches of the white birches twisted grotesquely toward a sky that would have been the color of lead if one could have seen it through the hazy opaqueness of the steadily falling snow. On the grounds, beyond the barrier, it was also grim, the branches of the white mulberry trees silent, naked, and unreal.

On the narrow parkway were piles of dirty snow and ice, the grime and soot rapidly disappearing under the new snow. Large drifts had made themselves at home on both sides of the barrier and against the sides of the six-story building; and since the bottom of the wide, smoked glass was only a foot above the ground, much of the snow was piled against the outside of the windows. No one was worried. The thick glass was reinforced.

"I'll put on the handcuffs just before we get out," Rykov turned and said, several moments before Tsola Nekliv stopped the BTR in front of the gates.

"Make damn sure you don't snap them shut," warned Winkler, who, on Camellion's orders, had exchanged places with Pekko Vardikiv and was seated directly behind Nekliv—close enough to the side window, by the driver, to hear what the guards might say and then translate to the Death Merchant.

The short pause before the gates was customary and only long enough for one of the guards in one of the white sandstone watchtowers to open the gates. Slowly the two steel sections parted, sliding back silently on hidden rollers moving over hidden rails.

Nekliv put the carrier in gear and moved the armored vehicle forward, stopping right behind the gates, which silently began to close. Immediately, a DS guard, in blue cap (earflaps down), blue wool greatcoat and boots, and carrying a Zeff AKM assault rifle, approached the BTR, moving in toward the driver's side.

Ivan Baev muttered something to Vard Kurdzhali in Bulgarian. Kurdzhali shook his head up and down—meaning no.

Fifty feet ahead, on the wide drive, was another barrier: a wooden framework hinged to a large square post set in concrete. In front of the white barrier were three more security guards, two in the blue of the DS, one in the dark brown of the militia, the DS men armed with RKZ submachine guns, the militiaman with an AKM.

Tsola Nekliv was pressing the button that automatically lowered the glass of the windshield to his left and Fedor Rykov was pulling his leather identification case from inside his greatcoat, when very suddenly the Death Merchant knew that something was very wrong. He *knew*—and not in case the guard, or guards ahead, might order the rear doors opened. Sometimes they did, sometimes they did not—so the NFC leadership had learned. If the guards did, they would find everything in order—three prisoners being brought in for questioning, two officers of the *Nersko-Tsopska,* and five *zhelali*. Should the guard, or guards, demand that the two suitcases be opened for inspection, the guards would die on the spot. Camellion had attached the Larand suppressor to the Beretta and the weapon was just inside his *chivva*, all ready to be fired.

No! The danger was not in that the guards might order the rear doors to be opened. Camellion only knew that disaster was about to explode. It was a matter of a finely honed sense of intuition based on years of experience, on years of partnership with the Four Horsemen. And it was more! It was that silent warning from reality that the Cosmic Lord of Death was not, for the time being, playing any favorites, even with a man who knew how to kill in seventy different ways and make any death look natural. *Hoc est corpus meum!* It was the *da-ra-Mut* of the Egyptians, the *yetzer ha-ra* of the Hebrews, the *fomes peccati* of the Latins. It was the feeling of falling in love with the wide-open jaws of a hungry alligator. . . .

No use to excite the men, not yet! Camellion waited, feeling the cold wind blowing in through the open window to Nekliv's left.

The secret police guard, his AKM shouldered on its sling, leaned down, put his face close to the open window, and said something in Bulgarian to Tsola Nekliv, who gave a brief reply. Leaning closer to Nekliv and looking at the guard, Fedor Rykov held out his identification folder and spoke to the guard in a louder, more authoritative voice.

The guard accepted the ID case, opened it, and read for a moment, then looked at Rykov, comparing his face to the photograph in the ID and passbook. He leaned closer to the opening and rattled out a stream of Bulgarian, his tone polite and respectful. Rykov replied, sounding insulted and angry. Still courteous, the DS guard again spoke . . . civil but firm. Nor did he return the identification case to Rykov, who shrugged, spoke a few words, and leaned back. Even though Camellion did not speak Bulgarian, he would have had to be blind and deaf not to know that something was not quite right in Sofia.

The instant the guard turned and departed, Rykov swung around in the bucket seat, an expression of fear on his far from handsome face. He was too slow. Carey Winkler was already translating to the Death Merchant, speaking very rapidly. "It's what we feared. They've increased security, which means the targets are in the building. Any incoming vehicle must be first cleared with DS Central and Militia

Central before it can proceed. The guard has gone to phone, to check out 'Captain Harkiv Maksolov.' We know there isn't any 'Captain Harkiv Maksolov,' and soon the guards and DS and Militia Centrals will know. We've blown it. We can't back this baby through closed gates, and we can't fly. So—we do it the hard way!''

The Death Merchant was not unduly surprised. What was now happening was a realization of one of his worst fears—and one of his first. He had planned accordingly.

There were several loud sounds—metal on metal. Belad Freidliv and Vard Kurdzhali had placed 7.62mm. cartridges in the firing chambers of their AKM assault rifles.

''Make sure the S levers are on nonfiring,'' Camellion ordered sharply. ''We're going to have a short but very bumpy ride. We don't want any weapons going off accidentally.'' He then said to Tsola Nekliv, who, while he was shifted into neutral, had kept the engines idling, ''The front of the building is seventy meters ahead of us. The front entrance is roughly six meters to our right. Get up speed, ram anything in front of us, and we'll take this P-carrier into the building the way Winkler said—the hard way!''

There were gasps of surprise from some of the men, the loudest from Nekliv, who had to do the tricky driving.

He said in an incredulous voice, ''With the big wheels we have, I suppose we can move up the steps and smash through the front doors. We'll have the speed, and we have the weight for momentum to carry us through.''

''No, not the doors of the main entrance,'' Camellion admonished in a sharp voice. ''The steel framework around the doors would stop us. Go straight up the driveway, then cut to the left and aim for one of the windows. We'll slam through a window the way a brick would tear through toilet paper.''

Nekliv's young face lit up with new hope, a flame of enthusiasm that burned instantly into the ash of a new fear. ''But the windows . . . the bottom of the windows are forty to fifty centimeters above the ground. Suppose we become hung up?'' he stammered.

''You're forgetting the severe winter Sofia's had!'' Camellion said gently. ''There must be twenty-five centimeters or more ice and snow packed around the outside of the windows. It will be like a ramp. We'll roll right in. Get going—fast!''

Nekliv got! He shifted gears, stepped on the gas, and the Soviet BTR personnel carrier charged forward, engines roaring.

Toward the top of each thirty-foot tower, on either side of the closed gates, there was a DS guard, behind a ZPU-2 heavy machine gun, looking down lazily at the vehicle. BTRs were a common sight. The two guards were stunned when they saw the personnel carrier suddenly shoot forward. Such a thing had never happened before. They knew that the vehicle had not been cleared because the buzzer in each tower had not sounded. *Vecherya!*[3]

The two DS security officers and the militiaman in front of the wooden swing barrier were even more astonished to see the BTR coming straight toward them. They didn't have time to raise their weapons. All they could do was jump frantically to one side as the vehicle roared by, slammed into the gate, splintered the wood, and kept on going, all the while increasing speed.

The BTR was hitting forty mph when the two guards in the tower opened fire with the heavy machine guns, a rain of 14.5mm. projectiles hitting the top and the rear of the P-carrier, giving the Death Merchant and the others the feeling that they were in the middle of a hail storm. All the slugs managed to do was make a lot of screaming noise and put several hundred tiny dents in the armored steel. None of it mattered to the Death Merchant and his men, who were doing their best to prepare themselves. Camellion had managed to remove his heavy *chivva* and, weaving from side to side against the other men, open the two suitcases and take out the three Viking SMGs, the nine spare magazines, and the silenced Beretta autopistol.

From the left-side watchtower a siren began to scream, its *awoo-ah-awoo-ah-awoo-ah* chopping into the ordinary street noise of the afternoon.

Perspiration crawling down his cheeks, his hands firm on the steering wheel, Tsola Nekliv stared through the driver's windshield, guessing the distance to the DS building that was looming larger and larger. A former driver for KINTEX, he now proved his ability to drive in emergency situations. He began turning the steering wheel to the left when the BTR was 110 meters from the front of the headquarters building. In only ten seconds the wide, solid rubber tires were crushing

[3] Impossible!

through the snow of a lawn that, in summer, would be decorated with marigolds, violets, and periwinkles. But on this day, no gentle breeze wound its way through a riot of color and lush green grass. There was only the uneven snow through which roared the Soviet personnel carrier—straight toward one of the wide smoked-glass windows.

The Death Merchant had done his homework well—with the help of the three NFC leaders. The width of the BTR was nine feet three inches. The width of the wide windows was an even ten feet. Camellion had relayed this information to Tsola Nekliv, warning him that he would have to make an approach that was perfectly straight.

Nekliv did. He aimed the BTR at one of the windows, cut his speed slightly and yelled *"Bikh zhela"* excitedly.

"Hang on, the man says!" yelled Winkler, translating and hanging on to the back of Nekliv's seat. "What the hell else can we do! Damn it! Speak English!"

Fedor Rykov, who was looking through the other front windshield, yelled out, "That's it! You have it centered! Another ten meters!"

There was no stopping the BTR personnel carrier. Its wide wheels ground into the packed snow, its slanted front and ram bumper centered on the window. The Death Merchant was proved correct. There was almost three feet of packed snow and ice pushing itself against the outside of the building and the bottom portion of the window. The eight wheels, however, did not sink deeply into the frozen surface. For one thing, the snow had, over the months, turned into almost solid ice. In spite of the heat only eighteen inches away, inside the building, the sharp cold wind had kept the mess frozen. For another thing, the wheels of the BTR didn't have time to sink. The instant the front of the vehicle began to tilt upward on the "ramp," Nekliv pressed down on the gas.

At forty-five mph, the personnel carrier crashed through the window, the sound of its engines mingling with the loud sound of falling glass. . . .

CHAPTER THIRTEEN

13.25 hours

The three tractors and their long trailers rumbled along the snowy streets of Sofia, their destination the headquarters building of the Bulgarian secret police—the *Komitet Darzhavna Sigurnost*—at 66 Boulevard Anton Ivanova. The three persons who would drive the last few hundred feet were snuggled down in the seat next to the NFC drivers.

It had not been difficult for John Zladko, Paul Gora, and Poytr Mikhailovich, the three NFC men posing as DS agents, to pull weapons on the SOMAT drivers and force them to drive to the three different points of transfer where the SOMAT employees had been taken in tow by other NFC rebels, and the two men and one woman, whose days on earth were numbered, had gotten into the trucks. The only really time-consuming task was opening the rear doors of the trailers and tossing in 118 sticks of dynamite in bags—twenty-two sticks in five bags, eight sticks in one bag. In all, eighteen bags. A cap was in each stick of *pjâsaci*, wire running from each cap to the detonating "spark" station in each bag. Asparuch Meszaros had worked overtime in assembling the eighteen receiving stations and the remote-control timing units.

A system had been worked out by means of which the suicide drivers would change places with Zladko, Gora, and Mikhailovich. The NFC drivers would turn the trucks toward the barriers and, at the last moment, just before the tractors would crash through the wooden fence, switch on the remote-control timers, set the metal brace bars against the gas pedals

159

and the seats, open the doors on their sides, and jump out as the "sacrificial" drivers slid over and took control of the steering wheels.

There was another danger, one over which the Death Merchant and the NFC had absolutely no control: the possibility that, at the last moment, one of the three suicide drivers might change his or her mind and decide not to go through with "self-execution." After all, life—if only a few minutes more—is precious to average people who have no concept of reality. Should that happen, the truck would have to be abandoned and the suicide driver and the NFC driver taken from the scene by one of the NFC cars following the three tractor and trailers.

At one point, the SOMAT rig being driven by Pyotor Mikhailovich, with whom Ludmilla Ilyina was riding, was spotted by two DS agents who wondered why the huge rig was moving on Aleksandar Stamboliski. SOMAT trucks never moved on Aleksandar Stamboliski and on Ruski Street, a fact not known to Mikhailovich or to the Death Merchant, a fact that had been overlooked by the three leaders of the NFC.

"That truck doesn't belong on this boulevard," one of the secret police agents said. "We should make him pull over and demand an explanation from the driver."

"Don't be an ass," said the other agent. A member of the *Komitet Darzhavna Sigurnost* for six years, he was the senior agent in the car. The other man was ten years younger and had been in the DS for only a year. "It's the snow. The driver must have canceled his trip and is headed back toward the depot."

The younger agent leaned forward and stared through the windshield at the SOMAT rig approaching on the other side of the road. He cleared his throat.

"I still think we should turn around and question the driver. He is breaking a regulation. And with that Soviet big shot in town, we can't be too careful."

The SOMAT tractor and trailer roared by in the other lane and the older DS agent gave a little laugh. "Don't be silly, Josef. Who do you think is driving that truck—a member of the NFC?"

CHAPTER FOURTEEN

Just as a spoonful of tar can spoil a cask of honey, sixteen Russians can ruin an afternoon that is already dark and dreary. Especially could sixteen pig farmers destroy an afternoon for the director of a secret police organization who suspected that he was about to be replaced.

After the usual hypocritical pleasantries had been exchanged between Colonel General Grigor Shopov and his group and Commissar Oleg Sharbovenko and his people, the Bulgarians and the Russians took their seats at the large conference table: Shopov, the three chiefs of the DS Directorates and four Bulgarian secretaries; Skarbovenko, his four KGB bodyguards, the five Soviet Uncles, Skarbovenko's aide-de-camp, and five Russian secretaries.

Settling down in his chair and pretending to listen to Skarbovenko's praise of *kisselo mleko*,[1] Shopov felt that personal disaster was about to smother him. Skarbovenko was a good friend of Lieutenant General Frein Cherfesky, and Cherfesky and Boris Chubenko, the first secretary of the Bulgarian Central Committee, were drinking and whoring buddies. Boris Chubenko hated Shopov's guts.

"It was one of the best lunches I ever ate," Skarbovenko was saying heartily. "That *kisselo mleko*, it was so thick and creamy . . . so tasty. I'll have to take several kilograms back to Moscova for my family."

As bald as a stone but with large tufts of gray hair sticking/

---

[1] "Yogurt"—especially good in Bulgaria; it is fermented with a bacteria, whose name, *Lactobacillus bulgaricus*, confirms its national origins.

out over his ears, Skarbovenko was short and heavy and had a peasant's rough face: flat, broad, with cheeks worn as smooth as the wood of a well-used washboard. Underneath his expensive gray pin-stripe suit, his chest and sides appeared to be too thick, too heavy. Shopov and the other Bulgarians knew this was due to the bulletproof vest the Soviet official was wearing.

At the head of the table, Shopov first looked at his wristwatch—five minutes after two—and then called the meeting to order, standing and saying, "Comrades, let us begin the discussion of security and mutual cooperation between our respective organizations."

No sooner had he spoken than the siren from one of the watchtowers began to shriek. Shopov and the other men at the table were still expressing surprise when the firing of two machine guns was added to the screaming sound.

"What is going on out there?" demanded Commissar Skarbovenko. He pushed back his chair, stood up, and looked harshly at Colonel General Shopov. The other Russians looked grim; the Bulgarians, including Shopov, worried and confused.

Before Shopov could even form a reply in his mind, the telephone next to him, on a small table, rang. Shopov picked up the phone. "This is Colonel General Shopov. Report."

He tried but couldn't keep the nervousness out of his voice.

The men at the table stared at him, anxiousness and impatience in their eyes.

"I see . . . A BTR. Very well. Turn off the power to the elevators—all elevators—and try to take prisoners. Keep me informed." Shopov returned the handset to the cradle, anger replacing his previous expression of confusion.

"Gentlemen, a BTR personnel carrier has gotten past the guards at the main gate and is headed directly toward the building. It's a stupid suicide attempt on the part of the *Narodno Gorsiku Rakigladenov* to disrupt this meeting and to make the *Komitet Darzhavna Sigurnost* appear ineffective."

"By God! Isn't it?" snapped Commissar Sharbovenko. His voice was so loud he was on the verge of shouting as he glared venomously at Shopov. "The personnel carrier got past the guards at the gate, didn't it? What kind of security service are you running, Comrade Shopov? In the Soviet Un—"

The distant sounds of a crash and falling glass from below cut him off. He didn't have to be told what had happened. No one had to be told. The carrier had slammed through one of the large glass windows in the lobby.

"Comrade Commissar Skarbovenko, I suggest we go to the roof and take one of the helicopters to the hotel," suggested Vladimir Badayev, the chief KGB bodyguard. "The helicopters are only one floor above us and pilots are always stationed on the roof."

For a moment, Skarbovenko stared at Badayev. He then swung his angry gaze to Shopov, who stared back at the high Soviet official, his own face expressionless. The other Bulgarians, their heads lowered, avoided looking at Skarbovenko and the other Russians.

"Comrade Shopov, how many men can ride in a BTR carrier?" inquired Skarbovenko imperiously.

Feeling foolish, Shopov didn't reply. He didn't know how many men could be contained in a BTR personnel carrier.

"Sixteen troops, plus a crew of two," announced Paul Lukomsky, another KGB man. "If the traitorous swine crammed in more men, there couldn't be more than eighteen rebels, Comrade Commissar Skarbovenko."

"Comrade Skarbovenko, I assure you that we are not in any danger whatsoever," Shopov said in a firm, clear voice. He had regained his composure and was determined to stand firm. "It is absolutely impossible for those terrorists to even reach the third floor, much less this meeting room on the fifth. There are easily several hundred DS and militiamen in the building."

Colonel Georgi Kraisin said grimly, "Those traitors will be cut to pieces before they even reach the second floor."

"Tch, tch, tch . . . Such inefficiencies could never happen in the Soviet Union," commented Lieutenant General Cherfesky in a sad voice. "Imagine revolutionaries getting into the headquarters of the *Kah Gay Beh!*" He added slyly with a straight face: "If the Soviet Union had any traitors. It hasn't. The people of the Union of Soviet Socialist Republics are happy and contented with their democratic form of government."

"Comrade Shopov, your assurances are worthless in view of your lax security methods." Skarbovenko curled his lip, his face scornful. "But in this case, I must agree with you and Comrade Colonel Kraisin. A dozen or so maniacs in the lobby could hardly get to the fifth floor. Also, how would it look if a handful of rabble, a handful of gunmen indulging in

murderous *khuliganstvo*,[2] chased us from this building? We
will continue the meeting.''

Shopov thought of picking up the telephone and ordering
more DS agents to take up positions outside the meeting
room. There were already a dozen uniformed DS agents
stationed outside the meeting room. Shopov decided against
calling for reinforcements. To do so would be to exhibit to
the Russians a lack of confidence in his people, a lack of
confidence in himself.

It really didn't make any difference what Skarbovenko
believed, reasoned Shopov. The BTRs invading the lobby had
taken care of that. As easily as night follows day, Boris
Chubenko would not have the slightest difficulty in recom-
mending to the politburo that one Grigor Nikolai Shopov be
replaced as director of the *Komitet Darzhavna Sigurnost.* . . .

---

[2] ''Hooliganism.''

CHAPTER FIFTEEN

It could have been worse. The Death Merchant did have one consolation. *We could have crashed an airplane into the tenth floor of a twenty-story building! Or I could be a citizen of Mexico!*

With the clink-clink of broken glass falling on its roof, the personnel carrier shot through the window. The men inside braced themselves and hung on to handholds and on to each other, feeling as if they were riding inside a rocket that had gone out of control.

A master driver, Tsola Nekliv braked all eight wheels the moment the P-carrier was halfway through the opening. He knew the momentum of the vehicle would carry it through the window and then some. For a moment, after the rear of the BTR had cleaned the inside of the window opening, all eight wheels, spinning furiously, were two and a half feet above the white marble floor. Coming down on all eight wheels, the BTR bounced crazily on its shocks and continued to move west in spite of Nekliv's having turned off the two GAZ-49B six-in-line engines and having applied the brakes to a full stop.

"Stop this damned thing before we're all crushed to death!" Grisha Dyuni yelled. He fell forward, almost crashing into Vard Kurdzhali, who was being knocked about on the bench across the aisle.

Careening crazily, the BTR was halfway across the wide lobby when its rear end skidded around on the slick marble floor that had been made slicker by the snow on the eight tires. Inside . . . it was almost like being on a runaway merry-go-round. The left rear side of the BTR smashed into the decorative rounded green brick ring surrounding a large fountain, in the center of which, above the streams of water, was a statue of Georgi Dimitrov, the Communist revolutionary leader. As the men on the left-side bench of the BTR fell into the men on the right bench, the big vehicle rebounded from the half-crumpled portion of the ring wall and—the rear end swinging violently toward the right—spun completely around so that when the P-carrier came to a full stop, the front was pointed toward the shattered window through which snow was now blowing.

Donkey dung! Triple fudge and damn it! The Death Merchant had counted on his force getting past the guards at the gate without any difficulty, on his men entering the building from the garage belowground. He had counted on the element of surprise. That component of unnoticed entry was now last year's news and as useless as an air conditioner in Antarctica.

It had taken only several minutes for the BTR to roar up the wide drive, turn off to the left, head west over the snow, and crash through the window. There were DS career agents, clerks, and other employees in the lobby, but they had not detected the vehicle until a minute or so before it smashed through the glass. Nor had the people on the five floors above the lobby. The screaming siren had been the first warning, and many people had looked out curiously. But not in fear. What could happen to them inside the headquarters building of the powerful Bulgarian state police? On all six floors most people heard the BTR being chased by 14.5mm. slugs from the two ZPU-2 machine guns. However, due to its speed and the angle of its approach, the P-carrier was quickly lost from the line of sight of people on the upper floors. Only by people on the first two floors could it be seen as it closed in on the building—a mass of metal roaring straight toward one of the windows in the lobby. And it was clear that the charging monster had no intention of stopping.

Seeing the vehicle, panic-stricken men and women scattered in the lobby, some running to the stairs and elevators, others to the other side of the lobby, to the small restaurant and visitors' lounge.

"Is everyone all right?" Camellion asked, patting his body to make sure the two Berettas and spare magazines for the Berettas and the Viking submachine gun were in place.

There were grunts, muttered curses, and affirmative replies as the men straightened up and checked their equipment.

"I'm fine," said Aleksei Izogyi, whose nose was bleeding. "I only hit my nose against Pekko's AKM." He had removed his greatcoat, but some blood had fallen onto his blue tie.

"Now that's what I call a grand entrance!" Winkler said. "Except that we've screwed ourselves. We've lost all tactical surprise, and retreat is out of the question. We'd be cut down before we got halfway to the fence." He turned and looked directly at the Death Merchant, the two small overhead lights, their circuits damaged by the grand slam against the fountain wall, flickering on his face. "We don't dare take the elevators, not now. We'll have to hoof it—and no grenades, no smoke, no gas, no nothing! Shit! We might as well try to swat flies with a sledgehammer. Shit! This is worse than having a dog named Sex!"

"Don't tell me your troubles," Camellion said. "Take it out on the DS. Rykov, you and your three men know what to do."

"Yes, we know." Rykov reached for the handle of the small door on his side of the BTR carrier.

"Good enough," said the Death Merchant. He switched off the safety of the Viking SMG. "Let's go do it—get to the stairs. Try not to kill any women unless they get in the way."

"Yeah, let's not forget to be gallant," mocked Winkler.

Fedor Rykov opened the door on his side and Tsola Nekliv left the stranded vehicle via the door on the driver's side, while Camellion, Winkler, and the six other men jumped out from the rear, after Belad Freidliv had unlocked and pushed open the two doors.

Only three shots were fired at the group, three rounds from a single Bidja auto, the shots coming from the door of the small restaurant. All three slugs missed, although two bullets came close to Rykov and one even closer to Aleksei Izogyi, both of whom were in militia officer uniforms; Pytoe Djilas, the only DS agent in the restaurant, was determined to kill them. He shouldn't have made the attempt.

On the run, Winkler swung to his left and raked the doorway with a short burst of 9mm. boat-tailed projectiles. Slug-chopped from testicles to the top of his torso, Djilas went down, his blood spreading slowly on the marble floor.

Moments later, Winkler had caught up with the others who had reached the west section of the lobby that was set apart

from the main area and contained seventeen self-service elevators and the wide marble stairs that twisted upward and ended
on the sixth floor.

Out front, the Death Merchant saw several women and
heard them scream. The two clerks had taken refuge in an
elevator and were terrified. The two DS agents and one
militiaman in another elevator, while not exactly happy, knew
where their duty lay and were not cowards.

They leaned out from either side of the open doors and
tried to get into action, one agent with a 9mm. Helwan pistol,
the other DS slob with both hands around a Soviet Stechkin
machine pistol. The moron who was a member of the militia
was using a Bidja autoloader.

Part of survival is the ability to detect almost imperceptible
movements. One is born with it, then increases it by experience.
The Death Merchant had lots and lots of experience at keeping healthy.

Detecting the three men, he pulled up short, went into a
low stance, and fired as the three Bulgarians were about to
pull triggers. The Viking chattered its dirge and did its job of
spitting out a stream of 9mm. slugs that tore off one man's
hand, caught the militiaman in the left side of his chest, tore
off the second DS agent's face, and decorated the rear of the
elevator with part of his brain and scalp.

Those three goofs couldn't outdraw a crayon!

Camellion turned, ran to the first flight of steps, and
started up, the rest of the small attack force racing after him.
It was the area between flights that worried him. The stairs
were arranged so that after you climbed one flight, you had to
move ten feet, either to the right of the left, to reach the next
set that led to the next floor.

The Death Merchant, Aleksei Izogyi, and Grisha Dyuni
were the first to reach the top of the stairs from the lobby and,
on the way to the next flight, see that the enemy was approaching from the middle of the north corridor and from the south
hallway, the group from the south only thirty feet away.
Every one of the Bulgarians was armed with a RKZ submachine gun.

Two of the uniformed DS men from the south managed to
get off short bursts that, fired too quickly, missed. While a
stream of 7.62mm. projectiles hissed close to Camellion's
right shoulder and missed the other two men by nine inches,
the projectiles did accomplish something: ten of them ripped

into a DS agent in the north corridor and came within a hair's breadth of hitting two more men. Another flow of hot 7.62mm. projectiles struck the AKM of an agent and knocked the weapon out of his hands. Four slugs zinged against one wall; another hit a man in the left arm, eliciting a loud yell of pain and fright. The others in the group dove to the floor.

Camellion, Izogyi, and Dyuni fired as they ducked to one side, the Death Merchant yelling, "The north side—watch it!" to warn the rest of the men still on the stairs.

The Death Merchant's own flow of 9mm. metal hit four of the secret police agents in the south hall, the vicious impacts knocking them into their comrades and creating more dread and confusion among the Bulgarians, who found it incredible that NFC revolutionaries had even reached the building. Their surprise lasted only a micromoment and was ended by Dyuni and Izogyi's roaring AKMs. The two had only to rake the rest of the group for a few seconds with a hail of slugs; two of the jokers howled in agony before crashing to the marble to join their comrades who were also corpses, including the four Bulgars that the Death Merchant had snuffed.

It was a combination of panic and tactical stupidity on the part of the DS that made it possible to waste the Bulgarians in the north hall with the ease of shooting packed fish in a small barrel.

Vard Kurdzhali, Ivan Baev, Winkler, and two of the remaining four on the attack force hosed down with slugs the Bulgarians on the floor to the north, firing before the enemy had time to reorganize their logic and swing up weapons. Four AKM assault rifles and one Viking SMG roared, the combined chattering a wall of pure noise. The Bulgarians yelled and jumped, several jerking in reflex after they died. Suddenly it was over and there was only an intense silence, the roaring of automatic weapons a fresh memory, and the air thick with the clinging odor of burnt gunpowder.

Camellion looked at his wristwatch: 14.12. *I'll take the chance!* "Some of you grab those RKZ subguns," he said, turning to the group. He looked up and down both sides of the hall. "Don't bother with the dead meat to the north. They're too far away."

It took only several minutes for four of the men to pick up the SMGs and spare magazines, three mags to each leather pouch.

Camellion said, "Carey, you and Ivan and Grisha watch our rear when we go up the next flight. Let's do it!"

The group charged up the next flight of steps, the Death Merchant, in the lead, thinking that their only chance for escape was the helicopters on the roof, provided Rykov and his three men could even get to the roof; and for some odd reason, he remembered what Winkler had said about a dog named "Sex." *Ridiculous! Ah well, even if Winkler "buys the farm," he'll not die unhappy. He should be a brother to Vernon Cole.*

They reached the third floor and to their surprise and delight found that the area between the stairs was empty. There were, however, a group of women employees at the end of the south corridor, two of them with folders in their hands. One of the women uttered a little scream when she saw the Death Merchant and his men, thinking that the "NFC murderers" would kill them all. She turned and ran with the other clerks.

"The Russian is clever but always too late," panted Pekko Vardikiv, his words a Bulgarian proverb that meant that good fortune was favoring them. Only in this case, it was not only the Russians but the Bulgarian DS that was too late.

"It's the luck of the Irish, me boy," Winkler said as they reached the next flight of stairs.

"What's the catch?" The Death Merchant searched the top of the stairs. Nothing. But sooner or later the Russians and the Bulgarians would have to wise up and have men waiting.

"My grandmother was Irish."

Up the steps they raced—and received one of their biggest shocks of the afternoon. On the fourth floor there were three long corridors meeting in the vicinity of the stairs area: the south and the north hallways and an east-west avenue, this latter intersecting the much longer south-north hall. Sixteen agents of the DS had formed a group, eleven plainclothesmen coming from the radio section off the east-west corridor, five, in uniform, from the file section in the north passageway. Armed with pistols and four RKZ SMGs, the group intended to go down the stairs and intercept, on the third floor, the tiny force of invaders. Their mistake was in not taking into consideration the speed of the Death Merchant and his group. Camellion and Company practically collided with the DS agents, whose astonishment was far greater than the surprise of the Death Merchant and his men, who had expected the DS and the militia, even if they hadn't anticipated bumping into the enemy.

The proximity of the two groups made it impossible for either side to open fire. Camellion found himself almost eyeball to eyeball with two incredulous DS agents in uniform, both young, muscular, and mean looking. Faster than a tiger shark[1]—but still too close to level down with his Viking SMG—Camellion attacked, using his left hand to speer the man with the thick black mustache directly in the celiac plexus, the soft spot just below the stomach.

A powerful first blow, delivered straight in, can injure portions of the liver and stomach, produce internal bleeding, and shock much of the thoracic ganglia. A four-finger *Yon Hon Nukite* stab, particularly when it is delivered by an expert, means certain death. Camellion was a first-degree black belt in *Tae Kwon Do Hyung*.[2]

Serge Korolev was dying and didn't know it. He gave a kind of muffled cry, staggered back, dropped his RKZ chatterbox, and, with a hideous expression on his flat slab of a face, began to wilt on legs that could no longer support him.

Mastislav Hurok would join Korolev within seconds. Idiot that he was, he tried to move in closer to Camellion and let him have an old-fashioned upper right hook, a fast swing that Camellion ducked with ease merely by pulling his head back. Hurok was trying to step back far enough to point the muzzle of his RKZ at Camellion's belly at the same time as Fedor Rykov jammed the RKZ he had picked up from the floor of the second story into the stomach of Aram Gvishini.

Hurok failed miserably. The Death Merchant first blocked the DS man's RKZ with his Viking. And then came the main reason why Hurok was a flop. When his uppercut missed, his momentum carried him forward—right to where the Death Merchant wanted him. Camellion brought his right heel down hard on Hurok's left instep, and when the tarsus bone shattered and the man yelled in agony and reflexively jerked his head up, Camellion used the short barrel of the Viking to stab

---

[1] The average person thinks that a cobra strikes fast. It does, but not half as fast as a diamondback rattler. A mongoose wouldn't have a chance with a rattler. Killer sharks are even faster.

[2] The more important aspects are the *Hyungs*, a set series of attacking and defensive movements that follow a logical sequence.

him in the throat, the end of the barrel smashing the trachea. Gurgling, gagging, and choking to death, Hurok dropped his submachine gun and began the quick process of dying, sinking to his knees, his frantic fingers tearing at his throat.

Fedor Rykov was having some slight problems. His short burst of 7.62mm. slugs had blown out the stomach and part of the spine of Aram Gvishini, the six projectiles zipping right through the Bulgarian and striking Vasily Ikonov in the left side, tearing through the coat of his business suit and taking up residence in his lungs. Then Rykov's RKZ was out of ammo and he didn't have time to pull his holstered pistol, switch off the safety, and fire. Another DS officer was swinging his weapon toward him. A cursing, snarling Rykov quickly reversed the RKZ in his hands and, with his right hand, swung it viciously at Abez Alkhimov's head. The blow would have crushed the DS officer's skull if he had not ducked, his quick motion making him lose his balance and fall backward, right into the path of Aleksei Izogyi, who carried a hunting knife in a leather sheath inside his lieutenant's uniform coat. He had jerked out the knife, wanting to save ammunition, and now he put the ten-inch gleaming blade to good use. Alkhimov, as he fell back, stumbled to within several feet of the long-faced Izogyi, who brought up the knife with an underhanded motion and buried the blade in Alkhimov's back, the razor-sharp steel slicing into the man's kidney.

"Uhhhh!" Alkhimov jumped like a speared fish, his feet and legs moving back and forth as though he were attempting to roller-skate. Izogyi pulled out the knife and let the dying, bloody fish flop to the floor. He didn't, however, have time to congratulate himself. Another DS agent was preparing to throw RKZ slugs at him. Izogyi was faster. He fired his own SMG, a short blast that made a bloody mess of the man's chest and carried him back toward Carey Winkler, who was struggling with Yuri Bukarim, a DS agent in a gray suit. In his excitement, Bukarim had forgotten to switch off the safety of his own RKZ and in desperation had dropped the weapon and grabbed the Viking before Winkler could pull the trigger. A born survivor, Winkler had no intention of wasting time in a contest of strength. In the first place, he wasn't that strong. In the second place, Bukarim outweighed him by almost thirty pounds. Piss on a pineapple! You don't put out a man's lights by playing tug-of-war with him.

Winkler did the unexpected as his hands and the Bulgarian's

were wrapped around the submachine gun. He suddenly released the weapon, letting the DS agent have full possession. Winkler had only several seconds to do what he had to do, and what he did was clap Bukarim's ears with both hands, the heels of his palms smashing inward with speed and great force against the sides of the Bulgarian's head.

A tornado roared inside Bukarim's skull and he had the feeling that his brain had become a balloon that couldn't expand fast enough and was about to burst. Intense nausea welled up in his stomach and it was with effort that he prevented himself from vomiting. His legs felt like rubber that had lain in the sun too long. For an instant, the sudden shock of a bombshell booming in his head pulled all his strength from his hands and arms. Almost helpless, he let the Viking slip from his fingers and tried to bring reality back into proper focus. He did not have the time. Winkler hit him in the stomach with a terrific right fist and, when he doubled over, chopped him across the back of the neck with a *Shuto* sword hand, the blow so devastating that the third intervertebral space was ruptured. With a loud *uggg* jumping out of his mouth, he dropped to the floor.

But Winkler was still in trouble, or rather he would have been if he hadn't been nimble-footed, in spite of his high instep that was making his feet and calves ache—he had left his arch supports in Rome!

Winkler's problem was that another DS agent had moved in close, both his hands around a Vitmorkin machine pistol. Georg Coastaskis was only a split second from pulling the wide trigger when Winkler used a high *Mae Geri Kekomi*[3] front thrust kick and knocked the MP and Coastaskis's hands upward, the meeting of foot with hands and weapon causing the machine pistol to roar and spit out a stream of thirteen 9mm. projectiles that shot upward at a steep angle and ripped into the ceiling, shattering the white plastic and three of the concealed fluorescent light tubes.

It was lights out for Georg Coastaskis. Winkler grabbed the long barrel of the Vitmorkin with his right hand, pushed the weapon to his right, and, all in the same motion, utilized a short knee kick against the Bulgarian's groin. He followed through with a left *Seiken* forefist that slammed into the man's glabella. Often misidentified as the "bridge of the

[3] From the school of Shito-Ryu karate.

nose,"[4] the correct area to strike is above the nose between the eyebrows. The *Seiken* slam was all that was needed. The shock of the blow had been transmitted to the frontal lobes of the brain, the result a severe concussion and unconsciousness for Coastaskis, whose legs were already crumbling.

In an instant, Winkler had picked up the Viking submachine gun and was seeking recipients for his slugs. He saw that Ivan Baev was in trouble, but he couldn't fire without hitting Baev.

While Baev, who had smashed one man's skull with the barrel of his AKM assault rifle, was struggling with two DS agents, Zhores Tverdokh got behind Baev and locked his arms around his neck. Tverdokh was working with Yevgeny Loskos, who had had his left wrist smashed by the barrel of Baev's AKM and, in pain, was at a disadvantage. Loskos had managed to hang on to the stock of the Zeff AKM with his right hand while Tverdokh had wrapped his left hand around the barrel and was trying to pummel the chunky Baev with his right hand.

It was the Death Merchant who came to Baev's aid. He only had to use a Shuto sword hand against the side of Loskos's neck to put the man to sleep. Another sword-hand chop to the back of Tverdokh's neck sent the man spinning into the dark world of unconsciousness. As this went on, Winkler and Grisha Dyuni began sending the rest of the DS force into eternity. The Viking SMG and Dyuni's Zeff assault rifle began their furious snarling and in only seconds the rest of the DS agents were dead and sprawled out on the floor. For good measure, Winkler and Dyuni, after Camellion and the others had stepped back, raked the entire group with a tornado of slugs, the 7.62mm. projectiles making slight thudding sounds as they stabbed into flesh.

Vard Kurdzhali sighed loudly, his eyes roving around the corpses on the floor. "I suppose God has to make great sinners in order to accomplish His purpose." In spite of being a firm believer in Collective Socialism, Kurdzhali was also a religious man.

"Don't kid yourself!" Winkler was acrimonious. "God didn't have anything to do with this, and if you think prayers are going to help, you're out of your tree!"

---

[4] The actual bridge of the nose is the middle of the nose. A blow here will shatter the thin nasal bones—very painful but not all that serious.

"All of you reload," ordered Camellion, who was thinking that Winkler would have made an excellent Nazi. "We've lost almost five minutes with these chicken-brained biological disasters. Let's dip the bread in the gravy and get to the fifth floor."

First looking up and down the halls, Camellion hurried across the area to the next flight of steps, reflecting that the fourth, fifth, and sixth floors had halls that, laid out from east to west, merged with the south-north corridors. On the sixth floor, the stairs that took one to the roof, to the helicopters, were in the east end of the east-west hall.

Privately, the Death Merchant was in complete agreement with Carey Winkler. The people who prayed the most were always the ones least prepared. Man made his own miracles, frabricated his own impossibilities, and won his own earthly battles. *In spite of the ETs[5] who would surrender us to Soviet imperialism. The clerics who are "positive" what God wants! The well-intentioned but unrealistic morons who can't even manage their own children! The celebrity circus from Holly-wood—that world capital of mediocrity—who are "experts" on peace! All babbling about "The Bomb." Yet not one word about Soviet military buildup. Nor do they ask why Soviet Embassies are never attacked, or why Soviet government officials are never kidnapped, held hostage, or assassinated. . . .*

Yet all of them—the entire population of this planet—have only another sixteen years at the most. If they think the H-bomb is a threat, wait until they learn about the photon bomb!

The Death Merchant paused at the bottom of the stairs, stood to one side, and looked upward.

Winkler, who felt so bad he would have to die to feel better, also looked up the stairs. He too could see that the area around the top of the stairs was clear. "They have to be waiting at the top," he said, and for a refreshing change sounded deadly serious. "By this time they have to be. The meeting room—if the targets are still there—will be ringed with guards. Frankly, I don't see how we're going to do it."

Camellion stared toward the top of the stairs, a strange glow in his icy blue eyes. "They're there, waiting," he said. "Not thirty feet from us."

---

[5] The "Emotional Terrorists," who would destroy will and freedom, the price they are willing to pay for "peace"

"You sound positive." Winkler gave him a curious sideways look.

"I can feel them. They're waiting to waste us."

Fedor Rykov, who had lit a cigarette, eased up to the Death Merchant and whispered, "It is eighteen minutes after two. Are we not going up? If those trucks got through and are on time . . ."

Logic circuits clicked in the Death Merchant's mind. "If the targets are still there!" Winkler had said.

He turned and faced Winkler, Rykov, and the other men. "We'll use the stairs in the east end of the shorter hall. I have a hunch that route will be safer. Let's do it. Let's shove the cornbread in the mush."

The RKZ slung over his left shoulder, a Beretta autopistol in his right hand, Camellion started for the east-west hall. Winkler and the rest of the men sprinted after him, Belad Freidliv, who had once taught English in the Sofia school system, thinking more of American colloquialisms than of the danger facing him and the other men. "Dip the bread in the gravy," "shove the cornbread in the mush." No doubt both meant to proceed on course. But why "bread" and "gravy"? Why "cornbread" and "mush"? A strange language, English, especially when spoken by Americans.

Time: 14.21 hours.

CHAPTER SIXTEEN

Commissar Oleg Yuli Skarbovenko found it difficult to believe the report of the DS major who had just rushed into the meeting room. The tiny band of revolutionaries had reached the fourth floor and, apparently, had killed Captain Chervos Raeskoti and the group of agents with him.

Skarbovenko and the rest of the men had heard automatic weapons firing yet had not realized that the noise was coming from the floor directly below them. Sound could be very deceptive when coming through double panes of glass.

Commissar Skarbovenko, Colonel General Grigor Shopov, and the rest of the men in the glassed-in meeting room stared incredulously at Major Bovan Vordorbov, who was in command of the DS men guarding the fifth-floor area.

"Comrade Vordorbov, could there be some sort of mistake?" Grigor Shopov's voice quivered slightly. "Are you certain of the disaster?"

"*Dai,* Comrade General," Major Vordorbov said without hesitation. "Neither Captain Raeskoti nor any of the men with him have answered on their walkie-talkies. We must assume they have been killed. However—"

"*Was macht ihrda, piski na levorka-skie ertura?*" ["What are you trying to do, get us all killed?"] thundered Skarbovenko, the rage in his voice matched only by the fury in his eyes as he glowered at Shopov. "A sprinkling of scum! A begger's purse full of traitorous trash who were not even supposed to get past the lobby! Already they are on the fourth floor!" His fat face became even more choleric. His voice grew louder, his double chins shaking. "The disgrace! The shame of it! For it to take place within the very nerve center of the Bulgarian security service! *Vn Bogom!* [By God!] Suppose this debacle leaked out to the West! We would look like idiots! I can tell you right now, the *Komitet Darzhavna Sigurnost* needs a new director!''

''The scum were not even supposed to get past the lobby,'' said Anatoly Tretyakov, the Soviet Uncle who was a political theorist. ''And already they are on the fourth floor.''

''Colonel Kraisin assured us that the swine would be cut down before they could even reach the second floor!'' Lieutenant General Cherfesky spit out. He had dropped his grandfatherly pose, and for the first time, Shopov and the other Bulgarians were face-to-face with his true nature—vicious, savage, sadistic.

Colonel Georgi Kraisin, wondering how he could save his own neck when the shake up came, remained silent. Major Ivan Mikolov, sitting next to Kraisin, became very busy opening a pack of cigarettes. Major Stanko Divuncha kept himself carefully detached, his head tilted back, as though there were a spot on the far wall he was studying.

Lieutenant General Shopov was actually embarrassed. He couldn't refute Skarbovenko's charge that the DS was ineffective since revolutionary gunmen had succeeded in invading its headquarters. Worse, the DS could not stop the traitors once they had entered.

Feeling the muscles in his cheeks and neck quavering, Shopov turned to Major Bovan Vordorbov. ''Comrade Major, you were interrupted. Continue with what—''

''I would like to know why you haven't sent men to the fourth floor to investigate and find out what's going on?'' Colonel Evgeny Tovma, the expert on violence, demanded of a highly nervous Major Vordorbov, who was standing ramrod straight. ''What are your men doing, looking the other way? Or perhaps they're afraid of the traitors of the *Narodno Gorsiku Rakigladenov?*''

''Your insult was uncalled for, Colonel!'' Shopov said angrily. Knowing he would very soon be replaced as chief of the DS, he no longer felt the need to be cautious. He signaled Major Vordorbov with his eyes.

''I was going to say there isn't any danger to anyone in this meeting room,'' Major Vordorbov said. ''We have men in position around the top of the center stairs on this floor. The other door in the shorter hall is being watched by other agents. Comrades, I can assure each and every one of you that the terrorists cannot get to this floor. It's absolutely impossible for them to do so—impossible.''

Commissar Skarbovenko put his hands on his hips, thrust out his pumpkin-shaped head, and glared at Vordorbov. ''I'm not interested in your 'assurances,' Comrade Major Vordorbov. Pledges of the DS are worthless.''

Major Vordorbov surprised Skarbovenko, as well as Shopov and everyone else, by saying, ''Comrade Commissar Skarbovenko, I would stake the lives of my family on my conviction that the terrorists cannot even get close to this meeting room!''

Skarbovenko stared in surprise. ''And suppose the terrorists use grenades or other kinds of explosives? What then, Comrade Major Vordorbov? Can you give 'assurances' against such weapons?''

''The terrorists have not used explosives,'' Major Vordorbov said stubbornly. ''There isn't any indication that they will!''

''We're going to leave this meeting room and this building,'' Skarbovenko said to Lieutenant General Cherfesky and the four other Soviet advisers. ''We'll fly back to the hotel in one of the helicopters on the roof.''

''Splendid! Splendid!'' said Cherfesky. ''We can't depend on the DS to protect us from their revolutionary barbarians.''

''We'll continue the meeting after your people have killed the terrorists,'' Skarbovenko said to Shopov, scrutinizing the director of the DS with furious eyes. His face was one big smirk as he addressed Major Vordorbov. ''I assume, Comrade Major Vordorbov, that it is possible for your men to get us past the sixth floor to the roof?''

''*Dai,* Comrade Commissar Skarbovenko, we will get you and your people to the pads safely,'' Vordorbov said mechanically, his face reddening.

Biting the left side of his lower lip, Shopov did not speak. The three chiefs of the DS's three Directorates remained mute. They, Shopov, and the Bulgarian secretaries watched Skarbovenko, his aide, the five advisers, and the five Russian secretaries put papers into their briefcases and prepare to leave. The four KGB bodyguards went to a side table, picked up PPS-43 submachine guns, and switched off the safeties.

Major Bovan Vordorbov led the way, then Commissar Skarbovenko and the rest of the Russians, the KGB guards moving to one side, watching all approaches. Colonel Grigor

Shopov and his people followed, although Shopov waved a hand toward the DS secretaries and shook his head, silently telling the frightened women to remain in the room.

The group walked quickly down the corridor, moving north, the sound of their footsteps on the marble floor echoing loudly in the unnatural quiet. Civilian workers in the various departments were behind closed doors and down behind desks.

Arriving at the area close to the top of the stairs, the Russians and Colonel General Shopov and his three Directorate chiefs saw that several dozen DS agents—all in civilian clothes—were spread out in a half circle at the top of the stairs that led down to the fourth floor. They had piled metal folding chairs, one on top of the other, and were lying prone behind the stacks, the barrels of their assault rifles and submachine guns protruding between the piles.

Major Vordorbov called over his shoulder, "As you can see, Comrades, it is impossible for the enemy to get past the top of the stairs." There was a major note of satisfaction in his voice.

No one bothered to answer.

The group came to the T, the corner where the hall merged with the corridor. A Vitmorkin machine pistol in his hand, Vordorbov stopped and carefully looked down the hall. He then made a forward motion with his right hand and stepped into the hallway. The group headed toward the door at the end of the hall. It would be a simple matter to go up the steps behind the door to the sixth floor, and from there to the roof and the Mi-4 helicopter. Twenty feet from the steel door were six DS men flat on their bellies, two with Zeff AKMs, four with RKZ submachine guns.

Major Vordorbov and Commissar Skarbovenko were stepping around two of the agents on the floor when a submachine gun roared from the other side of the door.

Major Vordorbov's eyes widened and he jerked erect.

Commissar Skarbovenko's mouth fell open and he stepped back, almost stumbling over one of the DS agents on the floor.

CHAPTER SEVENTEEN

The tractor-trailer rumbled along Dimitar Bue Avenue, fumes pouring from the twin stacks to the rear and on each side of the cab. The snow had slackened, making it easier for John Zladko, the NFC driver, to handle the rig. The road was slick with snow, and it would take only one mistake to create disaster. Once the big tractor-trailer began to slide, there would be no stopping it.

"How do you feel, *tosvarkish* Likostri?" Zladko gave the other man a quick, fearful glance, marveling how a seventy-two-year old man, suffering from cancer of the liver, could still have so much energy. To look at Josef Likostri, one would never suspect that he was dying.

"I'm somewhat tired," the old man said, yet his voice was strong. "I will tell you something, young man. I did a lot of thinking before I agreed to what I am about to do. At the present time, there is only a dull ache in my side. A few months from now the pain will be—would be—intense. I prefer to die this way—quickly, and I'll be helping my country, the real Bulgaria, the Bulgaria of our grandparents. Any thinking person knows what Communism and the DS are—instruments of the Devil."

"*Tosvarkish* Likostri, you do know how we will do it after I turn toward the barrier?" Zladko asked. He glanced at the bent metal brace on the floor.

"*Dai*, I know. How soon will we be there?"

"Within the next ten minutes, I'll be turning into Boulevard Anton Ivanova."

Zladko looked at the long rearview mirror mounted on the outside of the cab. He hoped the pickup car was close by.

Only the fifth-floor door in the west hall had been locked. The fourth- and sixth-floor doors had not been locked, the reason being that the meeting was being held on the fifth floor and that no one had even considered the possibility that the terrorists might reach the fourth level, much less the sixth—or for that matter, the door on the sixth floor that led to the roof.

Ordinarily, the elevators would be used to get to all the floors, including the roof, but Lieutenant General Shopov had ordered their power turned off. The stairs in the west ends of the halls were fire stairs, escape stairs—one long spiral supported by a central column, a small landing in front of each door.

The Death Merchant and his small force had not had any difficulty opening the door on the fourth floor and rushing up the steps to the fifth-story landing, every second expecting some kind of ambush.

On the fifth-floor landing, the Death Merchant studied the door, calculating how many slugs it would take to shatter the large electric lock. He was aware that the electric lock was controlled, from the other side, by a series of buttons. The door on the fourth floor had been open, but who was to say that the door to the fifth floor was too?

Winkler whispered, "Look! If they have DS watching this door on the other side, they'll see the knob move when you turn it. If the door is *locked*, all you'll do is warn them and let them know where we are."

The Death Merchant did some hard thinking. Once they had reached the fifth-floor landing, Fedor Rykov and three other men had kept right on going up the stairs. Camellion now reflected on how Rykov and his men had disappeared through the door above, on the sixth floor. That door had also been unlocked.

"All we can do is shoot off the lock and hope for the best," offered Grisha Dyuni, who was standing on the other side of Camellion.

"Maybe so, but we can narrow the odds," Camellion said, after which he proceeded to tell the other five how the attack would be made. Aleksei Izogyi would watch the area above, Belad Freidliv the steps below. "Once the lock is wrecked,

I'll push open the door. Carey, that's where you and Grisha come in.''

"We go with you?" Winkler said.

"No—and yes." Camellion went on to explain that once the door was shoved open, Winkler would shove the barrel of a RKZ around the edge of the doorway on the left side and rake the area with a full magazine of 7.62mm. projectiles. "Only you'll do it at floor level. Oh . . . say not more than five to six inches above the floor—twelve to fifteen centimeters. If there are any DS on the other side, the slugs will catch them, whether they're down on the floor or standing."

"You hope!" Winkler said dryly.

"I hope! Anyhow, that's the theory. In fact, fire two full magazines. Grisha, after he exhausts the ammo in his SMG, hand him your weapon. It will save him reload time. You can reload his while he's getting off the second mag."

"What will you be doing while I'm sweeping the floor with slugs?" Winkler sounded as skeptical as he looked.

"The instant you exhaust your second mag, I'll go in," Camellion said. "The rest of you follow—unless I get blown up! Comments?"

"We're in the hands of fate," sighed Aleksei Izogyi, who had dried blood on his chin. "I keep thinking of the three trucks. If they got through, they must be very close by now."

"I suggest we do it," urged Belad Freidliv. "The quicker we find the targets, the quicker we can get to the roof."

"All of you stand back," ordered the Death Merchant, amused at Freidliv's use of the word "target." *He's beginning to think like a pro!* "There'll be some glance-offs. Carey, get set."

"Go ahead, shoot!" Winkler said.

Camellion raised his own RKZ to waist level, aimed by instinct at the housing of the lock, and fired, the SMG roaring, the sound reverberating up and down the long shaft of the stairwell.

Commissar Oleg Skarbovenko had only one thought when he heard the submachine gun firing on the other side of the door: flee, in the opposite direction. And that's what he and the rest of the group did. However, Major Bovan Vordorbov dropped down on one knee by two of the DS men. Skarbovenko and the other Russians and Lieutenant General Shopov and the three Directorate chiefs turned and began to run east.

They were almost sprinting by the time the Death Merchant kicked open the door, and ten seconds later, Carey Winkler opened fire.

It was that ten-second lag time that saved Skarbovenko, the other Russians, and the four Bulgarian DS officials from having their ankles shot out from under them—ten "1000ls," plus the angle of fire. Since Winkler was on the other side of the door and firing from the left side, he could move the RKZ only so far to the left, his kill zone being limited.

While all of Winkler's 7.62mm. projectiles missed the Soviet officials and the Bulgarian DS chiefs, the rain of deadly metal became executioners for Major Bovan Vordorbov and the six DS agents on the floor. Three of the agents were killed instantly, one right after the other, slugs stabbing into their chests—and one man was struck in the head—before they could roll over from their stomachs and get to their feet.

Another agent fell into eternity as he tried to lie perfectly flat and a bullet struck him in the trapezius muscle to the right of his neck, the bullet entering from the top. Traveling downward, leaving a bloody tunnel along the length of his chest and viscera, the bullet finally stopped when it struck the top of the right ilium or hipbone.

Major Vordorbov and the last two DS agents alive did have a five-second reprieve, the lag time when Winkler ran out of ammo and prepared to fire the RKZ that Grisha Dyuni handed him. Winkler pulled the trigger only a split second before the Death Merchant and the others heard distant firing above them—higher than the sixth floor. Proof positive that Fedor Rykov and his three boys had run into trouble.

A lightning-quick thinker, Bovan Vordorbov deduced instantly, even while he had still been on his feet, that his only hope for life lay in silencing the deadly RKZ submachine gun spitting out death only ten to fifteen centimeters above the marble floor. He and Vasil Bogoraz and Nikolai Yakut were squirming around and trying to aim their weapons at the barrel of the RKZ when Winkler cut loose with the second subgun. A 7.62mm. slug struck the Vitmorkin machine pistol in Vordorbov's left hand. A second projectile struck him in the top of the left shoulder, shattering the knob of the humerus. A third slug cut off the tip of his nose, sliced through the end of his chin, and, zipping almost half the length of his body, bored high into the front of his left leg;

and when he jerked violently in agony, the fourth bullet hit the top of his head, exploded his brain, and killed him.

Nikolai Yakut took a slug right below the nose, the bullet tearing across the roof of his mouth and blowing out the back of his head. In the right side of his neck was where Vasil Bogoraz caught the slug that ended his life. Gurgling, he flopped to his face, blood spurting from severed carotid arteries.

Click. Winkler had run out of ammo. By the time he had gotten to his feet and had unslung the Viking SMG from his shoulder, the Death Merchant had stormed through the doorway, a 9mm. Beretta M92SB autopistol in each hand, the Viking music box, its sling strap over his left shoulder, flopping against his back.

Camellion was just in time to see Oleg Skarbovenko, Rikil Igkuliv, Skarbovenko's aide, and one of the Russian secretaries disappearing around the corner of the hall. The fire of triumph flared in the Death Merchant's eyes. He had never seen Skarbovenko, Igkuliv, or the dumpy woman, but instinct told him the three were Russian—pig farmers! Could the other big shots be far behind? *In this case, far ahead? They were going to take one of the choppers and escape. We changed their minds!*

Camellion raced after the frantic Russians and Bulgarians, Winkler, Dyuni, Nekliv, and the two other NFC men tearing after him.

The tractor-trailer moved north to Boulevard Anton Ivanova, John Zladko's face wolfish as he prepared to slow the huge rig, turn to the left, and take the large front wheels over the curb and through the snow piled on the parkway.

Zladko and Josef Likostri could see the headquarters of the DS building. The structure was like a tremendous gray tombstone in the afternoon snow, growing larger and larger, a misty yet evil thing that would soon come tumbling down.

"How soon, my young friend?" asked Likostri.

"Right now," Zladko said, his voice shaking with tension. "Get ready to slide behind the wheel. Wedge the brace against the gas pedal and the seat when I tell you to."

Zladko eased up on the gas and slowly and carefully began to turn the steering wheel to the left, moving the cab toward the curb. Close to the curb, he increased speed, and with only a little effort the wide, rubber tires rolled over the curbstone and plowed through the snow, the diesel roaring, the twin stacks throwing out more fumes. Then the rear wheels were over the curb.

"Now, the brace!" said Zladko, who noticed that several people on the sidewalk, bundled up in heavy clothes, had stopped and were staring in awe at the rig, wondering what was going on.

Josef Likostri bent down, picked up the curved brace, and jammed one end against the gas pedal, forcing the pedal all the way down. The other end of the brace he wedged underneath one of the metal bands embracing the front seat. At once, as the front wheels of the trailer rolled over the curb, the engine began to roar with a new life and the cab began to move faster and faster.

Zladko knew he had only a minute, if that long. Holding the steering wheel steady with one hand, he reached down, found the small metal box on the seat, opened the lid, and pushed the toggle switch upward. The box began to hum. The remote-control device was in operation. The sticks of *pjâsaci* and the hundreds of sacks of ammonium nitrate in the trailer would explode in exactly four minutes.

"I'm going to jump," Zladko said. "Start moving over. Be careful of the device, old one."

"I am ready," Josef Likostri said, his voice remarkably calm, even peaceful with that eerie tranquillity of one who has accepted, even welcomes the Cosmic Lord of Death.

Zladko, saying prayers he had learned in childhood, his right hand holding the steering wheel steady, opened the door and began to slide on the seat. Josef Likostri picked up the remote-control detonator and placed it on the seat. All the while he continued to slide until he was almost behind the steering wheel.

John Zladko pushed open the door all the way and flung himself from the cab, landing heavily in a pile of snow.

Josef Likostri, both hands on the steering wheel, began to pray.

Landing heavily in the snow, Zladko didn't even have time to stand up and brush snow from his heavy *chivva*. He was staring up at the side of the trailer, moving by him, when the front of the cab struck the wooden barrier with a loud crash, the big slam sending splintered boards flying. The crash didn't even slow the rig, which had moved through the fence as though it had been constructed of wet tissue paper. Breathing heavily, Zladko stared after the rig. All he could see was the rear of the trailer moving rapidly away from him, becoming smaller and smaller. At fifty-five mph the tractor and trailer roared toward the east side of the DS headquarters building.

Zladko stumbled to his feet, his quick breathing turning to steam in the cold air. He was now concerned for his own safety. A couple on the sidewalk stared at him, the woman's eyes wide. Then the man said something to her and both of them started running toward Dimitar Bue Avenue.

Zladko didn't know what to do. Where was the car that was supposed to pick him up? It was supposed to have been trailing the tractor-trailer? Where were the other two trucks? Or had something gone wrong? His hands in his *chivva*, he switched off the safety of the Bidja pistol and started toward the sidewalk. He was positive of one thing: the police would never take him alive, never.

A gray Zaporozhets swung around the corner, pulled up to the curb, and honked. Zladko saw that the driver was Martin Kigzervosky. Thank God. He hurried toward the car.

Reaching the end of the hall, the Death Merchant looked around the corner and saw that the Russians and the Bulgarians were halfway to the main steps, with the heavyset pig farmer yelling at the top of his lungs, "Behind us! Behind us! Shoot! Shoot!"

The Death Merchant was more than slightly amused. "*Do zvidaniya, druk!* Farewell, my friend," he muttered, stepped out from the corner, and began firing the two Berettas, knowing that he and his men had the advantage in that the targets were between him and the DS security people ringing the top of the stairs from the fourth floor.

His first two 9mm. FMJ projectiles stung Oleg Skarbovenko and Rikil Igkuliv, the commissar's assistant, between the shoulder blades. Igkuliv, blood trickling from the corners of his mouth, did a quick one-two step forward, half turned, and fell.

But Camellion's 9mm. slug only knocked Skarbovenko forward, and so did the second and third projectiles. *It's that damned bulletproof vest!*

The Death Merchant aimed higher. This time the projectile made flesh fly from the back of Skarbovenko head and from his forehead, the bullet taking bits of brain and bone with it. Stone dead, the slob slumped to the marble.

By this time, Winkler, Dyuni, and the rest of the men had arrived at the corner and were firing their submachine guns, the roaring a tidal wave of noise. Colonel Josef Gavva and Major Stanko Divuncha went down with blood pouring out of holes in their backs and chests. Amid the screams of the Russian secretaries, Colonel Mikhail Isakov, Colonel Evgeny Tovma, Colonel Anatoly Tretyakov, and Lieutenant General Frein Cherfesky tried to drop to the floor so that the DS agents ahead could fire across them at the attackers who had outsmarted them. But the Russian Uncles couldn't outrun slugs. Projectiles exploded Tretyakov's head, parts of his skull and brain splashing over Tovma, who died with 9mm. Beretta metal in his heart and lungs. Cherfesky, finding it difficult to believe that this was happening to him, let out a short cry when Belad Freidliv's 7.62mm. projectiles stitched him up his spine. He died before his legs stopped running. A few feet away, Colonel Mikhail Isakov fell against Narda Lebsenko, one of the secretaries who had been killed by Grisha Dyuni. Isakov had received slugs in the head, neck, and back and was a bloody mess of dead flesh.

Two of the KGB bodyguards, Vladimir Badayev and Georgi Kabulov, had managed to stop and turn around. However, they didn't get a chance to fire their Stechkin machine pistols. Kabulov's flat-featured face flew in all directions and pieces of his coat fluttered out into space from Aleksei Izogyi's projectiles that popped all over him. Badayev fell next to him, almost decapitated from Belad Freidliv's blast, the flying 7.62mm. metal stabbing through him, some of the slugs then striking Paul Lukomsky, another bodyguard, in the right temple. Lukomsky spun like a top, tripped over one of the bodies on the floor, and fell.

Colonel General Grigor Shopov had, somehow, almost reached the top of the main stairs. His luck, and the good fortune of two DS security agents, ran out when two of the Death Merchant's Beretta slugs sliced into his back at the same time that Tsola Nekliv's chain of 7.62mm. projectiles tore into the back of his bright blue uniform coat and ripped it to bloody shreds. Killed within a tenth of an eye blink, Shopov dropped into the other side of hell. With him fell the last of the Russian secretaries and two of the DS agents who were part of the intended ambush at the top of the stairs.

"Get back! Get back!" yelled the Death Merchant—not at Winkler who, running out of ammo, had run back to the corner and, to Camellion's right, was inserting a full magazine into his Viking submachine gun.

In their excitement and haste to kill the Russian and the Bulgarian high officials, the four NFC men had forgotten that once the targets were dead and down on the floor, the DS gunmen by the stairs would have a clear field of fire. Aleksei Izogyi was the farthest from the safety of the corner. To his right, spread out in a sort of crooked line were Freidliv, Dyuni, and Nekliv.

Elated at trapping the Russians and the chiefs of the DS, Izogyi placed his last three 7.62mm. slugs in Lavrenty Strokash, the last KGB bodyguard, the projectiles stabbing into the Russian's midsection and making him the only corpse in the building with four navels. In snuffing Strokash, Izogyi had, in a sense, boxed himself in; now there were only dead bodies on the floor between him and his comrades and the DS agents twenty-five feet to the south. Not all the DS agents had remained in the hall. Although eight had been machine-gunned by Camellion's group, the more perceptive of the Bulgarians had crawled across the wide hall and rolled over onto the upper steps of the stairs, out of the line of fire. Ten agents were still in the hall, rattled and confused by the attack that had happened with the speed of lightning.

With his vast experience, the Death Merchant sensed the danger and realized that his shouted warning, only fifteen seconds earlier, had not been heard because of the snarling of machine guns. Unless a miracle happened, the four freedom fighters were as good as dead.

"Cover me," he yelled at Winkler, and just as five of the DS agents began firing leaned around the corner of the hall and cut loose with the Beretta in his left hand. Each Beretta held fifteen cartridges and he estimated he had used twelve to fifteen in slaughtering the pig farmers. He still had an adequate supply of ammo for what he intended to do.

Camellion fired almost simultaneously with six of the DS agents and with Grisha Dyuni and Belad Freidliv. Out of ammo, Tsola Nekliv made a dive for the corner, 7.62mm. slugs screaming all around him.

It was mutual assassination. Dyuni and Freidliv fired with sweeping, horizontal motions, realizing, during those last mercurial moments, that their only salvation was to kill the DS security men before the DS snuffed them.

The NFC men failed. Twenty-six 7.62mm. spitzer-shaped projectiles struck Belad Freidliv in the stomach, chest, and head, a hurricane of slugs that turned the front of his body into chopped hamburger and literally exploded his head into nothingness. Freidliv's own slugs, and Dyuni's, had cut into five of the secret police who started the short journey to the floor, falling in tempo with Dyuni and Freidliv, the former of whom had been almost cut in two by enemy metal. Aleksei Izogyi had grasped at the last straw. Knowing he was trapped, he was trying to drop to the floor and pull his semi-automatic Bidja when a flood of steel-cored projectiles rained all over him. He died as quickly as a light bulb is turned off.

It was the Death Merchant and Carey Winkler who saved Tsola Nekliv, who, crawling on his hands and knees, was still six feet from the corner. The Death Merchant had not dared to expose more of his body than was necessary. For this reason, he could only use the Beretta in his left hand. He had fired rapidly, four times in quick succession, four 9mm. slugs that sent four DS agents spinning into eternity. But he couldn't waste the fifth and the last agent in the hall *and* the two DS men lying on the steps aiming at him. He couldn't kill all three men with one shot!

Moments earlier, Winkler had shoved another magazine into his Viking and then had gotten down in back of Camellion on one knee. Now, he leaned outward, raised the Viking SMG, and tapped the trigger—only a single tick of any clock ahead of the three DS security agents.

The Viking snarled, jerking in Winkler's hands. The DS agent in the hall fell backward, his body slightly heavier from the four slugs in his chest. Finger reflex action made him pull the trigger of his RKZ, but the projectiles went wild, most of them striking the ceiling.

The two DS agents on the stairs also missed the boat. One of the men had his left hand butchered by two slugs and half his face blown off. The second man—Winkler's projectiles having bored into his right shoulder, upper chest, and neck—jerked and fell back, blood gushing from his neck, the thick stream weakening in proportion to the last beats of his heart. Unrecognizable as a human being, he jerked, sagged, and lay still, as lifeless as a stone.

Tsola Nekliv got shakily to his feet, his face the color of

chalk. He sensed by that intuitive process that all men have that never again would he be that close to death without dying, that he had been only a microsecond from eternity.

He finally managed to croak, "M-my God! Only three of us! Only three of us left alive. And I forgot to bring my weapon. It's still over there on the floor."

"Don't go after it," warned Camellion, who was reloading his Berettas. "Pick up one of the weapons from the six we wasted by the fire-stairs door."

"It doesn't seem right to leave Grisha and Belad and Aleksei up here," muttered Nekliv sadly. "I know we must."

"Don't talk nonsense," Winkler said impatiently. "You might as well ask why we don't rust!" He looked straight at the Death Merchant. "None of us are going to live long if we keep hanging around here. Some of the DS in the south hall escaped. They know we came by way of the other stairs. Right now they're sending men to the fourth-floor steps to cut us off, and they might start using the elevators. We either beat them to the fifth-floor landing or we're dead!"

"Run for it," Camellion said, and started running toward the metal door at the end of the hall, jumping over the dead DS agents when he came to them. Seconds later, he had jammed one of the big Berettas into a shoulder holster and, with his left hand, was carefully opening the door, beyond which was the stair landing of the fifth floor. He wondered why he hadn't heard any more SMGs firing on the roof. *Or were they firing when we were terminating the Russians and the Bulgarians? They could have been and we didn't hear them.*

Behind Camellion came Winkler and Nekliv, the latter pausing long enough to pick up a Zeff AKM assault rifle and pull a three-magazine shoulder pouch from one of the dead men.

BERRRRRRUUUUUMMMMMM! It was the explosion that prevented Camellion from stepping through the opening onto the landing, a titanic blast that, although five stories down, was very loud. The marble floor shook violently beneath their feet, a wave of quick motion that made them lose their balance for a few moments. From all sides of the building, they could hear windowpanes cracking, plus the sound of tons of broken glass hitting the ground far below. There were other ominous sounds: the structure creaking and groaning, and from below and toward the center of the building, numerous shrieks and screams, most of the wails of misery and agony coming from the east.

"One of the trucks succeeded in getting through," said Winkler, feeling his heart pounding extra hard within his chest. For the first time, he sounded very worried. "Assuming that the two other rigs made it, they can't be far behind!"

Nekliv whispered in awe, "Listen: glass and other stuff is still falling. I wonder how much damage was done?"

Dominus Lucis vobiscum! "We're going to have to be marathon runners to reach the end of the sixth-floor hall and get to the roof—and death is going to have to look the other way! Let's go."

Both Winkler and Nekliv gave Camellion an odd look. His tone had been calm, level; yet there had been a mocking solicitude, a contempt for life itself.

Camellion stepped through the doorway onto the landing. . . .

CHAPTER EIGHTEEN

If Tsola Nekliv had been in one of the watchtowers by the main gate, he would have seen and felt what the DS and the militia guards experienced when the tractor-trailer crashed through the wooden barrier. The security people had at first assumed it was a freak accident, that the cab had slipped on the icy pavement of Boulevard Anton Ivanova and the driver had lost control. Only moments later did they realize that even in thick snow the driver would be applying his brakes, but this vehicle was roaring toward the center of the building—straight as an arrow—at top speed. This was no accident. This was deliberate. This was a suicide attack.

For several seconds the security men were stunned by the sheer audacity of the attack. Then they leaped into action and swiveled their ZPU-2 heavy machine guns around. Immediately they opened fire, but the streams of slugs fell short of the rig by three to four meters. The tractor-trailer was beyond the maximum angle at which the ZPU-2s could be depressed. Some of the guards frantically fired submachine guns and assault rifles at the cab, knowing they would be held responsible if the rig crashed into the building. They realized that the truck had to be loaded with high explosives. Merely crashing a truck into the building would be a waste of time.

Predictably, the guards also fired at the long, rectangularly shaped trailer. It was a total waste of good ammunition. The Death Merchant had instructed the four leaders of the rebel National Freedom Council to give specific orders to the drivers and the other NFC men who would intercept the trucks. "Make sure the dynamite is placed at the bottom of the

193

trailers and covered with sacks of ammonium nitrate.'' Hundreds of slugs from ARs and SMGs ripped with ease through the comparatively thin metal side of the trailer, yet every one was stopped by and buried in the sacks of fertilizer.

Scores of slugs tore through the roof of the tractor, some scattering Josef Likostri's skull and brain all over the dash, the seat, and the windshield. More slugs ripped into the seat next to the butchered Likostri. None, however, struck the remote-control device Likostri had placed on the floor between his feet. Far more projectiles found the engine of the tractor. Slugs wrecked the distributor and the carburetor. Bullets cut into the fan belt.

Time was on the Death Merchant's side. By this point, only God could have prevented the catastrophe that within half a minute would befall the headquarters of the Bulgarian *Komitet Darzhavna Sigurnost*—and God was not the least bit interested. . . .

It didn't matter that slugs had wrecked the engine and that the large rig was losing speed. The momentum of the vehicle, loaded as it was with tons of fertilizer, was more than ample to carry the rig forward. All the guards could do was helplessly watch the truck roll through the snow and tear toward the building.

Ten seconds later the cab hit the DS headquarters building, the contact of metal with stone sounding like an explosion in itself, the grand smash breaking not only the window directly in front of the tractor but dozens of others as well.

Struck dumb with disbelief, the guards stared at the destruction, at the tractor that had broken not only scores of windows but had also crushed a section of wall so that half the tractor protruded into the lobby. There it hung, looking ridiculous. Inside the lobby, fifty feet away, was the BTR that DS explosive experts were examining.

''Get back!'' one of the explosive technicians yelled at other DS agents as he and two other technicians jumped from the top of the BTR. ''The truck must be loaded with explosives.''

As for the security men in the watchtowers and on the ground below, all they heard, for the next twenty-three seconds, was the moaning of the cold wind and the various hunks and chunks of broken masonry falling on top of the cab, on the ground, and on the floor of the lobby.

"We'll all end up in Darvo over this," mumbled one of the guards. "We'll get the blame."

BERRRRUUUUMMMMMMMMM!

Even though the guards in and around the watchtowers had expected the explosion, they hadn't thought it would be of such magnitude. All they saw was an instant's flash of dazzling bright white, red, and yellow, a fireball sixty feet in diameter. All they heard was the thunderous blast and the sound of stone and glass and furniture falling—the sound of destruction. The concussion knocked the guards, facing the explosion from open windows in the towers, off their feet. Glass panes were blown from windows that were closed.

"Oh my God—look!" croaked one of the guards, picking himself up.

The other guards looked and gasped. Unbelievable! The handsome white stone building resembled some kind of living creature with a gaping raw wound in its side. The monstrous blast had demolished 150 feet of the east-side wall of the first and second stories, another eighty feet of the third floor, sixty feet of the fourth floor, and twenty-five feet of the fifth floor. Through the thick, swirling dust and smoke the guards could see the exposed rooms on the various levels, offices in which furniture and equipment had been tossed about and now lay in a profusion of disorder, some of the desks, tables, and filing cabinets dangerously close to the ends of the floors, ends that were broken and snaggled, the concrete and marble of the floors held in place only by twisted reinforcing iron rods and grotesquely bent steel I-beams. Ceilings hung in tatters, the plaster suspended by interlacing wire.

Glass in every window had been shattered, either by the concussion or by the violent shaking of the entire building; the vacant spaces, staring out bleakly at the snowy world, resembled the empty eye sockets of battered skulls.

Most of the mirrors in the shaft of the heliostat lighting system had been broken. Others had been cracked. One hundred and six people had been killed outright by the terrible blast that had been heard not only all over Sofia but also in some of the suburbs. Scores of people had been severely injured; many, still alive, were buried under rubble, as was the BTR, which had been lifted up and carried thirty feet before being buried under rubble and debris.

The tractor-trailer no longer existed.

*   *   *

It was the explosion that prevented Lieutenant Vasil Zorkosobog and seven other DS agents from reaching the fifth-floor landing of the spiral fire stairs. Zoekosobog had been in charge of the agents waiting around the top of the stairs on the fifth floor. The tall, broad-shouldered officer with the thin lips and freckled cheeks had survived the ambush-in-reverse by snaking across the floor to the shelter of the main steps. A clever man who resented being only a lieutenant, Zorkosobog had deduced that the enemy had outfoxed the DS by using the fire stairs; he had also surmised that the mission of the terrorists had been to assassinate Commissar Sharbovenko. The escape route? He guessed incorrectly, believing that Camellion and Company would retrace their steps, try to fight their way out of the building, flee across the grounds, get over the wooden barrier, and be picked up by waiting cars. *Dai!* The small band of terrorists were on a suicide mission. Zorkosobog had toyed with the possibility that the traitors might try to reach the roof and use one or two of the helicopters to effect their escape. In his pride and arrogance, he then assumed the rebel trash would not have the technical ability to fly sophisticated aircraft. With typical DS presumption, he was convinced that the rebels were inept.

Zorkosobog had first alerted other DS men on the second, third, fourth, and sixth floors, using his walkie-talkie and informing them that the terrorists were on the fifth floor and would, no doubt, try to get to the ground floor by means of the fire stairs.

An RKZ subgun in his hands, Zorkosobog and the men with him were only fifty feet from the door to the fourth-floor fire steps when the explosion knocked him and the other men off their feet.

"More terrorists!" one man said, in a near panic. "They're trying to blow up the building."

"Don't talk like an idiot!" raged Zorkosobog. "That explosion was the result of a diversionary tactic carried out to help the scum inside escape. Right now, they're trying to get to the ground floor. Hurry! Get to the door."

Zorkosobog rushed ahead. The other DS men ran after him, none voicing his real thoughts, all thinking that the situation was far worse than Zorkosobog believed. The agents had seen that all the windows had been blown out. Much of the glass around the offices had either shattered or was cracked.

*   *   *

Once the Death Merchant was on the landing of the 5th floor, he glanced upward, then downward. The fourth and the sixth landings were as empty as the mind of a pig farmer *kulak*.[1] Feeling that success was composed of both attitude and aptitude, Camellion motioned to Winkler and Nekliv, saying, "Carey, you watch the fourth floor as we go up."

The trio proceeded up the stairs toward the sixth-floor landing, the Death Merchant and Nekliv staring at the door on the landing above, Winkler, moving up backward, watching very carefully the door on the fourth landing.

They were almost to the sixth landing when Winkler detected the fourth-floor door move outward, only an inch or so. "They've arrived," he said, something subtly merciless in his expression. He sighted down on the door with his Viking music box and waited. Presently, the door was pushed outward a few inches, then a few inches more as Lieutenant Vasil Zorkosobog prepared to step out. He never completed this act. Winkler's Viking chattered and a short stream of slugs shot through the three inches between the door and the wall. Zorkosobog's face and head exploded with all the force of a melon hit by a blast from a double-barrel shotgun, much of the blood and flesh, bone and gray brain matter splattering on the shoulders of two other DS agents. It didn't make any difference to the man on Zorkosobog's right. Two of Winkler's 9mm. FMJ projectiles caught him high in the chest. He followed the corpse of Zorkosobog that was spurting blood and sagging to the floor.

"Let's get out of here before the building falls and us with it," one of the DS said, visibly shaken. The others were quick to agree.

The six men left the door, turned, and raced down the hall. The hell with the terrorists.

The sixth floor was laid out differently from the fifth floor. There was the large north-south hall and the intersecting east-west passage, plus another east-west passageway toward the north end of the building. The door that opened to the roof stairs was in the east end of this latter corridor. To reach that vital door, the Death Merchant, Winkler, and Nekliv would have to use the center east-west hall, turn and go north up the main corridor, then turn again, and move east through

[1] "Peasant."

the hall at the north end. It was the only available route—an impossible journey under prevailing circumstances.

The trio stood before the metal door on the sixth landing.

"They'll be waiting," Winkler said with cold ruthlessness. "How do we play it, the same way we did below?"

"But with one difference." Camellion spoke with quiet deliberation. "Carey, you fire from the floor. Tsola, you keep standing and fire at normal level around the left side. Make sure you expose only the barrels. One long burst and then I'll go in." He glanced downward. The stairs were empty.

Once Winkler and Nekliv were in position, Camellion holstered one of the Berettas, put his right hand on the doorknob, turned the knob all the way to the right, and pushed slightly. The electric lock was unlocked. He shoved open the door and jerked back.

Eleven DS agents were waiting, and they weren't lying on the floor either. After receiving the report from Lieutenant Zorkosobog, they had worked quickly to move six filing cabinets to the hall and arrange them in a semicircle not far from the door. However, six ordinary metal filing cabinets of five drawers each cannot adequately protect eleven men, especially when four of the men are two-hundred-pounders. The DS agents were determined that the terrorists would never reach the main hallway. For that reason, they were overanxious. They should have waited until Camellion darted through the door. Instead, the instant the door was open and they saw a few inches of the barrel of Nekliv's Zeff AKM assault rifle, they opened fire with four RKZs, three Zeff ARs, two Vitmorkin machine pistols, one Hungarian 9mm. FEG semi-A-pistol, and one Czech CZ-75 autoloader.

A stream of projectiles, winging from the left at a sharp angle, burned through the doorway, two striking the left side of Nekliv's barrel, the slugs glancing off with loud *zings* and almost jerking the SMG from his hands. Except for those two projectiles, all the others struck the far wall of the stairwell.

The Death Merchant, a mean snarl on his lips, pulled the second Beretta pistol.

Not used to looking for weapons firing only inches above the floor, the DS agents didn't notice the barrel of Winkler's Viking until a raking burst struck the right foot of three of the agents and the right ankle of two other men. They cried out in pain, dropped their weapons, and fell to the floor. The DS

agents standing next to the wounded were uninjured, due to
the positions of the filing cabinets and the angle of Winkler's
stream of projectiles. Instead, the slugs cut into the lower
fronts of the cabinets.

Tsola Nekliv had not fired a shot. During those seven
seconds, he was too busy checking the barrel of his assault
rifle to make sure the enemy projectiles had not dented the
steel. The slugs hadn't. There were only the bright marks of
ricochets. As Winkler scrambled to his feet, Nekliv, a gooney-
bird stare in his eyes, charged through the door behind the
Death Merchant, his Zeff AKM spraying out slugs toward the
filing cabinets, the roaring of his AR mingling with the loud
cracks of Camellion's two Beretta M92SB pistols.

A line of 9mm. JHPT Vitmorkin slugs burned smoky air
very close to Camellion, some of them tearing across the thick
shirt on his right arm, one bullet leaving a deep inch-long gash
in his biceps. Another chain of 7.62mm. RKZ bullets ripped
viciously along his left side, slashing through the shirt and
leaving several red-purple burns on the flesh of his rib cage.

The DS gunman who had fired the Soviet Vitmorkin machine pistol didn't have time to realize that he hadn't wasted
Camellion. One of the Death Merchant's Beretta slugs streaked
into his throat. His brain circuitry didn't have the speed of
Camellion's high-velocity bullet, which sent the agent spinning into the darkness that was forever.

Karlsi Tsipiv, the agent who had tried to blow up Camellion
with his submachine gun, died with equal speed, three of
Nekliv's 7.62mm. Zeff projectiles popping him in the chest
and almost lifting him off his feet.

Like Camellion, Winkler had a sixth sense for threat and
lethal attack. He didn't storm into the hall; he only stepped
around the left of the doorway and began firing his Walther
P-88. His first slug took out the lone DS agent who was
behind a filing cabinet that was only a few feet from the wall,
a position that afforded Yevgeny Polkovsky complete safety
from machine guns poked around the sides of doorways. He
wasn't safe from Winkler as he leaned out to one side and
tried to aim down on Camellion with his Hungarian FEG
pistol. Winkler's 9mm. slug struck him in the right eye, dug a
long deep ditch through his skull and brain and rocketed out
the back of his head.

Nekliv's short deadly bursts had killed Nikolai Ykutov and
Seymon Bikjokk and now went to work on the men who had

been shot in the feet and ankles. Simultaneously, Camellion put a 9mm. Beretta bullet into Jarvo Michael Batjir. Winkler, moving from side to side, ducking and weaving, killed one of the men lying on the floor, moaning from the agony in his foot that had been almost shot off.

The Cosmic Lord of Death often comes with a roar that shakes the world. World War II is a prime example. There are other times that he comes as quietly as the flight of a butterfly. Very often, he wraps his bony arms around a soul with unexpected suddenness. That is the way he came to Tsola Nekliv.

Valentin Pazardin, in agony and weak from being shot in the ankle, was determined not to die without a fight. Pazardin had managed to twist his body around and pick up the CZ-75 pistol he had dropped. The last enemy agent alive, during the final two seconds of the one-sided firefight, he raised the pistol, jerked the sights to a figure his dimming eyes could barely discern, and pulled the trigger twice. The two 9mm. Parabellum projectiles hit Tsola Nekliv, who had just stitched Seymon Bikjokk from knee to neck with the last slugs in his AKM. At a very steep upward trajectory, one 9mm. struck Nekliv high in the neck, knifing in right under his chin, tearing through his lower throat and taking its leave by way of the back of his neck. The second 9mm. cut into his chest, zipped through the aorta, and came to an abrupt halt against a rear rib. Nekliv was dead while his finger was still on the trigger of the AKM. His expression frozen firm in death, his eyes wide open, he toppled backward and hit the floor. At once, a pool of blood began spreading under his head.

Winkler and the Death Merchant, both dodging and ducking and weaving, fired at the same time. Camellion's Beretta bullet banged Valentin Pazardin in the forehead and snapped back his head. Winkler's Walther slug stabbed the already dead Bulgarian in the chest, the impact completing the job of knocking him to the floor.

Winkler glanced down at the dead Nekliv and darted to the front of one of the filing cabinets. The Death Merchant was getting down in front of another cabinet.

"I have almost a full mag in the Viking," Winkler said, taking the SMG from his shoulder. He then looked around the filing cabinet and quickly jerked back, making himself as small as possible behind the metal. "Oh boy! Look what's coming at us. They have to be desperate!"

There were nine DS agents in plain clothes and four uniformed militiamen. Camellion had seen the thirteen leftovers from a genetic garbage dump. The Bulgarians had come around the corner of the main hall and were approaching slowly, their hands full of RKZs and Bidja autoloaders.

"You're four filing cabinets away from me," Camellion whispered, his tone mocking, gritty. "I'll toss one slug at the butt faces and make them think I'm the only 'terrorist' alive back here. When—"

"You had better hope that cabinet is full of files!"

"After they fill this cabinet full of assorted holes, waste them on lag time. Use the Viking. Tell me when you're ready."

"Let's go for it."

Go, went, gone! The Death Merchant sent a 9mm. Beretta slug at one of the approaching Bulgarians. As the man doubled over, Camellion pulled back behind the filing cabinet and lay flat, keeping his body perfectly in line with the sides of the case. He was positive he had a foot of safety, at least. Enemy slugs, fired toward the bottom of the case, would strike the sprawled-out corpses in front of it.

The DS and militia agents reacted instantly. Weapons roared, filling the hall with such a blast of sound that glass walls and windows shook and shivered. Six windows, already cracked by the explosion, shattered and fell to the floor.

Only four enemy projectiles passed all the way through the steel filing cabinet, and these missed Camellion by eighteen inches. Lag time came next, those few eyeblinks of time in which the Bulgarians had to reshift their thought and recycle their reflexes for the next move.

More than ready and anxious, Winkler leaned out and cut loose with the Viking submachine gun, moving the snug little weapon back and forth. Five seconds was all it took, five seconds during which men yelled, screamed, fell to the floor, and died.

"Hot diddle damn!" mused Winkler, a happy lilt to his low voice. "As easy as stepping on an old cockroach that was half asleep. But we have a long way to go, and if Rykov didn't succeed . . . well . . . I think we have more of a chance of converting Ronald Reagan to Communism than we have of getting out of this mess!"

We'll get out, my friend. We are both members of the Kingdom.

"I'd be beholden if you'd watch the hall," Camellion said.

"Will do—Zeke!"

Camellion crawled over to the dead Nekliv, pulled two Zeff AKM magazines from the pouch slung over the corpse's shoulder, picked up the AKM, moved to the filing cabinet to the right of Winkler, and reloaded the assault rifle. The other magazine he shoved into his belt.

Winkler sighed. "We still have to go down this hall and—"

BLLAAAAMMMMMMMMMMMMMM!

The colossal blast, from the southeast, was similar to the first huge explosion. And with the thunder bang came another wave of motion, a heavy rippling of the floor, walls, and ceilings. Double-paned glass walls and windows, enclosing offices, crashed to the floor. Plastic ceiling sections fell in the halls and offices and everywhere was the smell of smoke and death, along with prophetic grinding and grating sounds, subtle creakings that were reminiscent of noises one would hear below decks in an ancient sailing ship.

The filing cabinets shook violently.

"Finally—the second rig!" Winkler said hoarsely, licking the corners of his mouth. "And hear those noises? This building is going down. Should the third truck hit before we're going bye-bye in one of the choppers, we'll go down with it! Shit! Who wants to 'go west' while in Bulgaria? Let's make a run for it."

"Wait!" The word jumped from the Death Merchant's mouth. "Take a look, and listen to those yells. A few more minutes and we'll have a clear field."

The DS employees were in a panic, many of the women screaming. Men and women were running down the main hall, racing south, shoving and pushing each other in a frantic effort to reach the wide steps that went downward to the fourth floor. Patriotism was fine. But being buried alive under tons of stone and steel did not have anything to do with love of one's country.

The Death Merchant consulted his wristwatch: 14.37 hours. He was not worried about Winkler's doing his part. He was a kill expert and would most certainly die in bed . . . *Or when World War III starts*. Winkler never turned the other cheek and he never forgot an injury—two qualities that told the Death Merchant Winkler was no hypocrite.

The Death Merchant felt good about Winkler. It took a particular and peculiar kind of individual to get certain kinds of jobs done.

Within three minutes the crowd ahead had thinned out, and there were only stragglers running north.

"Watch the offices to your left," Camellion said as he and Winkler prepared to race to the vital door to the roof. "I'll take the right."

They moved from behind the filing cabinets and raced down the hall, Camellion ready with his own Viking, Winkler with the AKM that the dead Tsola Nekliv had used. The empty Viking was strapped to his back.

They didn't stop when they came to the wide hall. Instead they turned and began to to run, at once seeing that there were still several dozen people between them and the corridor leading to the door to the roof.

Camellion and Winkler fired on the run, bursts of 9mm. and 7.62mm. projectiles that cut down the terrified men and women with all the brutal effectivness of a summer's fire destroying a parched prairie.

Still, there were the fanatics, those crackpots who were determined to stop the terrorists at all costs, even at the expense of their own lives. Two of the zealots were in a nearby office—Boris Cheszinsky and Raissa Katushev. Both were members of the KGB and had been placed in the DS's Map Analysis Section by Colonel Anatoly Tretyakov to keep an eye on the Bulgarians working in that department.

An attractive blonde in her late twenties, Raissa Katushev was confident that she would not miss with her 9mm. Makarov pistol. All the glass windows were broken and she and Boris could see the hall very clearly. Furthermore, she had practiced pistol shooting on Soviet GTO ranges[2] since the age of twelve and was so good that, in 1979, she had come close to going to the world Olympics.

Davin Rikoajok, the third nut, was a Bulgarian. With an RKZ SMG, he waited by the northeast corner at the end of the north hall.

The last man, sent to his "reward" by Winkler, was still falling when Cheszinsky and Katushev reared up from behind

---

[2] The Soviet Union encourages young people to learn to shoot. Everything is free, including ammo. Ranges have full-time instructors and are open nine hours a day, six days a week.

a desk and tried to aim down on the Death Merchant and Winkler. The two Slavs were far from being novices, especially Cheszinsky who had once been a "blood-wet" agent. They were good, but still not a match for the Death Merchant, who spotted their first movements, swung the Viking around, and raked their chests with a dozen 9mm. projectiles. With looks of great surprise on their faces, Cheszinsky and Katushev fell back and slid to the floor, lifeless.

Davin Rikoajok was next to go. Full of hatred and determination, he was leaning around the corner and bringing up his RKZ when Winkler's Zeff 7.62. slugs blew open his stomach and chest at the same time that Pekko Vardikiv fired from the doorway at the end of the east hall, the doorway facing the steps that led to the roof. For a space of an eyeblink, the square-faced Rikoajok, his eyes rolling back in his head, resembled a man who grabbed a 30,000-volt high-tension wire, his body jerking first one way and then another as he received a double dose of slugs, Winkler's trying to knock him one way, Vardikiv's another. Shot to pieces, he sank to the floor.

"We had help on that last dummy!" Winkler shouted, springing forward. "You heard. It came from the end of the hall. Rykov made it."

There was a fairly loud ripping noise, and Camellion and Winkler suddenly found they were running on a floor that seemed to have jerked upward to the north and tilted downward to the south. The two explosions had destroyed many of the supporting I-beams of the building's overall framework. With many of the supports gone on the first floor, the building was out of kilter, its framework struggling to hold up the tons and tons of rock, furniture, and other materials . . . and gradually failing.

Knowing they were in a wild race with death, in which each second counted, Camellion and Winkler tore up the north hall, their feet pounding the marble floor, large sections of which had cracked. They sprinted around the corner, ran east, and saw Pekko Vardikiv waiting anxiously by the open door, a Zeff AKM in his hands.

Quickly, Camellion and Winkler were at the bottom of the stairs and going upward, Vardikiv leading the way.

"The others, they are dead?" he said, his voice strained with tension.

"It was their time to go," Camellion said. "They died

bravely. Without them, we never would have gotten to the Russian Uncles and the DS officials. They're all dead. How about Rykov and the others?''

Vardikiv explained that there had been a dozen men in the operations station on the roof. ''We attacked. They spotted us only moments before we went in. We killed them all, but they got Fedor and Ivan. Vard is waiting by one of the helicopters. He said if all of us died and he was the only one left alive, he would kill himself.''

''He won't have to, not now,'' Winkler said, and started up the final six steps of the shaking stairs. The twisting and the settling of the building had snapped several bolt heads and loosened a few large nuts. Winkler pushed open the door and stepped out onto the roof, fighting the cold wind blowing snow in all directions.

The roof area was as bleak as the surrounding grounds. Off to one side was the square building containing the air conditioners. Next to it was the operations station, a long building where pilots, co-pilots, and technicians waited in comfort. Toward the center of the roof were the aluminum mirrors of the heliostat, five having fallen from their frames; they looked out of place lying in the snow. The wind was everywhere, fierce and forceful at this height, its power responsible for the vortex of snow that made it impossible to see more than a hundred feet in any direction. It was like being suspended in the center of a gray-white nothingness.

Moving toward the three helicopters on round concrete pads against which snow had drifted, the Death Merchant felt his imagination receiving data—forms, images, impressions from some source other than the three-dimensional world, parts and pieces that instantly formed reasons and logic in a strange and completely alien fashion. Quick flashes of twisting rivers and shadowy trees and irregular shapes flashed across his consciousness, along with a riot of colors, skin sensations, odors, all in the rhythmic pattern of a drunk trying to tap dance on a tightrope; and with all of it came a new awareness—and knowledge. There was only the Will, the Will, the Will of the Kingdom. Camellion wanted to roar with laughter. *Indeed! How could civilization have gotten along for 7,000 years without plastic garbage bags—or indoor toilets!*

Keeping an eye on the closed door of the small housing of the steps, they came to the Mi-4 Soviet-built helicopter and a happy Vard Kurdzhali, who was wearing the overcoat of a Bulgarian air-force chopper pilot and the gloves and cap of a militiaman.

Pekko Vardikov told him in a loud voice, because of the crying wind, "The others are dead. We four are the only ones alive."

"And we'll freeze to death if we don't get the lead out of our butts," shouted Winkler, his teeth chattering. "Let's get the hell out of here."

The Death Merchant, not exactly warm himself and with snow blowing in his face, motioned with his left hand. "We're not going to use this one. We'll take a Hare, one of the Mi-1s. It's smaller, faster, and easier to handle. Get aboard and I'll lift us off."

Camellion turned to go. Winkler grabbed him by the arm. "Hold on. I'll pilot the bird," he shouted, each word weighed down with determination. "I can fly a chopper a lot better than you can. We have enough problems as it is. Even with the heading we have, we'll still need fate's smile to get to the woods close to Dragalevtsti. And if some wise-ass DS puts out the word and we meet jets from the airfield north of Sofia, we'll be lucky if we reach the ground in fifty pieces. No way, baby! I'm flying the bird."

A realist, Camellion yelled back, "Fly it!"

It took only a short while—seventeen times the length of time it takes to stab a pig farmer in the eye with an ice pick—for the four men to board the green Hare (trimmed in red and white) parked on the pad to the right of the large Mi-4, Winkler settling in the pilot's chair and fastening the safety belt.

The Death Merchant shoved a full magazine of 7.62mm. ammunition into the Zeff AKM that Winkler had used, not failing to notice that Vardikiv and Kurdzhali, sitting down, were extremely apprehensive, having never before flown in a helicopter.

Winkler started the Ivchenko A1-26V piston radial engine. "How do you want to trash the other two birds?" he called back to Camellion, keeping his eyes on the gas producer tachometer—assuming it was the GPT. He could not read Russian.

"Lift off to fifty feet, swing to port, and I'll do the rest," Camellion said. He listened with relief as the transmission and mast assembly locked in and the three-blade rotor began to revolve and the powerful whine of the engine increased in volume.

The craft shuddered and tilted slightly toward the south. The building had dropped, a six-inch incline, and with it the roof and the pad. The loud straining sound of tortured I-beams had been lost in the roaring of the chopper engine.

Winkler may not have been a pro in the cockpit of a chopper, yet he lifted off with a smoothness that surprised even the Death Merchant. Expertly, Winkler worked the cyclic and collective controls, his feet just right on the antitorque pedals. He had switched on the cabin heat and the defog system, which for the time being was useless. All the heat was escaping through the right-side door that Cammelion had left open.

Main rotor revolving, tail rotor spinning, the Soviet eggbeater soared up, Winkler swinging to the left and hovering at 16.8 meters, keeping the whirlybird as steady as possible—not an easy job in the unrelenting wind.

The Death Merchant directed a stream of Zeff AKM slugs at the hub and blade assembly of the tail rotor of the Mi-4, the projectiles wrecking the mechanism. He couldn't see the tail rotor of the second Mi-1 because of the intervening Hound. He could see the main rotor, however, of the Mi-4 Hound. He finished off the 7.62mm. magazines by wrecking the Hound's pylon installation[3] and transmission-and-mast assembly.[3]

"Hell, why didn't you blow 'em up?" yelled a disgusted Winkler.

The Death Merchant closed and latched the starboard side door, grateful for the heat now blowing into the small cabin.

"Why tip off the DS with double explosions?" Camellion put to one side the empty Zeff AKM. "There's the worst kind of confusion down there and all the people who can make decisions are dead. We could be halfway to the woods, or even in the school bus, before they realize what is really going on. Another thing: don't fly low. Low flying could be suspicious. Take her up to about two thousand."

"Shit!" Winkler worked the controls and the chopper shot

---

[3] The "hub" of the main rotor.

upward and to port. "If we don't get out of this mess, I'm going to become a pimp in Pomona!"

After we crash through the gates of the American Embassy in Sofia!

EPILOGUE

The Embassy of the United States
1 Boulevard Stamboliisky[1]
Sofia, Bulgaria
Four days later
15.00 hours

If good manners are the happy way of doing things, Carey Winkler was being a barbarian. He was telling a smutty joke to Robert Bernard Beall, a stiff-necked CIA officer who was the chief of station's assistant. Sitting a short distance away, glancing through *OMNI* magazine, Richard Camellion could tell at a glance that Beall was not the kind of man who enjoyed off-color jokes, and he suspected that Winkler knew it, that Carey was only telling the story to annoy the prissy Beall.

Winkler was saying, "Every guy names his dog Prince or Rover or whatever. Not me. I called my dog Sex. It was a mistake, but I didn't want to change the name. You see, when I went to city hall to get a license for Sex, I told the clerk I wanted a license for Sex. He said, 'Who in hell doesn't?' I said, 'But this is a dog.' He said, 'I don't give a damn what she looks like!' Then I said, 'But I've had Sex since I was twelve years old.' He grinned and said, 'You must have been quite a kid!'

"When I got married and went on my honeymoon, I took

---

[1] Boulevard Stamboliisky is not the same as Aleksandar Stambolijski. The two are different streets and should not be confused.

209

the dog with me. I told the clerk at the motel that I wanted a room for me and my wife and a special room for Sex. He said that every room in the place was for sex. I said, 'Look, you don't understand. Sex keeps me awake at night.' He said, 'Me too!' ''

Beall cleared his throat uncomfortably.

Winkler continued. ''One day I entered Sex in a contest, but he ran off before the judging started. Another contestant asked me why I was just standing there looking around. I told him I had planned to have Sex in the contest. He laughed and said I should have sold my own tickets. 'But you don't understand,' I said. 'I had hoped to have Sex on TV.' He said I was crazy.

''When my wife and I separated, we went to court to fight for custody of the dog. I said, 'Your Honor, I had Sex before I was even married.' The judge said, 'Me too!' I told him that after I was married, Sex left me. Again he said, 'Me too.'

''The other day, Sex ran off again. I spent hours looking around town for him. A police car pulled up, a cop got out and asked me what I was doing in the alley at four o'clock in the morning.

'' 'I'm looking for Sex,' I replied.

''My case comes up next Friday! Now, what do you think of that?''

Beall smiled feebly. ''Yes . . . yes, very amusing. Now you must excuse me. I have things to attend to upstairs.''

''I'll go with you,'' Winkler said merrily. ''I want to get something to eat.''

''Very well.'' Beall turned and started toward the door of the basement lounge. Winkler turned and winked at Camellion, then tagged along after Beall, leaving the Death Merchant with his thoughts.

The headquarters building of the Bulgarian *Komitet Darzhavna Sigurnost* had not collapsed. It had, however, sagged ten degrees, at an obtuse angle, to the south. For all practical purposes, the building had been wrecked and would have to be torn down.

Such a catastrophe could not be kept a secret, neither from the Bulgarians nor from the world at large. *Gas!* It was a ruptured gas main underneath the building that had caused the two explosions, which had killed 240 people and injured another 186. Unfortunately—stated the media and all the Bulgarian television commentators (reading from scripts prepared by DS specialists)—the "beloved" Colonel General Grigor Shopov, his aides, and "some guests from the Union of Soviet Socialist Republics" had been on the first floor and had been "killed by tons of rock."

Not a single word about the BTR or an explanation of how escaping gas could have managed to explode twice! The stolen helicopter was not mentioned either. Nor had DS surveillance increased around the U.S. Embassy—in actuality a good sign that the KGB and the DS suspected that the CIA was the prime mover behind the disaster.

It had not been luck. It was knowing what to do and when and how, and that special intuition from the superconscious zone of the mind. Cybernetics from another time continuum! The escape to the woods near Dragalevtsti had gone as planned, with one exception: the school bus, on the road from the village to the woods, had almost become stuck in the snow. The DS and the militia still had not found the helicopter in the woods, or if they had, they had not released the information . . . naturally.

The second SOMAT tractor and trailer had reached the DS headquarters building and had exploded. It had been driven by Pytor Mikhailovich, its final suicide run by Ludmilla Ilyina, the elderly woman dying of cancer. The third rig's luck had been all bad and black. There had not been anything in the papers or on the air. The only report had come by way of the two NFC men who had been trailing the rig in the pickup car. Either the rig had had engine trouble or it had been stopped by the *Jokka* for some reason. All the two NFC men knew was that they had driven by the tractor-trailer—it had been parked on Kirili Motdi close to Patriarh Park—and *Jokka* vehicles were all over the place, hemming in the rig, *Jokka* traffic militia swarming over it. The NFC men had driven three blocks, doubled back, and once more passed the rig. This time they had seen two sheet-covered bodies being loaded into the rear of a meat wagon.

"We will never know what really happened," Stephen Traikov had told Camellion, Winkler, and Harry Cross. "Perhaps the *Jokka* became suspicious for some reason. The SOMAT rig could have had engine trouble. We feel that Paul Gora, our NFC driver, first shot Johnko Lisma—Lisma was the suicide driver—and committed suicide. Paul had no choice. He and Lisma died for freedom."

They died for nothing. It was a waste. . . .

The third day after his and Winkler's escape from the roof of the DS building, Camellion had contacted the American Embassy on the Gould PCS-20001 transceiver and, using the special "Sixfix" code, had explained his scheme to Leapfrog.

Leapfrog was flabbergasted. Impossible. Oh, no! Never! It couldn't be done. There would have to be special 16Y-4 comfirmation and—

SCREW THE RED TAPE, Camellion had tapped out. THIS IS A PRIORITY 4. YOU KNOW WHAT THAT MEANS, PINHEAD!

Indeed Pinhead knew. Priority 4 meant that the sender of the message—in this case Richard Camellion—had the permission of the CIA home office and that Leapfrog had damn well better comply.

WE'LL CRASH THROUGH SOMETIME TOMORROW, Camellion had radioed. MAKE SURE THE GATES ARE UNLOCKED, AND MAKE DOUBLE-SURE THE MARINES DON'T FIRE ON US. MAKE SURE THE MARINE GUARDS KNOW WE ARE NOT TERRORISTS. CONFIRM.

CONFIRMED.

It had been a terrible risk (but perferable to taking the long-way route out of Bulgaria and going through the mountains into northern Greece).

09.00 hours. Three elderly men, dressed in *chivvas,* cheap fur caps, and boots, walked slowly north on Aleksandar Stambolijski. They were well armed but without any identification. To be stopped by the police could mean only discovery and death. They were elderly for only one reason: the Death Merchant's talent with cosmetics.

10.30 hours. Camellion, Winkler, and Cross had—at gunpoint—taken over a Kalota being driven by a minor official of the Bulgarian Ministry of the Interior. Fifty, fat, and frightened, Josko Jisosva ended up in the rear seat next to Harry Cross, who told him if he so much as blinked the wrong way, he would blow his head off.

10.58 hours. Winkler was driving the Kalota on Boulevard Stamboliisky while Camellion and Cross carried on a conversation in German, every now and then dropping the name of Mischa Wolf, the chief of the East German *Ministerium für Staatssicherheit*—the *Mfs*—the Ministry for State Security in East Germany, the East German intelligence apparatus.

When Winkler spotted the United States Embassy ahead, he said, "Now!", looked in the rearview mirror, and swung the vehicle toward the curb. Cross motioned to the door with his pistol, telling Josko Jisosva to get out. As soon as the astonished man was out of the car and on the sidewalk, Winkler speeded up and headed straight for the U.S. Embassy. He didn't stop, either, before the double gates. He crashed right through them and stopped a hundred feet inside the compound. Moments later, seven U.S. Marines were pointing M-16s at the vehicle, one of them ordering the occupants to get out—and keep their hands high in the air!

Ten minutes more and the Death Merchant and Winkler and Cross were standing before Thomas Joseph McLean II, the undersecretary who was so nervous he could hardly speak. Ambassador Hazlouw was at an official function and McLean was afraid he could not handle the job properly. *Damn these spooks!* He tried to give the Death Merchant an argument: "Who are you? Blah, blah, blah . . ."

11.21 hours. Camellion and his two companions were standing in the Operations Room of Leapfrog, the CIA network covering Bulgaria, Leonard Haver, the chief of station, Robert Beall, and a small knot of "U.S. government employees" staring at them.

The Death Merchant, never one to waste time, turned to Harry Cross.

"Cross, you're one of the Fox's watchdogs and a good street man! He sent you over to keep an eye on things, so tell—"

"How did you know? How did you find out?" Cross was genuinely surprised.

Camellion's eyes became a dustless depth of expanding space, with fire burning in the blue. "You were too good with a weapon at the Slavyanska. A mere 'messenger' couldn't have the survival talents you have. You've been in a lot of firefights, my friend. Now tell these jokers the score."

"What score?" Leonard Haver demanded angrily. "The three of you contact us on a Priority 4, crash through the gates, and expect us to be happy about it. Do you realize that this embassy is now faced with the paradox of 'harboring' three supposed Bulgarians who want protection? Whoever you are, sir, I can assure you our State Department will not be happy with the problem you have created."

"Harry," Camellion said, and glanced at Cross.

"He's C-16-D on FK-27B," Cross told Haver. "I suggest you do as he says or you'll end up as some minor official in a two-bit gorilla nation in Africa."

11.31 hours. The Death Merchant was speaking what could

have been gibberish into the mike of the powerful station transceiver that had a frequency hopper—2,000 per second—and a black box double scrambler. The transmissions, both ways, would be impossible to decode, even with computers.[2]

At the other end, thousands of miles away in the United States, Courtland Grojean was ecstatic about the elimination of the targets and anxious about the files.

DID YOU DESTROY THE FILE SECTION?

WE COULDN'T. IT WAS IMPOSSIBLE TO GET TO THE FILES. I HAD A CHOICE TO MAKE. IT WAS EITHER THE FILES OR THE RUSSIAN UNCLES AND THE DS BOSSES. I REASONED THE FILES WOULD BE DESTROYED WHEN THE BUILDING COLLAPSED. I FAILED. THE BUILDING WILL HAVE TO BE TORN DOWN, BUT THE FILES ARE STILL THERE.

Surprisingly, the CIA operations chief accepted the explanation. Came back the question: WHY DESTROY THE DS BUILDING? WHY NOT KINTEX HEADQUARTERS?

BECAUSE YOU DON'T KILL A SPIDER BY CUTTING OFF ONE OF ITS LEGS. YOU STEP ON IT. YOU CRUSH THE BODY.

Grojean then wanted to know how the Death Merchant, Carey Winkler, and Harry Cross intended to slip from the embassy and get back to the United States. He added that the U.S. State Department was in an uproar over "three Bulgarian refugees," but that the problem would be resolved.

Camellion replied that he had assumed it would be. AFTER ALL, CARDINAL JOSEPH MINDSZENTY LIVED FOR YEARS AT THE U.S. EMBASSY IN HUNGARY. He then explained the escape-to-the-States plan. His master makeup kit would be brought to the embassy in Sofia by three diplomatic carriers. ONCE I HAVE THE COMPLETE KIT, I'LL DO A JOB ON WINKLER, CROSS AND MYSELF AND MAKE US IDENTICAL TO THREE MEN AMONG THE PERSONNEL ALREADY HERE AT THE EMBASSY. WE'LL USE THEIR IDENTIFICATION AND DIPLOMATIC STATUS TO FLY BACK TO THE U.S. WHEN THE THREE MEN, WHOSE FACES WE HAVE BORROWED, DO SHOW THEMSELVES IN PUBLIC, SAY A FEW DAYS AFTER WE LEAVE, THE BULGARIANS WILL KNOW WE'VE SUCKERED THEM, BUT THEY WILL BE HELPLESS TO DO ANYTHING ABOUT IT, UNLESS THEY WANT TO MAKE FOOLS OF THEMSELVES IN FRONT OF THE WORLD COMMUNITY. THE KGB WOULD NEVER ALLOW THAT. . . .

Camellion put down the copy of *OMNI*, leaned back on the couch, and told himself that man lived in an exquisite bedlam,

---

[2] Only half true. A computer could decode the conversation, but it would take years.

a brutal asylum in which everything was tinged with death. A wise person learned to speak the language of reality and to see through the misty veil. He danced with the tango of life and enjoyed the tantalizing possibilities of the paradox, of the riddle of consciousness. The lover, the mystic, and the scientist discovered the very same things on different planes. The people's thirst for liberty and the martyrs' hymn of faith mingled in a madness of worthless solutions that lasted only for the moment. The world has always washed the corpses, wiped up the blood, and prayed over caskets about to be lowered into holes. . . . The world always would—but for only a very short time. . . .

The Death Merchant frowned. What could be so "extremely important" in the United States?

Camellion analyzed what Grojean had said, AN EXTREMELY IMPORTANT MATTER THAT REQUIRES THAT YOU GET BACK HERE AS QUICKLY AS POSSIBLE.

Why? What was so vital, so pressing?

What did he mean by The Soul Search Project?

Watch for

THE SOUL SEARCH PROJECT

next in the DEATH MERCHANT series
from Pinnacle Books

coming in March!

CELEBRATING 10 YEARS IN PRINT
AND OVER 22 MILLION COPIES SOLD!

the EXECUTIONER by Don Pendleton

Relax... and enjoy more of America's #1 bestselling action/adventure series! Over 25 million copies in print!